Helena
Campbell

MICHAEL'S WIFE

MICHAEL'S WIFE

Marlys Millhiser

G. P. Putnam's Sons
New York

For my husband, David

MICHAEL'S WIFE

1

A SCREECHING CRY made her roll over. The hawk circled above her in a light gray sky, swooped lower to take a final check, and then silently folded itself into a nest on top of a strange tree.

No. Not a tree.

She closed her eyes tightly and then opened them just enough to peer through dark lashes. It was a tall cactus, weird and distorted, with three spiny green arms reaching upward as if signaling a turn in traffic. Others like it were all around her, and still others without arms, that were short and stubby, shaped like barrels. She shut her eyes again trying to make sense of what she'd seen.

Something she couldn't identify nagged at one corner of her consciousness.

Birds—it sounded like hundreds of them—trilled and chirped somewhere close and a light but heady sweetness scented the air. The pain at the base of her skull tightened the skin under her hair, spread to her forehead, pulling up on her eyelids, forcing them open.

The sky a lighter gray now.

Cold. She raised first one bare arm and then the other; both felt leaden and prickly with sleep. Flexing numbed fingers, she examined her hands curiously and finally forced cold, stiff muscles to let her sit up.

Nausea. It pushed up from her middle to her throat and brought sickly sweat to her face. Shivering, drawing the sweet air into her lungs in deep measured breaths, she waited it out.

She sat in a miniature stream bed without water that twisted away through cacti, small trees, and clumped bushes until it was out of sight. Around her night shadows lingered still, but the edge of a red-orange sun peeked over a dark mountain range low on the horizon. It rose to sit on a mountain crest, bringing a strange world into sharper focus, drawing out the colors around her as she waited for the sense of it all to come to her.

She was sitting in a desert at dawn, but for the moment she couldn't think why.

The tranquil, familiar sound of flies. Three buzzed past her to settle on a hardened cow pie nearby. A bee scuttled into an opening purple-red blossom crowning a small paddlelike cactus. The nagging something was growing stronger, creeping up through the haze of her thoughts.

Carefully now, not wanting to disturb her aching head more than was necessary, she got to her feet, placing her weight on one tingling foot and then the other. She searched the ground around her, not knowing exactly what she looked for—a purse, a jacket, some belonging. But there was nothing.

Her body had left no impression on the packed sandy earth. The desert stretched vast and endless in every direction, repeating the same scene over and over.

And then it hit her, with almost a physical blow. Fear, full-blown, unmistakable.

She was racing down the stream bed away from the mountains, blindly following its twisting course as if something monstrous were at her heels, one small part of her trying to analyze what it was she feared, the rest consumed with the fear itself till she was breathless with it, weak.

At one point the stream bed made a wide curve and she overran it just a little. Just enough to step into a nest of lime-green bristles beneath a lime-green bush that glistened in the strengthening sunlight. As she hurriedly stooped to extract the painful barbs from her sandals, exposed foot, and

10

then from her fingers she saw the track, a double car track with a feathering of grass and short weeds in the middle just a few feet from the edge of the stream bed.

Rubbing a sore foot, she tried to push down the panic and to assemble her confused thoughts into a pattern that would help her remember what had happened. That momentary loss of being that sometimes comes in a dream or between sleeping and waking was still with her. But she was fully awake, had been for some time. She must know how she had come to be here and what caused her to be afraid, if only to know that she was running in the right direction.

The feeling of urgency, or danger about to rush around that curve in the stream bed, was strong, but she forced herself not to look over her shoulder, to walk and not run down the double track, to give herself time to think this out.

Only one coherent thought surfaced, and when it did it was a shock. The very first memory she had of her life was that hawk screeching above her, as if she'd been born that instant. And she was running again.

She didn't notice the cattle guard that stretched across the track until it was too late. It caught her toe and she sprawled across it.

As she raised her head to spit the grit from her mouth she saw the paved road, undulating at first behind dancing transparent red and green splotches and then settling into a smooth ribbon-band of highway that stretched taut between either horizon. The early sun had washed away the night and left illusions of shimmering pools on its surface.

She couldn't believe that in all that vastness she'd been less than half a mile from a highway even as she crossed it, felt its hardness under her feet, heard the rumble of an engine in the distance.

Except for the blue pickup that rattled toward her, the road was empty. She stood at the edge of it, a willowy figure swaying slightly with the tall grass and flowers of a desert spring that crowded up from the ditch behind her.

The pickup slowed and came to a stop. Its driver leaned elbow and head out the window and looked her over twice from bottom to top. "Hey, you bummin' a ride somewheres or out picking daisies?" Blue eyes grinned over a swirl of cigarette smoke.

"Please, I'd like a ride."

"I'm just going to Florence." He pushed the door open and watched her climb in. "Where'd you come from?" He made no move to start the truck.

"From there," she said, pointing past him to the double track that led to a break in the barbed-wire fence and began again across the shiny steel poles of the cattle guard.

"There's nothin' up that road but a broken-down ranch house. That's a long walk this early."

"Oh. Well . . . I was lost." Despite the warmth of the truck she trembled with cold and fear. Or was it just reaction?

"Your car back there?" he asked, his expression good-natured, his curiosity obvious.

"No, I was walking."

Squint lines deepened at the corners of his eyes, and he managed to broaden his grin without losing the cigarette from his lips. "In sandals?"

"Can't we just go, Mr. . . . ?"

"McBride, Harley McBride."

They started down the road with a jerk, the truck smelling of raw gasoline and dust. There was a waiting silence as she tried to run her fingers through long matted hair and stared at the rip in her slacks.

"You going to tell me your name?"

A pleasant numbness began to dull the ache in her head, the insistent hunger in her stomach. The warmth and motion of the truck soothed the confusion in her mind. She studied the man next to her. Should she tell him? Ask for his help? Surely there was no danger here. Still she didn't answer.

Harley McBride, in faded denim jeans and jacket and a T-shirt so stretched at the neck that the sandy hair on his

12

chest curled over the top, slouched easily behind the wheel.

She was still wondering whether or not to confide in him when the truck braked to a halt so suddenly that she had to grab the dashboard to stay with it. And just that quickly her fear returned.

Harley turned to her, the easy slouch and grin gone. "You a hippie?" He finally removed the cigarette from his lips and blew the smoke between his teeth. "Because if you are, little lady, you can get out right here."

Her eyes followed his down her dirty sleeveless blouse, the awful orange slacks and sandals. "I'm not a hippie," she said quietly, wondering if she lied.

He studied her face and then threw the cigarette out the window and shifted the truck into gear. His grin returned. "I heard they was squatting around here, looking to get some sun. Papers say they're going to raise hell at the air bases." And he tapped the newspaper lying on the seat between them.

HIPPIES PLAN DEMONSTRATIONS FOR PHOENIX AIR FORCE BASES. HIPPIES FROLIC IN THE SUN—PICTURES, PAGE 12. She turned to page 12, more to forestall his questions than because she was interested in hippies. A tall, emaciated girl picked desert flowers, stringy hair hiding half her face. Another picture showed a rangy bearded boy with wire-rimmed glasses sitting on a sleeping bag. A full page of pictures was devoted to long-haired people eating, standing, sitting. She could see no sign of frolic.

Unwilling to face Harley or the alien world outside the truck, she hid behind the paper, wishing that this ride would go on forever.

"You come back to haunt me, Doe Eyes?"

His strange question brought her up from behind the paper to find him grinning at the tear in her slacks. "Have you seen me before?" Hope and fear mingled as she tried to adjust to this new thought.

Small even teeth gleamed behind his grin. "I was huntin'

once, up north in the mountains. Stopped at a stream to get a drink. When I looked up, there was this deer, not ten feet away, so still I hadn't seen her before."

Something inside her went very still, tense, as she pictured the deer standing in the sunlight, her head high, watching her hunter, her nose and ears quivering as she sensed the danger. "And you shot her, I suppose?"

"Right between her beautiful blank brown eyes!" More light curly hair escaped from the cuffs of his jacket and spread onto the back of his hands, and heavy blunt fingers.

"But you know"—Harley turned the truck onto a side road where cultivated fields replaced desert and trees grouped around buildings just ahead—". . . she's haunted me ever since. Had eyes just like yours." His grin was conspiratorial. "Never trust a hunter, Doe Eyes."

She decided to keep her problem to herself. Things would come straight any minute now.

On the quiet main street in early morning, the sidewalks sat at least a foot above the street; overhangs jutted from storefronts over the sidewalks forming an arcade and a shield against the summer sun.

"Can I drop you someplace?" Harley waved back at an old man in cowboy boots who leaned against a storefront picking his teeth.

Florence was small and they reached the end of the main street all too soon, pulling into a paved area in front of a tiny park where palm trees shaded picnic tables, sprinklers splashed carefully groomed grass and narrow sidewalks. A man in a tan shirt and trousers clipped casually at a bushy hedge. If Florence wasn't exactly an oasis in the desert, this lovely park certainly was. Still she hesitated.

"Look, lady, you must be going someplace."

She opened the door but couldn't quite get up the courage to step out and had to wipe the tears off her cheeks with the back of her hand. She didn't even have a handkerchief.

14

"Something tells me this is where I should ride off into the sunset, but. . . ." Harley sighed and reached across her to close her door. "You don't know anybody in Florence, right?"

"Just you."

"Uh-huh. And you weren't going here, were you?"

"I . . . wasn't going anywhere."

"Yeah, well. . . ." He rubbed his chin and considered her for a long moment over his hand. "I got an errand to do here and then I'm going into Phoenix. I don't suppose you know anybody there?"

"No . . . but I'd like to go with you." Time. Safe time to think, to plan. A reprieve.

"But can you give me one reason why I should take you?" Harley did his best to look serious, but the grin lurked in the corners of his eyes. He was enjoying this in spite of himself. "I mean, look at it from where I'm sittin'. It's plain you got trouble. You won't tell me your name, where you come from. I find you on a road in the middle of a desert without a car, not even a purse. And you ain't going no place. Now. . . ."

"Please?"

Her appeal caught him in midsentence counting off his reasons on his fingertips. Another long look and then he shrugged. "Oh, hell! Okay. You wait here and I'll be back for you. There's a head over there; you could clean up a little while you wait." He pointed to a small concrete building at the back of the park and handed her his comb.

"You will come back for me?"

"Sure."

She had to avoid glistening water from the sprinklers overspraying onto the sidewalks. The park seemed a lush green after the desert. She felt shaky, no headache now, just a frightening lightness.

The windowless building was clean and whitewashed. The

15

hot water spigot was gone from a disappointingly tiny sink. Avoiding the mirror, she wrestled with long hair and did what she could to her hands and face with soap that would not lather in cold water.

The stool sat behind a partition without a door, giving off the prickly ordor of disinfectant. It was there she found it, tucked into the tight waistband of her slacks. A slip of paper—"Captain Michael Devereaux, Luke A.F.B." handwritten across it.

Captain Michael Devereaux. She waited for something to happen, to click into place. Nothing did. She knew she should be relieved, but the nagging fear was still there as she faced the mirror over the sink. Oval face. Large eyes. Brown hair. Long neck. The face didn't reflect the confusion inside her, its expression stony, indifferent.

Sitting on the cold concrete floor, holding her head in her hands, staring at the slip of paper on her knee, she felt more lost than before because the name Michael Devereaux meant nothing to her.

When she finally stepped out of the concrete building, Harley McBride was waiting for her, arms folded, slouching against the truck.

"Harley, where is Luke Air Force Base?"

"Glendale, just outside Phoenix. That where you're going?" He looked relieved.

"Yes."

"Well, get in." Once in the truck he handed her a paper bag and a thermos. "Thought maybe you hadn't any breakfast." It was steamy coffee and a ham sandwich and tasted like a banquet after a fast.

They rode with the windows open, the air warming now, more heavily scented with the mingled fragrances of wild flowers. Patches of blue, red, yellow, and reddish purple waved in the ditches in rich shades that even a desert sun could not wash out.

16

"Do you live around here, Harley?"

"I grew up here. Got a sister in Florence—that's where the sandwich came from. And a brother in Phoenix. I sort of drift between the two." He drove with one elbow crooked out the window, squinting in the sun. A big man, with curly hair bleached by sunlight and long gristly sideburns.

"Do you know a Michael Devereaux?" A casual question, as if her whole world didn't hang on his answer.

It came after a hesitation and a curious glance in her direction. "I know a Devereaux family. Don't know if there's a Michael. Why?"

"I want to contact this Michael."

"At Luke?"

"Yes, he's a captain."

"Well, the Devereaux' I know live in Tucson. They lease some land around Florence. In fact they used to lease right where you say you got lost." There was something of the carefree high pitch of adolescence in his voice, but he appeared to be in his middle thirties.

"That ranch house up the road where you picked me up. Who lives there?"

"Nobody."

"Are you sure?"

"I was born there. You're sure long on questions and short on answers. What's your problem anyway?"

"I don't have any answers. I don't have . . . anything. Harley, please tell me about the Devereaux'."

"I don't think we're talking about the same ones. I can't see a Devereaux making a career of the service, too busy living off other people's sweat. I should know—my old man ran a ranch for them for thirty years. And anybody getting stationed that close to his family has got to be related to the President. I've been in the Navy twice myself."

The sprawl of city soon displaced desert and the truck was immersed in heavy traffic. MESA, TACOS, LIQUOR, MESA

17

NEW AND USED CARS, HAMBURGERS, DESERT PEACE MOTEL—the signs and buildings were somehow garish after the flowering desert.

"That ranch house where you were born was a Devereaux ranch?"

"A Devereaux house on Devereaux land where I lived with two parents, four brothers, and one sister. Between dying and growing up and leaving, the help was gone and my dad was working it alone. It stopped paying and the Devereaux' closed it down, and it broke my old man so he hung himself in that house he didn't even own." His grin tightened to a grimace, his voice muffled by barely parted lips. "The name Devereaux ain't my favorite topic. I'm nice enough to give you a ride, so leave it alone, will ya?"

It was no good alienating the only person she knew. She felt a strained, floating security riding with him, as though the panic followed somewhere behind the truck, as if it would catch up with her when they stopped, when he left her alone in Phoenix.

Her thoughts kept skirting reality and the impossibility of her situation, the growing dread of reaching Phoenix and Michael Devereaux. She knew she was deluding herself, that she would have to face things, and soon.

"Where are we now?"

"Tempe. Next stop, Phoenix. It's all grown together into one big mess. I have to stop at my brother's. Then I'll take you on to Luke. I don't know why. It's out of my way, but you don't look long on cash."

"I don't have anything."

"You said that. And that's about all you've said."

A sign read WELCOME TO PHOENIX AND THE VALLEY OF THE SUN. The street was lined with pickup trucks and trailer home lots, with swanky motels where palms hovered over swimming pools and where lavish restaurants waited for the dressed-up evening trade.

The truck pulled into the SUNNY REST MOTEL, AIR-CONDITIONED, TV, PHONES, CAFÉ, VACANCY. It squatted in shabby pink stucco between two magnificent glass and brick motels that sported two stories, balconies, pools, and palms. The Sunny Rest sat like an embarrassed poor relation in unaccustomed surroundings.

"Does your brother live here?"

"He owns it. Be back in a minute." Harley got out of the truck and went into the door marked CAFE, OFFICE.

The Sunny Rest was U-shaped, one story. The café sat at one end of the U, Venetian blinds drawn against the sun and a small handwritten sign, WAITRESS WANTED, stuck in the window. She sat looking at the sign seconds before she really listened to her thoughts. What she needed was a little more time to face her problem before she faced Michael Devereaux. She knew Phoenix was in Arizona, and she was almost sure she was seeing it for the first time. She hadn't really forced her mind to cope with reality, and given a little time, she might be able to solve her problem herself. She still could remember nothing. Was it because she didn't want to or really couldn't?

Following Harley into the café, she was relieved to find there were no customers, only Harley and the heavy sweating man in a smeared apron behind the counter.

"What can I do for you, ma'am?"

"She's with me, Ray." Harley perched on a stool at one end of the counter.

"Look, Harley, you ain't shackin' up with none of your dames in this place. I told you before."

"Raymond! *Raymond!* Now this gal got lost picking flowers in the desert and I just gave her a ride into town. Right, Doe Eyes? This is my nasty big brother. Sit down, might as well get a hamburger out of old Ray before we go to Luke."

"Not unless you're paying, you don't."

19

"Come on, Ray. Two hamburgers and two cups of coffee ain't going to break you. Looks like you could use the practice."

Raymond McBride started to answer but then shrugged and disappeared into the kitchen. When he returned with the hamburgers, a small fleet of flies came with him. Quickly, before she lost her nerve, she asked if she might have the waitress job for a room instead of wages for a day or two until he could find someone.

Raymond looked from his brother to her, his eyes interested but suspicious. "Harley, if this is one of your schemes to get bedded in town tonight. . . ."

"This is her idea, Ray. I'm leaving, honest. Thought she wanted to go to Luke."

"Well, I could use someone. What's your name?"

"Her name's Maggie, Maggie Freehope." Harley supplied this with a grin he tried to hide behind a napkin. "Now that's a good waitress name if I ever heard one."

"I got somebody coming in for dinner, but you can have a room tonight and start in the morning. We'll see how you work out tomorrow . . . but no men, understand?" Tiny red veins stood out on the bulb at the end of his nose.

"Men?"

"He means you shouldn't share your room with one. You see, Ray? She's all innocence. You don't have any worries."

"She's with you, ain't she? And you better mean what you say about leaving."

"I'm going now. What room does she get? I'll put her bag in."

"Number Fourteen, right across from here." He handed Harley a key from the board behind the cash register. "And, Maggie, bring your Social Security card with you in the morning."

Harley walked her to the truck and slammed the door on the far side. Keeping the truck between them and the café, they walked to Number 14, and he unlocked the door for her. "You wouldn't have got in without a bag. What made you change your mind anyway?"

"I wanted some time to think. Maybe I can call this Michael from here. Thanks for everything, Harley. Now if I only had a social security card."

"Can't help you there."

"At least I have a room for tonight. I don't know what I'd have done if you hadn't come along when you did," she said, wishing he'd leave, afraid that he might.

They stood in the open doorway, Harley leaning against the frame, looking down at her. "You'd have latched onto the first male in sight with that helpless look and had him feedin' you steak instead of hamburger. Women like you manage to get along real well in this world." And he leaned closer.

His closeness made her shiver. "Harley, I'm sorry if I took advantage of you. I didn't have any choice."

"Harley!" Raymond McBride yelled from the steps of the café.

"I'm leavin', I'm leavin'. Well, so long, Doe Eyes. Hope you get away from whatever you're running from."

She watched the truck pull into traffic and wanted to run after it. The panic that had been following closed in . . . *whatever you're running from.* She had the clothes on her back and a slip of paper with a man's name on it. Was she looking for him or running from him? But you didn't write down someone's name and address if you didn't want to find him.

The room had a bare floor of dark green tile with some of the tiles chipped at the corners. Bedspread, walls, and curtains were a grim beige and there was hardly enough room to walk between the bed and a desk.

I'm alone. I'm safe. Now what do I do? I could call the police. Instead she turned on the TV that sat on the desk. There was a picture, but the volume dial brought no sound. A newscaster mouthed words from some notes in his hand, the clock behind him reading 12:05. And then a grisly picture of wounded soldiers on stretchers . . . the men, their clothes, the ground they lay on, everything in varying shades of dreary. She switched it off and lay back on the bed.

Her mind was very clear. It didn't seem empty but full of images. Images of Harley's stubby blond hair and teasing eyes in a tanned face, of Raymond and his dirty apron, the truck with a dent running along its side, a vast desert with mountains in the distance. She would have looked but a speck from an airplane. She could see the pleasant park in Florence; even the deer Harley had spoken of seemed clear and real. But her own face was not clear, and anything that had happened before that morning was not there at all.

In her mind the picture of the gray men on gray stretchers fought with the image of the black telephone that sat on the bedside table just before she fell asleep.

She awakened more tired than before with her head aching again and an intense desire to soak forever in a hot tub. But there was no tub, only a shower stall with a curtain that wouldn't quite reach across. She showered, letting the water get as hot as she could endure it, and worked on her hair until the little bar of Ivory disintegrated. Wrapping herself in one towel and her hair in another, she washed her clothes and hung them around the little room to dry.

She must have slept most of the afternoon for it was growing dark when she stepped out of the bathroom. She pulled the curtains and switched on the lamp. In the large mirror over the desk she could see herself from the knees up, a very slender woman—girl? She couldn't guess at her age, somewhere between twenty and thirty? There was a mole on the side of her neck.

She found it embarrassing to stare at this stranger so intimately, and frightening not to recognize her. Rewrapping the towel, she turned from the mirror with the same depressed feeling she'd had that morning watching her reflection in the whitewashed building in Florence. She could be in terrible trouble and not know it or running from something she wouldn't recognize until it caught up with her.

Then her eyes rested on the telephone. *Why do I keep putting it off?* There was a phone book in the drawer of the little bedside table and in it the number of Luke Air Force Base. Dialing quickly before she could change her mind, she half hoped the phone wouldn't work. But the call went through.

It took some time to locate Captain Devereaux and she considered hanging up. She didn't know what she'd say. She really should rehearse something before she talked to him. . . .

"Hello."

". . . Captain Devereaux?"

"Yes."

"Captain Devereaux . . . I need your help. I wonder if you know of anyone . . . anyone who is missing. . . ." Her heart was pounding blood past her ears so hard she could barely hear herself.

"Who is this?"

"Would . . . would it be possible to meet you somewhere?" She sounded silly to herself; what must she sound like to him?

"What the. . . ." The voice was deep, resonant, impatient.

"Captain Devereaux, it's urgent that I see you. I know it sounds strange, but . . . I was given your name and I . . . have to see you. Please, I won't take much of your time."

The voice on the other end of the phone was silent.

"Captain Devereaux, are you there?"

His answer came after a long pause and was barely audible, as if he were choked with astonishment or disbelief. "Laurel?"

"Do you know me? Oh, thank God, you see I'm lost and I don't know who. . . ."

"Where are you?"

23

"I'm at the Sunny Rest Motel, Room Fourteen. I don't know the street. I can look it up; there's a phone book right here."

"Never mind, I'll find it. Give me half an hour. And Laurel?"

"Yes?"

"Stay there. Stay right there." And he hung up.

She replaced the receiver and drew her feet up onto the bed and off the dingy tiles. *Laurel, Laurel.* The name didn't make the face in the mirror any more familiar.

Michael Devereaux. She closed her eyes, waiting for a picture. None came. The voice on the telephone had sounded neither old nor young nor familiar. It had sounded surprised. No, stunned. And then angry.

Michael Devereaux. Father? Uncle? Brother? Husband? No, no ring. Casual acquaintance? No matter, he was her only tie to a world she'd temporarily lost. *He is coming to take me back to somewhere. Somewhere safe and familiar.* She shivered in a damp towel, still unable to convince herself that she was relieved, that this was all real.

He could be an enemy. She would have to chance it; there was no one else. Why should she have an enemy? Why was she left alone on the desert without food, money, memory?

There was only one door into this room and out of it.

Lying back on the bed, she pictured an angry faceless man standing in the doorway. He reached for her with one hand, a knife in the other. She ran to the bathroom—her movements sluggish, dreamlike—and managed to get in and lock it at the last agonizing second and the man pounded on the door yelling, "Laurel, Laurel, Laurel." She pushed the dream away.

A sharp knocking awakened her. She moved from the bed with dizzying suddenness, tugging off the grim bedspread to wrap around the bath towel that was all that covered her nakedness. Only the dim light of the desk lamp lit the room,

24

and she opened the door just enough to peer into darkness relieved by a white shirt collar and V-shaped front, divided by a black tie and enclosed in a dark uniform.

Improbable metallic eyes glinted in a swarthy face and widened as they looked down at her.

"Laurel." It was a statement spoken quietly, not a question.

So she was Laurel. How could anyone forget eyes like his?

Captain Devereaux yanked the door from her hand and stepped in, slamming it behind him, his movements forceful, deliberate. And with his entrance the little room changed, became overfull, suffocating.

There was no look of welcome for her, no smile of relief that she had been found. The veins in his neck bulged against the skin and he held himself still, rigid.

She stood clutching the coarse spread against her as if for protection. Under it her hair lay damp against her back, a sickening cramp tightened her lower abdomen, the breaths she took refused to fill her lungs, and she knew what that deer had felt staring back at Harley McBride. She couldn't turn and run. Those strange eyes held her. Like an animal, she felt the danger instinctively.

"You've got a goddamned nerve!" He spoke so quietly that she heard him only because of the deep resonance in his voice.

"I'd better explain. I called you because I didn't know. . . ."

The blow came so fast there was no time to dodge. It caught her full on the side of the head, the face of his wristwatch catching her cheek. She grabbed for the bed on her way down but missed and hit the floor on her chest and stomach.

She prayed that she'd pass out so she wouldn't feel the next blow. But it didn't come. He picked her up roughly and set her on the bed, tucking the towel back into place. The beige

25

bedspread lay crumpled and useless at his feet. Holding her shoulders so that her head would tilt back to face his, he leaned above her and spoke slowly, distinctly.

"Laurel, I once promised myself that if I ever saw you again I would kill you. Don't tell me where you've been all this time or what you've been doing. At least not yet. Because if you do I might keep that promise. Now get some clothes on."

She saw him through tears jarred loose by the blow. It was an arresting face that told her he meant what he said. She felt weak and sick, beyond panic. *If he killed me now,* she thought, *I would never have to know fear like this again.*

2

He drove violently, crashing to a stop for a red light and jerking to a start as it changed, sitting tensed over the wheel, his lips compressed and silent.

They were soon out of the city and racing over open desert, the car a sleek blue missile rushing her toward some terror she couldn't even guess at. Even at night there was an eerie glow on the desert, every cactus and tree with its own still shadow, distant mountains dark against the lighter sky. Her clothes clung to her with a chilly dampness and she clutched the armrest, pressing her feet against the thick carpeting as if to brake their frantic speed.

"Where are we going?" She had visions of his smashing them into the ditch in anger at the very sound of her voice.

"Tucson." He glanced at her as if to appraise her reaction. The car didn't swerve from its course.

Tucson was where Harley's Devereaux' lived. She longed suddenly for the safety of Harley's truck, his good-natured grin. She'd walked into trouble the moment she was left on her own, probably the very trouble she was running from. There was no doubt that this man was an enemy, and if she got the slightest chance to escape she'd take it. That's what she should have done when he went into the café to pay the bill; instead she'd waited in the car numb with shock.

"Captain Devereaux, will . . . will you tell me what this is all about?"

"Cut the Captain Devereaux bit. Look, Laurel, I don't

27

know what your masquerade is but just drop it. It won't work."

"What should I call you then?"

"Try Michael," he said, his voice steely with sarcasm. "If you're worried it'll create any intimacy, forget it. You may be my wife but I could damn you to hell for coming back!"

"Wife?"

"The church may mean nothing to you, but I was born in it, remember? I'm stuck with you." And the car did the impossible—it went faster.

Relaxing her hold on the armrest, she lay back against the seat, her ears ringing. *It's not possible! I've been mistaken for someone else. I'm not Laurel.* Her relief was mixed with disappointment; Laurel had at least been a name.

The dials on the dashboard glowed green and added an exotic tinge to his profile. His face was angular with the black hair starting well back at the temple and coming forward over a high forehead. A shadow of a beard showed around a thin but expressive mouth. No woman could forget a man like this, not so completely. But then she hadn't known herself in the mirror. He was the normal one with a memory. *I'm not normal. A man would know his own wife . . . he certainly saw enough of me.* Her plans for escape began to fade.

They drove through sparse traffic, the lights of an occasional town sparkling in the desert night. This man would not believe her if she told him she didn't know him.

Finally they came to the outskirts of a city that spread out on a broad valley floor, and the car turned onto a road that wound among the low mountains at the city's edge. It stopped in front of a high masonry wall set close against the road and showing a mellowed white in the moonlight. When Michael left the car to open the gigantic wooden gates, she made no attempt to bolt as she had planned but allowed herself to be driven through the gate to the graveled court-yard beyond.

Facing her was the front of a large building the same

mellow color as the wall, rectangular but for the wide arch-shaped bell wall that rose above the roof. Within the bell wall three arched niches were open to the moonlight beyond. The center niche held a bell. Great carved wooden doors were built low to the ground without steps, and intricate iron grillwork protected the narrow two-story windows.

Fine hairs prickled at the back of her neck. It looked more like a well-endowed private institution than a home. Of course, if she'd escaped from an institution he would bring her back. So that's why she couldn't remember. Insanity was the one thing she hadn't thought of.

In the center of the courtyard stood a low circular fountain, and they drove around it to approach the door from the side. When the car stopped, Michael made no move to get out but sat gazing at the windshield as if he too wanted to put off what must come.

"What is this place?"

"This, little wife, is the family home. I'd once dreamed of bringing you here, of showing you off. And now look at us."

"Then it isn't . . . an institution?"

"A loony bin? Let's say it's a private one. Come and meet the Devereaux loonies. They'll be overjoyed to see you." Taking her wrist, he pulled her across the seat and out of the car.

They entered the house through a smaller door set within the great paneled doors. The barnlike entry hall was lit by wrought-iron sconces and by moonlight at its far end. A staircase led up one wall to a balcony that ran the width of the hall.

Across from the staircase light poured through an open doorway and they could hear a woman's voice, low and husky. "When we have guests, Paul, I want you to be here. It was embarrassing to make excuses to the Johnstons. I won't have this happen again."

A man answered, a fussy feminine quality in the way he spoke. "My dear, you knew I had this lecture. You insist

29

upon arranging your little social events without consulting my schedule, and if you hadn't stolen my secretary I'd have more time for such things. Now, will you kindly leave and allow me to get to my work?"

They entered without knocking, Michael half dragging her behind him.

"Your work. It's . . . Michael, what on earth?" The woman with the husky voice stood next to the fireplace, a petite redhead in a green dress—the shade of green reminiscent of the painfully bristled lime-colored bush on the desert. "We . . . weren't expecting you." Her eyes widened under perfectly arched brows as she looked from Michael to Laurel, and Laurel felt awkward, shabby.

As Michael brought her forward into the room, a slight man rose from behind a desk, adjusting thick glasses to peer at them.

"My sister-in-law, Janet. My brother, Paul. I don't believe you've met them," Michael said. And then with that soft stinging reproach of his, "This is Laurel."

There was a long silence while everyone gaped at her as though wishing her to vanish under the rug.

"Laurel! Not . . . ? Oh, no." Janet sat heavily in the nearest chair. "I thought she was dead . . . or something."

"Do you think it was wise to bring her here, Michael?" Paul Devereaux had the same pale eyes as his brother but lacking the impact and magnified by thick lenses.

"What was I supposed to do with her?"

"Where has she been? Do you propose that she stay here?"

"I don't know where she's been. Right now I don't want to. She'll stay here until I decide what to do with her."

"Of course. I just don't want any. . . ."

"Any what, Paul?" Michael's grip on her arm tightened.

"I don't want any violence. You're obviously angry. You have every right to be. But you must be careful of your temper, Michael."

"Then don't sermonize! I'm taking her upstairs. She hasn't

met everyone yet." He dragged her from the room as suddenly as he'd dragged her in.

She hadn't said a word but, like a naughty child, had been talked about and not to. What was this about? There was no time to worry about it as she stumbled after him up the broad staircase and along a corridor.

He opened a door and pushed her through ahead of him, releasing her wrist and pressing a light-switch. It was a bedroom big enough to house Raymond McBride's café, with room to park Harley's truck. A deep red area rug spread over polished parquet. The giant bed with double headboards sat between two narrow windows, its coverlet red with outlines in white of wild horses and stolid conquistadores racing back and forth across it. She would have loved to stretch out on that bed and cry. But not next to Michael Devereaux.

He put his cap on the dresser, unbuttoned his coat, and turned to her, the pale intense eyes in the dark face looking enormous, almost hypnotic. "I think it's time you faced the music."

She backed away as he moved between her and the door.

"He's here, Laurel. He's in the next room."

"Who? I don't know what you're talking about."

"You're going to carry your little masquerade to the finish, aren't you? Well, let's see if you can keep it up. Move." The room was L-shaped and he motioned her around the corner past the bed where this fantastic room continued to another door. She moved swiftly to avoid a shove.

The adjoining bedroom was smaller and more crowded, with a picture of the Madonna over the bed. It was narrow and opened into an L about halfway between them and the bed. A woman came around the corner just as Michael Devereaux was closing the door.

"Claire, I've brought. . . ." But Michael was cut off by another figure careening around the corner, giggling and screeching.

31

"Daddy!" A little boy wearing only diapers lurched into Michael's arms. He hugged the child and the Teddy bear he clasped.

Laurel felt the floor begin to move under her feet.

"Claire, this is Laurel."

She was getting used to the shock her name caused in people, but Claire's was the strangest yet. A red blush rose up Claire's neck and onto her face through a funny mist that began to swirl around the swaying room.

"Well, aren't you even interested in seeing him? Haven't you ever wondered what he looked like? Look at him." And Michael shoved the little face close to hers.

"Lady, Daddy."

"This is your mother, Jimmy." There was no reaction from the child who began tugging at the medals on Michael's jacket.

Laurel grabbed a chair and sat in it before it could spin out of her reach. "There's been some mistake . . . this is all a mistake. I couldn't have. . . ."

"Oh, no, this is the same baby. The only mistake is that this poor kid was even born. Look at him." The child was blond and smelled of powder.

"You can't tell me that I had a baby. . . ."

Michael towered above her in the swirling mist, "What kind of a woman are you? Don't you even feel ashamed?"

"Pay truck me, Daddy?"

"No, son, I want you to meet this lady. She's your mother, Jimmy. God, doesn't he even know what that is? Hasn't anybody around here explained?"

"We thought it was better not to, Michael, not yet," Claire said from a long way off, her voice reverberating out of the roaring mist.

"Lady sick, Daddy."

"Michael, she's falling!"

And just as she hit the floor she was scooped up and carried back into the next room where Michael laid her on the bed.

32

The mist blended with red and green lights behind her eyelids and her head ached again. *Got to get out of here. Mistake . . . mistake.* She didn't know if she'd spoken out loud. They were talking about her as if she were unconscious, talking somewhere above her as she fought down the nausea and tried to open her eyes.

"Why did you bring her here?"

"I didn't know what to do with her, Claire. I guess I wanted to see her face when she saw Jimmy."

"Where did you find her?"

"She called me from some flea-bitten motel in Phoenix. Didn't even have a suitcase."

"Michael, she didn't want you or Jimmy. You've got every right to throw her out. You shouldn't even have brought her here." Claire's voice sounded shrill and possessive.

"She is my wife."

"She'll just do more harm. Take her back to Phoenix and dump her like she dumped Jimmy."

"She's sick. God knows what she's been doing. Let's get Jimmy to bed; he shouldn't be up so late, Claire."

A door closed and the room was silent. She kept her eyes shut in case they should return. There had been a terrible mistake. Or was it a cruel hoax? But these people seemed so sincere in their hatred. Their shock was real. Laurel had deserted her husband and child, and she must look very much like this Laurel. She'd almost been convinced that she was Laurel, had even started thinking of herself as Laurel.

But I've never had a baby. That much I do know.

When she opened her eyes, the lights were out except for the one in the bathroom behind a half-closed door. She'd slept and someone had covered her with a blanket and laid a frilly white gown across the bed. She turned her head, afraid she wasn't alone, but Michael Devereaux did not sleep beside her.

Sitting up, she found her headache gone and with it the dreamlike indecision. She was through being slugged and

33

dragged around, being introduced to another woman's past sins. *I'll go to the police. They'll find out who I am and keep me safe from Michael.* She should be able to walk into Tucson if she could get out that gate or over the wall. *I should have gone to the police in the first place.* It felt good to be taking positive action at last.

She crept to the door and was surprised to find that it opened to moonlight, a balcony of some sort. *More doors in this place.* She'd go out the way she'd come in so as not to lose her way.

Perhaps she'd take another look at the child just to be sure. He was not her child, but she hadn't really had a good look at him. All seemed quiet as she listened at the door of the adjoining room.

A miniature train and a stuffed giraffe lay on the bed, a small TV set sat on the dresser with a dimly lit lamp next to it. Around the corner of the *L* she found the crib and the sleeping child. Nothing had been done to make this a child's room; he'd merely been added to it as if he were a temporary guest.

He slept on his stomach, one thumb in his mouth, fine blond hair damp against his forehead. As she bent to cover him she disturbed his sleep and he mumbled something unintelligible, turning his head to the other side and switching thumbs automatically. The crumpled Teddy bear was pushed farther into the corner.

An appealing child, sturdy and healthy-looking. She guessed him to be two or three years old. How could Laurel have left him motherless? And if Laurel looked so much like her, how could she and Michael have had such a fair child? She reached down to touch a cheek the texture of warm silk. The eyes of the Madonna in the picture over the bed seemed to bore into her back as she left the room.

Well, he doesn't look like me, that's for sure. But it was funny how she kept forgetting her own image. She checked it again in the bathroom mirror. Every time she looked at herself it seemed a new experience. And the face never attempted to mirror her emotions. Her hair was dark brown and matched her eyes. Her skin was more pale than fair. There was a slight swelling around the scratch on her cheek where Michael's watch had caught her.

On an impulse she lowered her slacks and panties to her knees and examined her hips and thighs carefully. Faint white lines ran along the outer side of each pelvic bone.

She ran a finger over one of the lines as if to erase it.

I could have been very fat at one time, and she looked up into wide staring eyes, the mouth below them opening as the marble image finally cracked, *or very pregnant.*

3

Laurel crept through a silent house. Carved wooden doors moved quietly on massive hinges to display cool, echoing rooms that dwarfed even the heavy furniture. She found herself looking over her shoulder, closing doors carefully.

Thick off-white walls. High ceilings with dark stained beams. Archways. And all the windows barred on the outside by black metal grillwork. It could have been a palatial prison.

The sun had been high when she'd awakened in her borrowed gown. No one had disturbed her sleep or called her for breakfast. It was as if everyone had vacated the house in horror at her presence there.

Her feet made no sound on the lush carpeting of the staircase that broadened into a sweeping curve to meet the polished tile of the entry hall. An inlaid sunburst in oranges, pinks, yellows, disturbed the even pattern of the tiled floor and spread from the base of the stairs to the far wall. It looked as if it had been removed intact from some ancient temple across the border.

She hesitated at the bottom of the stairs, searching the shadows that lined the walls, created by carved chests or straight-backed chairs with dark tooled-leather seats. The fear of some unremembered thing that had sent her racing across the desert to Harley's truck had not left her. It was here, miles away, in this house, too. Why?

She had half-crossed the sunburst when she stopped again. Was it because this was Michael Devereaux's home?

36

There was no sound of life downstairs.

Moving to the double doors opposite the stairs, she entered a salon at the front of the house, its ceiling open to the roof, its two-story windows draped in dark green velvet. The smell of furniture oil hung in the air. Couches and chairs in rich brocades clustered around tables on thick-piled area rugs. Any one of the rugs could have carpeted a normal room from wall to wall.

A house the size of this one would soak up sound. That's why it was so quiet. She stood in the middle of the intimidating room and rubbed her scalp beneath her hair where the throbbing was hardest and again her mind seemed so full of memory. Nothing before yesterday morning, but every event since then bulged with detail. The way Michael's lips had curled when he'd said, "Laurel, I once promised myself that if I ever saw you again I would kill you!"

She hurried away from that memory to the fireplace at the far end of the room and forced herself to study the hunting scene above the mantel. The picture was too small and somehow inadequate for its place of honor.

Spiral stairs at this end of the room led to the balcony of the second floor, a narrower continuation of the balcony in the hall. Behind the stairs a small door opened into Paul's study where she'd met the Devereaux' the night before.

"You must be careful of your temper, Michael," Paul had said from behind that desk. . . .

She ran across the silent study and through the door to the entry hall. The house had that eerie quality of a museum at night. Nowhere did a book lie open on a table, a child's toy peek from under a chair. Everything was polished and in its place, ready for the curious visitor.

Doors stood open to sunlight at the end of the hall, and she assumed this to be the back of the house but found instead an open courtyard completely surrounded by more house. Arcaded walkways sheltered the rectangle of the courtyard, the arches and columns with their shadows giving a cloistered effect. Black iron pots filled with leafy plants hung in the arches. Earthen jars with flowering plants and ornamental trees interspersed with stone couches and wicker chairs lined the walls.

Out in the sunlight a fountain splashed in a near corner and at the other end was a full-sized swimming pool. Misshapen gnarled trees twisted toward the sun past the upper story, their roots humping and cracking the pink flagstone paving.

She turned a corner of the walkway and halfway down one side of the rectangle she was stopped by an unmistakable screeching. It was the kitchen, and Jimmy sat in a highchair carefully dumping the contents of a bowl onto the floor. *Am I really that child's mother?*

The woman, Claire, rushed across the room to grab it, but too late. She looked harried, lank hair falling across her face as she lifted him from the chair. "No more lunch for you. You did that on purpose; you're a bad boy."

"Bad boy," Jimmy repeated as if he'd heard it often.

"He is only a baby, Miss Bently." An old woman in a voluminous black dress appeared from the dark recesses of the kitchen and knelt to mop the floor with a rag.

"Don't spoil him, Consuela. He's a monster already."

Laurel stepped hesitantly into the kitchen from the doorway. "May I have some coffee?"

"Oh, you're up, are you? Well, lunch is about ready. You might as well skip breakfast," Claire said, her expression haughty, her eyes rimmed with red. "This is . . . Jimmy's mother, Consuela."

The old woman rose heavily from her knees and came toward Laurel. There were still streaks of black in her gray hair. "Michael's wife! So, you have come at last, Mrs. Michael. I have waited long for this day." Her dark eyes, lined with wrinkles, were expressionless in a sagging face. Roughened hands clutched and unclutched the sopping rag.

Another person to hate her in this house that did not

welcome her? Laurel couldn't blame any of them. If she was guilty of what they said, she deserved only hatred.

"It's a nap for you, bad boy." Claire carried Jimmy to the door and then stopped to look back, her small slightly pear-shaped figure unenhanced by the full skirt and rounded droop of her shoulders. "If you're wondering where Michael is, he went back to the base last night. He didn't trust himself to stay in the same house with you."

Lunch consisted of salads, at least six different kinds, with hot rolls and coffee. They ate at a small table out on the sun-warmed flagstone of the courtyard, where the swimming pool, lined in blue tiled patterns, reflected the sunlight so intensely that it hurt the eyes.

Consuela served them silently, staring openly at Laurel. Everyone else avoided looking at her. Paul leafed through a folder of papers, Janet studied the day's mail, and Claire concentrated on her salad. There was a kind of fidgety silence at the table as if they were all thinking the same thing and wanted to talk about it but were unable to find a civil way to do so. The statue of a half-dog, half-lion creature glared at her from the center of a nearby fountain, water trickling from its snarling jaws.

This was her first meal in twenty-four hours, but Laurel's stomach would tolerate only the rolls, a little fruit, and coffee. She felt out of place in her messy clothes. The tear in her slacks had widened and her sandals were still gritty from her desert walk.

Janet finally laid down a letter and looked directly at her. "Dear Michael will leave his little problems on our doorstep, won't he?"

"Janet!" Paul Devereaux's scanty mustache had acquired a quiver.

"Well, for heaven's sake. First Jimmy and now her. What else will he present us with out of the blue? I'm not running a home for bedraggled castoffs."

"This is Michael's home as well as yours; he has every right to house his family here."

"Of course. And how nice that we can care for them while he goes off to play soldier." Janet's polished fingernails tapped the glass-topped table and then pretended to rearrange burnished hair where not one of the elegantly chiseled ringlets was out of place. She wore button earrings and full makeup that could not hide the creases at the outer corners of her eyes or the lines on her forehead.

"I suppose we shall have to do something about your clothes, Laurel. We can't have the mother of the Devereaux heir parading around in tatters, can we? I'm afraid Tucson hasn't much to offer, but then anything would be an improvement. Claire will take you in this afternoon."

"Why do I have to do it?" Claire lifted a sullen face from her salad.

"She's right, Janet. Claire gets all the odd jobs around here. She was hired as a secretary, you know. Can't you do it?"

"Nonsense. Claire would just love to do something nice for Michael's dear wife. Wouldn't you, Claire?"

And Claire retreated to her salad, the blush once again spreading up her throat to her face.

"I . . . don't want to be any trouble."

"Trouble? Nonsense, Laurel. Long-lost wives drop in on us every day. Although I don't know how I'm to explain this to our friends. I had just let it be understood that you were dead."

Paul removed his glasses and wiped them on a cloth napkin, weakened eyes squinting in the sun. Replacing his glasses, he leaned forward and cleared his throat as if preparing to deliver a lecture. "What our friends think is of no consequence, but I do feel that the family has a right to know just what you've been up to."

"I can't tell you."

"Laurel, perhaps you don't realize the difficulties. Leaving

40

a husband is one thing, deserting a child quite another." He spoke quickly, impatiently, and Laurel sensed his irritation at having to be involved at all. "I shall have to inquire, but I presume there is still some case against you on the police records in Denver."

"Denver?"

"Of course, that's where the desertion took place. And I would imagine it is a state offense, a criminal offense."

Laurel could only stare at the top of his head, much of it shining in the sun through thinning hair. She couldn't meet his glance.

"Paul, you can't bring the police in on this."

"We'll do all we can to keep this as discreet as possible, Janet. But there's bound to be some kind of legal action and we must know all before we confront the authorities. Now Laurel, if we're to help you, you must tell us where you've been."

"I don't know. I don't remember. Please, I feel sick." As she left her place at the table, she collided with Consuela.

"You realize that you will have to answer to us, to Michael, the police, and someday to Jimmy? That is, if you intend to stay."

Laurel ran from the courtyard and Janet's insistent voice followed her. "What does she mean she can't remember? Paul, make her come back. That's all we need—a scandal."

There were stone stairs at the corner of the courtyard and she raced up them and along the balcony, the diners below watching her as she looked for the outside door to her room. But the room she entered was the wrong one and Jimmy sat up in his crib.

"Hi!"

"Go to sleep." She hurried to the connecting door to her own room and lay facedown on the big bed, tears soaking into the wild horses on the spread. These people were horrible. They'd be glad if she ran out into the desert and

41

died there. Where *had* she been? And how long had she been gone? *Am I really Laurel?* A criminal offense, Paul had said. Would she go to prison?

A Teddy bear landed beside her, and Jimmy stood next to the bed in a shirt and diapers. His hair was combed down over his forehead, almost covering his eyebrows.

"Doesn't anybody ever cut your hair?"

"Bad boy." Sober eyes looked into hers. They weren't Michael's eyes or Paul's. Brown, large, elongated, narrowing at the outer corners like buttonholes—so dark that iris, rim, and pupil almost looked like one—vaguely familiar eyes.

"You are not a bad boy. You're too young to be bad. Whatever you are, they've made you that way. And if I'm Laurel . . . I guess I have, too."

His meager vocabulary could only produce a "Hi" in answer to her little speech. She picked him up and went to stand before the double mirrors above the dresser. He was unbelievably heavy, and she wondered how the frail-looking Claire managed to tote him around. They stared at each other in one of the mirrors, Jimmy looking a little worried at being held by a stranger. There was a similarity in the shape and color of their eyes. But their skin and hair coloring was so different, and her lashes and brows were thicker and darker. How many colors and shapes did eyes have anyway? Surely there weren't that many choices.

"What do you think, Jimmy? Am I your mommy? You're a nice, handsome little boy. But I don't feel anything for you I wouldn't feel for any nice little boy I met in the park."

His answer was to shove the Teddy bear in her face and bite through her blouse into her shoulder.

"Ouch!" She put him down and he raced back to his room, screeching like an Indian with a new scalp. Pulling her blouse back to examine the wound, she found that sharp baby teeth had broken the skin. When she got to him he was standing beside his crib, backed up against the bars, rebellious eyes daring her to punish him.

42

"Easier to get out of bed than back in, I take it." She hoisted him into the crib before he could dart away, covering him and the Teddy bear.

True to Janet's word, Claire took her into Tucson that afternoon. It was embarrassing to enter small expensive shops in torn slacks and dusty sandals, needing everything from underclothes to a handbag. Janet had sent along an extravagant list of what she would need, with a note on the bottom, "We dress for dinner, you know." Salesladies with molded smiles tried hard to look through her, but the name Devereaux brought their eyes into focus. Little nifties began to appear from nowhere, "so much nicer" than those on the racks. A handwritten note from Claire and an occasional discreet phone call were all that was necessary—no money, not even a charge plate changed hands.

To have literally nothing and to be offered her choice of everything was frightening. She wanted almost everything she touched, but she felt a growing obligation to the Devereaux', to Michael. With each exhilarating new possession came a feeling that she was selling a piece of her freedom, a pair of shoes, a dress, an eyeliner at a time. The spree ended in a drugstore, where she bought the basics. Even a toothbrush and a comb seemed to Laurel a priceless treasure, an extravagant bottle of foaming bath oil the most precious of all.

"You could have had some of this delivered," Claire pointed out as they staggered back to the car, both loaded with packages and the car already heaped with previous deposits. She hadn't done justice to Janet's list, but even so it had been hard to leave behind those few things that had to be altered. She still wore her own clothes as if putting off a little longer her commitment to being Laurel Devereaux.

Claire Bently's thin lips maintained their tight disapproval as she drove home. But Laurel decided to try to pump her for information anyway. Perhaps if she knew more she would remember something of what had happened.

43

"How long have you worked for the Devereaux'?"

"I've been here nine years."

"That long? Then you were here when . . . when Jimmy came. Have you always taken care of him?"

"We tried some nurses at first, but they kept leaving. I'm Professor Devereaux's secretary, but I started helping with Jimmy and lately I've done nothing else. You can't imagine the surprise he was to all of us." Claire giggled nervously and without humor, a loud irritating sound she often made for no apparent reason, as some people unconsciously clear their throats out of habit rather than need.

"You didn't know Michael had a child?"

"Child? We didn't even know he was married."

"Did he bring Jimmy to Tucson from Denver?"

"Of course not. How could he? He was in Vietnam." Claire looked away from traffic to search Laurel's face. "He hasn't told you what happened after you left, has he?"

"No." She'd left her child while the father was in Vietnam. What had happened to make her do such a thing?

"Well, *I'll* tell you. Michael and Professor Devereaux had an argument about Michael's entering the Air Force. But Michael went off anyway, and we heard very little from him for about three years." Claire's speech was like her driving, full of nervous spurts of speed and interspersed with slower phrases when she attempted sophistication.

"Then all of a sudden we get a phone call from Vietnam and it's Michael. We had no idea he was seeing any action. But that wasn't what the call was about. Michael said that he was married and the Red Cross had notified him that his wife had had a baby and then walked out of the hospital and disappeared."

"I left Jimmy in the hospital . . . a newborn?" No wonder Michael was so furious with her.

"You know very well what you did. Don't try any of that 'I don't remember' stuff on me."

"Then what happened?"

44

"All I know is that Michael said your parents wouldn't take the baby and would we please take care of him until he got home."

"My parents?"

"Yes, they went to Denver to try to find out what had happened and then your mother brought Jimmy to us. Your mother was in tears. I think she wanted Jimmy, but your father would have nothing more to do with anything that would remind him of you. You can hardly blame him."

"When did all this happen? I . . . I've lost track of time."

"Jimmy will be two in June, which is a strange thing to be telling his own mother."

It was too much. She'd been gone almost two years. She now had two parents she couldn't remember and had deserted a newborn baby in the hospital while its father was halfway around the world in a war. . . . The one hope she could cling to was that she might not be Laurel.

After dinner she stood in the middle of a litter of packages and tried to comprehend what Claire had said. Why would Laurel leave her baby that way? What had happened since? *Am I Laurel?* It just didn't seem possible. And it didn't explain the danger that lurked in the corners of her mind, that refused to come out of hiding so that she could identify it. She felt so helpless not knowing in which direction to look for a menace she couldn't even describe.

The throbbing in her head drove her to action and she hung dress after dress in the empty wardrobe that stood against the wall. Another across the room held Michael's clothes. She filled drawers with lingerie, depressed at the wastefulness of a vanity that had told her she really needed every item.

How can I feel guilt about my extravagance and feel only numb about what I did to that child? She washed her hair again, this time with a creamy shampoo.

If I am Laurel, I'd feel ashamed of that desertion whenever I looked at him. Stifling an urge to go in to see if he was covered for the night, she lay back in a hot bath, scented bubbles filling it to the brim. She couldn't seem to get enough sleep or enough scrubbing. Was she trying to wash away dirt or guilt?

It was then that the obvious hit her and she sat up in the tub spilling frothy bubbles over its edge. *I must be Laurel! Why else would I have had Michael Devereaux's name on that piece of paper?*

The next morning she stepped again onto the thick carpeting of the staircase, but not so hesitantly as the morning before. Could the indescribable thing she'd feared then have been in her mind? Was it in this house because she had brought it with her? That made her even more uneasy than the thought of a danger outside herself. Or had her nerves quieted a little because she knew Michael Devereaux was not here?

This time her thoughts engaged her attention so completely that she didn't see the shadow near the upright chest in the corner by the salon doors until it moved.

4

The shadow detached itself from the shadow of the chest and became a man. He was almost to the doors that led out of the house when she must have made some sound, for he whirled to face her.

He looked as startled as she felt, his hand suspended toward the doorknob but not quite touching it, her foot suspended above the next step.

He finally lowered his arm and shrugged. "Hi."

Her foot settled on the step. She moved to the bottom of the staircase expecting him to dart out the door, but he stood so still he didn't seem to be breathing. His mustache curled down at the corners around his mouth instead of up like Paul's.

"Hi," he said again with more of a nervous twitch than a smile.

"Who are you? What do you want here?" She still had her hand on the banister, ready to turn and race back up the stairs.

"What?" He looked confused and suddenly boyish.

He's more afraid than I am! This thought made her slightly braver, but still the dull throb in her head sharpened and millions of tiny pins pricked her skin. "Who are you?" she repeated a little more gently this time. "What do you want?"

"What do I wa . . . oh . . . well. . . ."

"Do come in," Claire said behind her, as if she owned the place. And the secretary swept down the stairs to the man by

47

the door, ignoring Laurel completely. "I expect you're here to interview."

"Interview. . . ." he looked even more confused and glanced at Laurel as if for assistance. His face reddened.

"For the job in the lab."

"The job . . . yes," he said to Claire, but his eyes were still on Laurel, two vertical furrows creasing his forehead.

"Have you had experience in lab work before?"

"A summer job in a medical research laboratory is all . . . took care of animals and cleaned up . . . things like that. I have a reference."

"Good. Well, come along then." Claire started across the hall. "You're certainly quick. Professor Devereaux just placed the ad yesterday."

"I need work." He followed Claire. Soft, rather shy hazel eyes probed Laurel's as he passed her.

"It doesn't pay much, I'm afraid, and it's only temporary. . . ." They disappeared into the inner courtyard.

Laurel stood staring at the sunburst, not seeing it. That young man had been sneaking *out* of the house. And if he'd come for a job, why did he look at her in that odd way?

They ate lunch, as before, near the fountain where the hideous creature endlessly drooled water. Paul ate hurriedly with one eye on the papers by his plate. He looked up at Laurel once with annoyance but didn't speak. Finishing before anyone else was half done, he carefully placed the papers in a folder and turned to his wife.

"If you see a strange face around here, Janet, don't be alarmed. I've hired a young man to assist me in the laboratory. Just cleaning up, filing, feeding the animals and so on. He starts tomorrow. His name is Evan Boucher. And I've asked Consuela to prepare lunch for one more on weekdays. He'll leave before dinner. Now, if you'll excuse me, ladies, I've. . . ." Paul rose quickly but not quickly enough.

"You hired *what?*" The husky quality in Janet's voice held a potential roar.

48

"A lab assistant. With Claire so busy elsewhere, I am in dire need of help in the. . . ."

"You mean you're sinking more money into that ridiculous hobby of yours?"

"It is a profession, *not* a hobby. And I'll thank you to remember that." Paul stalked off across the courtyard, and Laurel heard a door slam violently behind her.

She looked at her plate and tried not to smirk. Wouldn't it be funny if he had hired a burglar? That was his problem. No one here would be interested in her suspicions anyway.

"Really, Mrs. Devereaux, your husband is a noted authority. . . ."

"Rubbish, Claire." Janet pushed her salad aside. "Evan what's-his-name will be just another mouth to feed." She turned to Laurel and the contempt in her eyes did not diminish. "At least you're looking more presentable today. Don't you think so, Claire?"

"I think she's overdone it." And the familiar flush brightened Claire's sallow complexion.

"Nonsense. A little grooming and decent clothes have transformed our ragamuffin into a rather enchanting picture. She's even managed to put some order into all that hair. I can't help wondering what a little polishing would do for you, Claire."

"Polishing the outside does not make up for what's inside, Mrs. Devereaux." Claire glanced at Laurel with self-righteous distaste.

"Oh, I see. You parade around with your hair half-combed, no makeup, and such dreary clothes because it proves something about your inside? How fascinating."

Laurel felt uneasy. These women didn't like each other and they didn't like her. "I wanted to thank you for the clothes . . . and everything."

"Oh, don't thank me. I shall present the bills to dear Michael. He can pay the piper for something around here."

Laurel stayed in the courtyard, soaking in the warm sun

49

long after the others had left. If she went to her room she might meet Jimmy again, and she wasn't ready for that—not just yet.

Consuela came out of the kitchen drying her hands on the black bib-apron that always covered her black dress. "Mrs. Michael, would you like for me to show you the house?"

"Yes, if you have time."

"Come, I show you."

The old woman moved with dignity despite her heavy body. Laurel was surprised to find Consuela as tall as she was herself. Some of the rooms she had seen before. The salon and the study were across the entry hall from a smaller sitting room and a formal dining room where there was an extension of the balcony that ran the width of the house. So many stairs and perilous balconies. Claire must have to watch her charge closely. Those four large rooms and the entry hall that divided them composed the first floor of the front of the house. The rest was one-room deep and two stories around the courtyard, many of the rooms accessible only from the courtyard.

Everything was placed to show off the rooms and their contents to the best advantage—to be looked at rather than for convenience or comfort. And Laurel wondered where Jimmy played, where he was allowed to run free.

The tour was a selected one, Consuela passing many closed doors without comment. Laurel had a feeling that the housekeeper was hurrying through it because she was leading up to something.

Next to the study off the courtyard was Paul's laboratory, where furry little animals slept in cages against the wall and small cacti sat in pots near the window. A door that led to the outside of the house was open and she could see Paul on his knees examining the base of a tall cactus with arms like those she had seen that first morning in the desert.

"Claire said Mr. Devereaux was a professor. A professor of what, Consuela?"

50

"Of the desert."

"Isn't that a rather wide specialty?"

"I don't know about these things. But he writes many books and keeps poor little animals away from their mothers and dirty bugs he keeps in there. He plants things inside that would grow better outside."

"Does he teach?"

But Consuela was hurrying her on her way. There were stone stairways at all four corners of the inner courtyard leading to the upper balconies. The back section of the house was mostly garages, and Consuela led her past them and up a stairway to a door which she unlocked.

"This is a place that I wanted for you to see, Mrs. Michael . . . so that maybe you would understand." Consuela's eyes were still expressionless as they studied her face, but there was something watchful about her. This must be what she'd been leading to.

"Understand what?"

"Come and see." The old woman stood aside for her to enter.

Laurel's first impression was that this was a storeroom for broken furniture. Dusty pieces of chairs, picture frames, wooden cabinets, and a table lay on the floor. She soon realized that it was instead a scene of ugly destruction. How could there be such a room in a house like this?

A drum with a jagged hole in its center . . . a battered toy truck lying on its side . . . books torn from their covers and scattered . . . a barred dirty window, the lower pane replaced with boards.

The room darkened as Consuela closed the door and locked it. And Laurel felt smothered in the dry, dusty air.

"Consuela, what is this place? I don't like it. Unlock the door."

Consuela lowered her heavy body into the one chair still intact, a wicker rocker that creaked as she rocked. "Here, sit." She motioned to the single bed which sagged at one corner. "Before you leave I want you to know of this. This was the nursery. He did it with an ax; he cried afterward and then he screamed. We had to call a doctor to quiet him . . . oh, poor baby." Tears dripped over pudgy cheeks. "Mr. Paul and I . . . we had to hold him until the doctor came."

"Are you trying to tell me that Jimmy did all this? He couldn't possibly. . . ."

"No, not Jimmy. Jimmy's father."

"Michael?"

"He was only ten, my poor Michael . . . such a big strong boy . . . his brother would not let me clean it up. He would bring him here and make him look at it when Michael was bad . . . then Michael grew too big to be forced to come . . . and now no one comes here." So much emotion in her voice, so little on her face, just the wetness of tears.

"Why did he . . . do this?" There was something wrong with a child who would do such a thing, and she thought of the burning metallic eyes against the dark skin.

"Because of the death of his mother. Did he never tell you of her death?"

"If he did I don't remember."

"My Maria and Mr. Devereaux and Michael were coming home one night in the car . . . and there was an accident. Maria, my lovely Maria . . . she died . . . and poor Michael was there and saw it. He was not hurt bad . . . a few scratches. He loved his mother. He was only ten."

"Mr. Devereaux—was he killed, too?"

"No, but for many months he was in the hospital. He was a big man. So handsome and full of spirit. But after he came home from the hospital he was never well. He grieved so for my Maria, he became suddenly an old man."

Sunlight filtered through what was left of the dirty pane and dust speckles floated through abandoned cobwebs.

"Your Maria?"

"I raised her from a little girl. I worked in her father's house and then she brought me here when she married Mr.

Devereaux." Rolls of loose flesh sagged from the house-keeper's arm as she raised it to wipe her cheek with her hand.

"Paul wasn't along when it happened?"

"They never took him with them. He was always in his books, that one. Maria did not like him."

"Her own son?"

"Oh, no. They were the same age, Maria and Paul. Paul was her stepson. His mother died before we came to this house. There is twenty years between Paul and Michael. Paul, he was never strong or big. He did not like to hunt or do man things with his father. When Michael came, his father was so proud of such a big healthy boy who could do such things. And Maria would sit in this chair and rock her baby, and she would play with him when he got older. They were so good together, those two."

"Consuela, why did you bring me here and tell me this?"

The old woman got up from her chair and unlocked the door. "Because you are Mrs. Michael and you should know what he can do when he is hurt inside. And because you too are a mother."

Laurel was glad to return to the sun. She felt cold.

5

The rest of the week went by with little comment about her dark past. They waited and watched her. Through it all—Janet's bickering, Paul's stuffiness, Claire's disdain—Laurel knew they were watching her and waiting for Michael.

He was due home for the weekend and it would be left to him to force the issue. Whenever she saw Consuela, she thought of the dusty debris in the old nursery and felt panicky at the thought of Michael's return.

The new lab assistant joined them for lunch in the courtyard. Even he watched her, fumbling with his silverware, looking away when she stared back. She grew to loathe salads. As she slept less it became more difficult to avoid Jimmy and her own thoughts. Her memory refused to budge, and everything she learned about herself made her hate this Laurel the more. She began to think of herself as having two identities—herself as she wanted to be and this Laurel everyone thought she was.

But Jimmy was the hardest to bear. At first he just seemed curious, but she soon suspected he was looking for a friend. His lot was not easy in this magnificent house with only adults for company. His needs were seen to, but he was expected to find love and companionship from toys too old for him and a TV set. Claire spent most of her time scolding him. Janet and Paul ignored him.

One afternoon she found Consuela rocking Jimmy in his room. There was no rocking chair so the old woman sat on the bed rocking her body back and forth, crooning something gentle in Spanish. And Jimmy who sprawled on her ample

54

lap, a thumb in his mouth, the other hand stroking her dress, gazed sleepily up at her face and looked as though this was all the heaven he would ever need. Laurel couldn't sleep that night.

Friday morning as she walked along the inside hall, she heard an enraged scream from Janet's room at the head of the stairs.

"Claire! Get that child out of here."

And Jimmy came running out the door his eyes wide and his plump little face white with terror. Laurel caught him before he could reach the stairs. He shivered in her arms but didn't cry.

Janet stood in the doorway and Laurel was startled at the change in her appearance. She wore a filmy peignoir, but her hair was in a net, a greasy mixture smeared over her face and a strap under her chin. She was a sight to scare any child.

"Don't you ever come into this room again, brat!" The strap made her speak through her teeth with a nasty hissing sound.

"Please, he's only a baby. You've scared him half to death. He could have tumbled down those stairs and...."

"Oh, gone all motherly, have you? Well it's more than a little late. Claire has orders to keep that ... child out of my way. I don't want to hear him, see him, or even think about him."

"But he's your nephew."

"Is he?" Janet sent her a knowing grimace and closed the door on them.

Laurel looked at Jimmy. He really didn't resemble his father much. She pushed the ugly thought from her mind; she had more than she could handle already.

She awoke early Saturday morning, her first thought that Michael would be coming home. He'd want to know what she'd been doing for the last two years and she wouldn't be able to tell him, and God only knew what he'd do then. A woman who'd deserted her baby couldn't have been up to much good. *God, I'm scared.* Her only hope was that she wasn't Laurel. She had no proof of this, just a feeling.

As she dressed she stood before one of the barred windows by the bed, the bars reminding her of another problem. Would they send her to prison for deserting a child she couldn't remember having? But no one would believe that she couldn't remember. Would a doctor be able to prove it? Would the Devereaux' pay for a doctor to cure an amnesia they didn't believe in? A cure might prove beyond a doubt that she *was* this hateful Laurel Devereaux. It might also identify the nagging thing she feared. She was afraid to regain her memory . . . and she was afraid not to.

Just before lunch Laurel sat on the stone edge of the fountain, trying hard to think of nothing at all, watching sunlight glimmer on the clear water as it ringed beneath the dripping jaws of the creature.

She looked up and Michael Devereaux walked across the flagstone toward her.

He walked with a rapid smoothness, a flowing control that brought him up to her with startling suddenness. She knew it was partly her fear of him that made him look so big in the black sweater.

"I see you're still here." He rested one foot on the ledge beside her and gazed down at the water. "Have you called your parents?"

"No." She realized she'd been holding her breath.

"You don't think they'd be interested to learn you've rejoined the world?"

"I . . . suppose I should call. . . ." She could sense the contempt under the gruff sarcasm in his voice and it added to her uneasiness.

"But you don't want to. You don't care a damn for anyone, do you?" He had a slight stoop to his shoulders she hadn't noticed before.

The anger in his half-lidded eyes had given way to cold indifference. She knew he was going to ask about the last two years, and she knew that either truth or evasion would bring back the fury. She was too afraid to lie.

Just then Jimmy came screeching from the kitchen, some of his lunch still on his face. When he saw his father, he did a mid-run left turn.

"Hi, Daddy."

Laurel felt reprieved as she watched the big body stoop to catch the small one and lift him onto broad shoulders with unexpected gentleness.

"Michael, be careful with him." Claire appeared in the kitchen doorway.

"He's a big boy, Claire. Aren't you, slugger?"

Jimmy drummed little fists on Michael's head.

"You two ruffians, honestly." Claire laughed as she joined them and they walked off, excluding Laurel as though she didn't exist.

A stranger would have thought them a happy family group—Jimmy on his father's shoulders going up the stairs—Claire fussing about, reaching up to pull Jimmy's pants leg down, touching Michael with a familiar nonchalance. And Laurel felt resentment. Her situation was impossible. No one wanted her or needed her here. They had been happy enough before she came.

That afternoon she lay on the big bed trying to make up a plausible story for the last two years. Michael had not brought it up at lunch, but he would. His clothes were gone from the wardrobe so she didn't have to worry about his sleeping here. But she must have a story, a story that would hold up in court as well. She worked on it until her head ached, tossing on the bed until the cover was rumpled. Everything she thought of sounded just as silly as the truth.

If I had someplace to go, I'd just leave. No one would really care. They'd be relieved to get rid of her. She couldn't be any more miserable someplace else or more degraded. *It's awful being Laurel!*

The sounds from the courtyard had been providing a faint

background for her thoughts for some time. It gradually intruded on her senses—the sound of splashing water.

Jimmy's scream brought her off the bed and to the door. She was on the balcony and then running down the stairs before she saw them in the pool.

Jimmy clutched Michael around the neck, his blond head thrown back, pudgy legs trying to crawl up his father's chest away from the water. Claire stood a few feet away in what looked like a black tank suit.

"For Christ's sake, settle down. Now, go to Claire. Just relax and let yourself float." Michael had to force the child's arms from around his neck and then pushed him toward Claire.

"Consayla." Jimmy choked down water before he reached the safety of Claire's arms.

"Now turn him around and send him back."

By the time she reached the edge of the blue pool Laurel's panic had turned to anger. "What are you doing?"

"I'm teaching my son to swim, obviously. Come on, Jimmy. You're doing fine." Beads of water clung to the black hair on his chest and arms.

"He's too young. Look at him. He's terrified."

"Consayla." And the sobbing child was passed back to his father, turned around, and sent skimming back to Claire.

"If he's going to live here, he'd better learn to swim."

"He's not even two. Stop it!"

"I was swimming by the time I was one." Michael hoisted Jimmy out of the water onto the flagstone. "That's all for now, son." He lifted himself out of the pool in one quick graceful movement, dripping water on Laurel as she knelt to pick up Jimmy.

She wrapped him in a towel and held him close. "Hush, baby, hush."

Michael stopped toweling himself and watched her, cocking

his head to one side. "Is there really a mother instinct in you, Laurel? Or is this for show?" The soft irony was back in the deep voice.

"I feel sorry for him. Anybody would—poor kid." She stared back with all the defiance she could muster. *I hate this man*, she told herself and then looked away. She didn't like the word "hate."

Claire had covered her ugly swimsuit with a towel; she had thick legs for a woman her size. "Come on, sweety. Claire will find some warm dry clothes for you," she said, taking Jimmy from Laurel and walking off with him. Laurel had never heard Claire call him anything but "bad boy" before.

"Let's get one thing straight, Laurel. There will be no interference between Jimmy and me. You walked out on that right two years ago." Michael followed Claire across the flagstone.

I've got to get out of here. Laurel fled to the shadows of the arcade and almost stepped on Evan Boucher.

"Hi." He wore a lab coat over rumpled blue jeans. His soft hazel eyes watched her expectantly.

"Is that the only word you know?"

Evan blushed and looked down at his dirty tennis shoes.

"I thought you were supposed to be in the lab." She hadn't been very nice to this boy, but she didn't trust him.

"I heard the kid screaming and came out to see what was the matter."

"And saw the whole thing, I suppose?" Laurel sat in a wicker chair and looked across the courtyard. Michael walked along the balcony and stopped outside Jimmy's room to watch them.

"Yeah. You don't seem to be everybody's favorite member of the family." He sat in the chair next to hers and she saw him stiffen when he noticed Michael. "How come your husband's so mad at you?" When she didn't answer he leaned

59

toward her and whispered, "Mrs. Devereaux, I know it's none of my business, but if you need help. . . ."

"Help?" Laurel giggled and then laughed. "From you?" Michael turned abruptly and stepped into Jimmy's room. "Do you think I'd go for help to someone who sneaks around other people's houses?"

"Sneaks. . . ?"

"You were sneaking out of the house when I met you the other morning, not walking in to see about a job."

"Oh, that." He sighed and leaned back in the chair. "I did come about the job, but, you're right, I was leaving when you saw me." Evan's shy smile moved the drooping corners of his mustache out. "I climbed that wall first thing in the morning so's I'd be the earliest to apply, and when I got to the door, nobody answered it, but it moved a little and I saw it wasn't locked . . . I peeked in . . . everything was so grand . . . I'd just never seen anything like this house before except in movies . . . please, don't tell anybody. I just looked in one room, I swear it—the one with all the couches and chairs and velvet drapes—and I just stood in the door."

"But why were you leaving?" He looked so sheepish, she half believed him.

"I realized the place was too much . . . you know what I mean? It was too grand for Evan Boucher, and I thought of what would happen if I got caught like that and I just chickened, I guess. And then you did catch me . . . when I saw you . . . please don't be offended, Mrs. Devereaux, but I've never seen anything like you before either."

Now they were both blushing.

"And then Miss Bently came along and . . . what else could I do? But Professor Devereaux's a nice old guy; I'm glad I stayed now." Although he'd let it grow to his shirt collar, his brown hair curled and waved around his face and gave him a boyish look. "But you haven't answered my question. Can I help you somehow?"

Laurel found herself smiling at him for the first time. His

60

story sounded silly enough to be true and not nearly as silly as her own. "Not unless you're a doctor, Evan Boucher."

"Are you sick?"

"I must be. My total memory of my life starts exactly six days ago." Laurel expected to shock him but he just nodded casually.

"Oh, amnesia. I wondered."

"Don't pretend that you believe it," she said bitterly. "Nobody would. I don't expect you to."

"Oh, I believe it."

"You do?"

"Sure. It happens sometimes. I should know."

She leaned toward him. "Have you had amnesia?"

"No, but I worked in an institution a year or so ago and they had a whole wing of just people . . . who couldn't remember."

"An institution. . . ."

"Yeah. I was an orderly type. But I didn't stay long. I couldn't take it . . . you have to be. . . ."

"What did they do to them . . . the people who couldn't remember?"

"Oh, hey. I didn't mean to scare you. They didn't mistreat them . . . just tried to help them remember . . . kept them there until they did . . . I better get back to my job . . . I seem to be making you feel worse . . . I always say the wrong things." He stood and almost tripped over his own tennis shoes in embarrassment. "My feet are as clumsy as my mouth."

"Evan, how long did those people have to stay there?"

"Some just a little while—few months—and others never did get out . . . sometimes it depends on whether your family wants you back. Good place to get rid of people you don't want hanging around." He laughed and his mustache straightened a trifle and then drooped as he sobered suddenly. "I . . . did it again, didn't I?"

"Yes, you did."

61

He shook his head and then slapped himself on the forehead. "Look, forget what I said. What do *I* know? Those people had wonderful treatment, honest."

Laurel walked slowly out into the sunlight to get warm and then just kept walking. She could hear Evan's plea behind her but she didn't turn.

"Please, it's not you. It's me. I always say the wrong things to the right people . . . Mrs. Devereaux? Oh . . . hell."

That night Laurel prowled. She put a coat over her nightgown and walked the covered walkways where hanging palms and leafy vines made weird silhouettes on the walls in the moonlight and the twisted trees in the courtyard created moving, menacing shadows. There seemed to be no darkness in this desert world with the harsh sun in the day and the moon at night sending its eerie glow through barred windows and wide archways. There seemed no place to hide in darkness and to nurse jangled nerves.

It was cold and the pool steamed, the steam wisping and writhing in the moonlight as if from a witch's caldron. She paced back and forth beside it, tense and writhing inside like the steam. She couldn't bear to stay here but couldn't think of any place to go. Evan Boucher had offered help, but she dismissed him. Whether he was a fumbly lovesick kid or a house burglar, he wouldn't be much help. She still couldn't bring herself to trust him. Her parents had been cruel enough to disown her and she didn't know them anyway. *It's hopeless.*

She walked toward the recess of the garages at the back of the courtyard, and in a corner under the stone steps that led to the old nursery was a door she had noticed before but never opened. A thick wooden door like all the doors in this house, but locked. A large old-fashioned key of wrought iron was still in the lock. The key turned easily and the door opened to the outside world, a world she'd scarcely seen since she'd entered this house and become Laurel Devereaux.

Laurel pocketed the key and closed the door behind her. The house was built on the slope of a hill and the city of Tucson spread out on the valley floor below her, its lights snapping like stars in the clear night, dark jagged peaks rising up behind it on the far side of the valley.

Below her she could see the patio of another lush home with a steamy pool. She'd forgotten how close the rest of the world was, once inside this self-contained house at her back.

The hill rose steeply behind the house and the giant branched cacti marched widely spaced to the top, their ghostly profiles standing out on the skyline. Toward the front of the house a chain link fence that must have been ten feet high enclosed an area of desert outside Paul's laboratory and sloped down the hill almost to the drive of the house below.

Rustling noises on the hill around her gave Laurel the creepy feeling that unfriendly night eyes watched her. She turned back to the door. And then a measured thumping from within the house caught her attention.

Not far from the door the ground fell away to expose a subbasement and another barred window that opened into a lighted room. She had to stoop slightly to see into it and wondered who else was awake.

She was looking down into a gymnasium with mats, barbells, hanging ropes, and a trampoline that thumped each time Michael came down on it. He had removed his shoes and the coat he'd worn at dinner. White shirt sleeves were rolled to his elbows and straight black hair flopped against his forehead as he landed. Keeping his eyes on the taut canvas beneath him, he measured each jump with a precision that brought him down at almost the same spot as before.

He rose higher each time, his head rising level with the window and then above it, his arms flung out for balance. She could see the sweat-soaked patch of shirt between his shoulder blades as he twisted and landed to face the opposite direction. He leaped again and twisted so that he was facing her, his lips pulled back to expose his teeth as he gasped in air.

On the next leap he brought his knees up to his chest and somersaulted, landing on his feet. Again and again and faster until the veins at his temples pushed out at the skin, and Laurel's pulse raced. He was a powerful man and an angry one and here was another release for a violent temper.

She could stand no more and turned to the door, her head thumping with the trampoline. She had one hope left, a small one. Harley. He wasn't much, but he was all the friend she had in the world and she had to get out of this house and away from Michael Devereaux.

6

"He ain't here." Raymond McBride sounded as though he were used to receiving calls for Harley and didn't like it much.

"Do you know where I might reach him?" Laurel spoke softly on the upstairs telephone.

"I don't know where he is. He should be in late this afternoon though."

"I'll call back about four. Will you ask him to wait for my call?"

"Well, I'll ask, but I can't promise with Harley. Who should I say called?"

"Laurel . . . no . . . just say Doe Eyes. He'll know. Thank you, Mr. McBride." She hung up before he could ask any more questions.

It was Sunday morning and she'd watched Paul, Michael, and Jimmy go off to mass. Claire had taken another car to her church. She didn't know where Janet was, probably getting her beauty sleep. It had been a perfect time to talk to Harley and she was disappointed not to have found him at the motel. There'd been no reason to think he would be there, but the motel was her only contact with him. She'd have to take her chances and hope to get a phone call out secretly that afternoon.

Laurel didn't know how she would talk Harley into coming to Tucson for her. There was the fifty dollars that Paul had given her for spending money, a preciously small stake for a new start but maybe she'd offer him some of it.

She was jumpy the rest of the day and especially through dinner, an elaborate but quiet affair in the small dining room. It was served about two-thirty. There were two brass candlesticks on the table, their candles unlit. Laurel worried about spilling on the red and gold brocaded tablecloth that looked as if it should be hanging at the windows instead of covering the table. She fidgeted like a child in the uncomfortable high-backed chair and tried to take courage in the fact that this was the last such ordeal she'd have to endure.

Paul discussed some family business with Michael, something about withholding land from a proposed subdivision. Their voices sounded strangely hollow in the high-ceilinged room, Paul's thin nervous tenor contrasting with Michael's rumbling bass. Janet was not up to her usual snide chatter. She picked at her food and secretly watched Michael. And so did Claire.

Laurel had to admit that he possessed a certain magnetism that attracted female eyes—his deep voice, his effortless assurance. And yet an occasionally abrupt movement as he reached for his glass or rubbed his forehead gave her an impression of violence, of energy barely contained. She wondered what it was that had attracted her to him once, the exotic good looks or the hint of danger about him that frightened her now? Out of the corners of her eyes she watched as his long fingers unconsciously twisted and untwisted the cloth napkin on his lap. What had it been like to sleep with him? *I must not be Laurel. I can't even imagine what it would be like.*

After dinner the family congregated in the warm sun of the courtyard. Michael and Claire played with Jimmy, throwing a ball for him to catch. Janet and Paul sat near the fountain and watched. Laurel wandered off and no one paid her much attention.

Once inside she slipped into the library where there was a clock on the mantelpiece. It was already 4:10! She decided

66

to use the phone on the desk where she could watch them through the glass doors that led to the courtyard.

She'd obtained the number of the "Sunny Rest" that morning from Phoenix information, and she put the second call through quickly. Raymond answered and she asked for Harley. The hand that held the phone trembled.

"Harley? Yeah, he's here. Harley, I think it's the dame that called this morning."

"Doe Eyes? I knew you couldn't forget me—they never do."

"Harley, this is serious. I need help." She pictured the good-natured grin with relief.

"What'd you do—get lost again?"

"No, I'm in Tucson and I have to get away. Harley, could you . . . would you come to Tucson tonight?"

"Tucson! That guy who came to get you live in Tucson? Devereaux?" He didn't sound as if he was grinning now.

"Yes. Harley, I can't talk now, but I have to get away."

"Why don't you just leave?"

"It's not that simple. I don't know anyone but you and the Devereaux'. Will you come? About midnight?"

"Look at it from my angle, Doe Eyes—this all sounds kind of weird. You know? You're going to have to tell me who you are and what this is all about."

"They tell me I'm Laurel Devereaux, Michael's wife. The rest I'll explain. . . ."

"What do you mean they tell you—don't you know?"

"Harley, I can't explain it now; I will tonight—please come."

He swore in a perfectly audible whisper and then chuckled. "I'm a fool but . . . okay. Never let it be said I passed up a chance to do the Devereaux' dirt. Where do I meet you?"

"Outside the wall, on the road in front of the house. Do you think you can find the house?"

"I know where it is. I'll park the truck down the road and

walk up. Never thought I'd get mixed up with a Devereaux woman. Wait a minute, I thought you didn't know them. You were asking all those questions about. . . ."

"I have to hang up now. Harley, please be here tonight."

They were all walking across the courtyard toward her, Michael carrying Jimmy on his shoulders. Consuela had joined them.

When they came in she was in the entry hall and everyone but Laurel said good-bye to Michael as he left for the base. He didn't even look at her. He brushed Consuela's forehead with his lips, hugged his son and was gone. It took Consuela to quiet Jimmy's sobbing.

That night Laurel filled a purse with a comb, a toothbrush, a tube of toothpaste, a lipstick, and the money Paul had given her. After changing into slacks, a sweater, flat shoes, and a warm jacket, she paced the big bedroom, waiting for midnight. She'd take no more of what belonged to the Devereaux' than she had to. She didn't need all those luxurious clothes. Wherever she was going, she wouldn't be dressing for dinner. The only thing she regretted leaving behind was the bottle of foaming bath oil, too large to fit into her purse.

Cautiously opening the door to the hallway, she peered at the clock on the wall above the telephone. It was only eleven. She took off the jacket and sat on the bed to wait it out.

She felt excited and yet depressed. It would be such a relief to get away from these people, from Michael. What she was doing was wrong. But everyone would be happier if she left and she'd be happier. Could it be so wrong to make people happy? Michael obviously didn't want her and Claire obviously wanted Michael. Well, she could have him. *Although what he can see in her, I don't know.*

And Jimmy would be better off without her. He had Consuela and his father to love him, Claire to take care of him, and a wealthy family to see that he would never want for anything. He definitely did not need a mixed-up mother.

68

*Besides, I'm not convinced I am his mother. And I'm scared
to death of his father. It wouldn't work out, ever.*

She started pacing the room again. *I don't want to be
Laurel. Laurel is no good . . . walking out on her own baby . .
. I don't want to be her!*

She found herself facing the double mirrors over the dresser
and the image she would never get used to. There was an
adolescent pout about her lips that she didn't like. Was it the
sophistication of makeup or had the once-blank expression in
her eyes grown wary and suspicious? *Look what they've done
to me in just a week.* She was beginning to look like a . . . a
Laurel . . . immature, selfish. *I could swear I didn't look like
this a week ago.*

On a hunch and to pass the time she began searching the
drawers of the dresser, most of them filled with the clothes
she had bought in Tucson. Two were empty. She looked
about the room. If Michael had kept any mementoes of
Laurel, they had probably been moved with his things. In the
carved wooden commode table by the bed there was nothing
but a small box containing rosary beads. He probably
wouldn't keep any hateful reminder of Laurel.

The wardrobe that Michael had used had two drawers
beneath and room above for hanging clothes. The drawers
were empty and she had to stand on the floor of the upper
section to reach to the back of the shelf above the hangers.
There were two shoe boxes in one corner, and she pulled
them out and laid them on the floor. Kneeling beside them,
she wiped the dust from her hands onto the red rug.

The first box held a small assortment of mementoes. She
felt guilty prying into Michael's life this way. A certificate of
graduation from a Catholic academy, another from the
School of Engineering at the University of Arizona, Tucson.
A yellowed newspaper clipping with a picture of a man and a
boy in a rubber raft on swirling water with the caption,
PAUL ELLIOT DEVEREAUX I AND SON MICHAEL 9
SHOOT RAPIDS ON COLORADO RIVER. The picture was

69

taken from a distance, and one could not recognize the figures without the caption. There were two small model airplanes, one with a broken wing.

Laurel opened the second box and found three rings, a billfold, and a woman's watch. She put all three rings in the palm of her hand. They were white gold or platinum, two bands and an impressive solitaire diamond, emerald cut. Laurel's wedding and engagement rings and Michael's wedding band. The diamond and the smaller band fit her ring finger. She slipped them off quickly and picked up the billfold.

There was a quarter and a penny in one pocket but no bills. The plastic fold-out held a sober picture of a younger Michael, a Standard Oil Credit Card, a Colorado drivers' license made out to Laurel Jean Devereaux with a colored picture of a woman's head. It could be a picture of her; she wasn't sure. The dark hair was short and long bangs came down to the eyebrows. Other details listed told her Laurel was 5 feet 6 inches, weighed 118 pounds, had brown hair and eyes, and had applied for the license three years before. The birth date would make her twenty-eight. *I feel younger than twenty-eight.*

She looked hard at the picture of a heavy woman with graying hair and glasses in a blue sweater. Laurel's mother? A Denver Public Library card. Another card from the State University of Iowa, Iowa City, Iowa . . . "This is to certify that Laurel Jean Lawrence was granted the degree of Bachelor of Arts; Major Area: History."

Lawrence . . . Laurel Jean Lawrence . . . Iowa City, Iowa. Even this did not stir her memory. Next on the fold-out was a Social Security card made out to Laurel J. Devereaux and last was an identification card from the Denver Public Schools allowing Laurel Jean Lawrence into school functions free of charge as a teacher.

She slipped out the Social Security card, put everything else back in the box, replaced the boxes on the shelf, and put on

70

her jacket. Laurel majored in history at Iowa and taught school in Denver before she married Michael. Her maiden name was Lawrence. *And I don't remember any of this.* If she were Laurel some of what she'd learned would bring back memories, surely. She couldn't be twenty-eight years old. But she might be able to use that Social Security card in a pinch.

A check of the clock in the hall told her it was a quarter to twelve. She turned off the lights and went to the door that led onto the balcony. With her hand on the knob, she hesitated, glancing reluctantly over her shoulder to the door of Jimmy's room. One last look.

The night lamp was on and her eyes went immediately to the picture over the bed. The woman in the picture had always seemed to stare at her, but now as she walked to the foot of the bed to look closer she realized that the Madonna was instead gazing down at the near-naked child in her arms. The face of the mother and body of the child stood out flesh-colored on the otherwise dark blues of the canvas.

She moved to the crib and covered Jimmy. He seemed to have grown so in just the week she'd been there, this baby changing so quickly into a little boy. Gently, she brushed the fine damp hair from his forehead and touched the soft cheek. What would he look like when he lost the roundness from his face? Would he have freckles? His mouth was open and a wet thumb had slipped out.

She hated to do this to him. She didn't know if she was Laurel or someone else. Either way she was no good for him. He was looking for a friend, but what he needed was a real mother. *I hope you find some happiness in life . . . God, let him be happy . . . somehow. None of this is his fault.*

Although Laurel knew it wasn't so, the Madonna still seemed to stare accusingly at her back as she left the room.

Crying softly, she crossed the courtyard, passed the steamy pool and turned the key in the old lock of the door under the stone steps.

This time she left the key in the lock and walked past the

window of the gym, now dark, toward the front of the house. She was looking down, watching where she stepped, when she walked into the chain link fence. She'd forgotten about Paul's outdoor laboratory.

A monster cactus within the enclosure rose above the fence, moonlight outlining the spiny ridges of its trunk and arms with a ghostly corona against the night sky. It stood like a warning sentinel about to set the alarm that a prisoner was escaping. The familiar headache started its pulsating rhythm.

She hurried back the way she had come and crossed the concrete aprons of the garages at the back of the house to the graveled drive and followed it to the road.

There were no trees or bushes here to hide behind and the cacti were too lean, so she stood in the shadow of the great wall that sat right up to the road. She was safe unless someone drove in the drive and then she would be hopelessly spotlighted by headlights. This wall that surrounded the outer courtyard was an extension of the walls of the house, one monstrous white fort defying desert and public.

Flattening herself against the wall, she peered around it. The road was empty as it passed the house and wound past her up the hill and out of sight. *He's probably decided I'm crazy and won't come. Why should he, he doesn't owe me anything.*

. . . The dancing colored lights . . . dimming then brightening . . . soothing her tingling nerves . . . slowing her breathing . . . dulling the pounding in her head . . . her body all but weightless as it sagged against the wall . . . slipping toward the ground . . . her back sliding down the wall.

"Doe Eyes?" The voice jerked her back to her feet. Harley stood in front of the gate.

"Harley. Over here," she whispered as loud as she dared and motioned him into the shadow of the wall.

"This is got to be crazy. You know that."

"Oh, Harley. I thought you weren't coming and something awful was happening to me. . . ." She held onto his arm,

72

unable to stop the tears or the trembling. "I can't take any more . . . I just can't."

"You don't know how close I came to not showing. Hey, come on now. What are they doing to you?" He put an arm around her shoulders, and she could smell his spicy after-shave.

"It's just that they think I'm Laurel . . . and I'm afraid of Michael . . . and Laurel deserted her own baby in the hospital . . . and Harley, something's happening to me . . . in my mind. Take me away from here, please."

"Wait now, who's this Laurel?"

"They think I am."

"But you're not?" He held her away from him and looked into her face.

"I don't know. Let's get out of here. I'll explain it all in the truck."

"Wait a minute, for all I know you're the family nut and running away from the headshrinker and. . . ."

They both stiffened as a creaking noise came from the front of the wall. One half of the massive gate was opening slowly. Laurel crouched in the shadows against the wall, Harley standing behind her and watching over her head. A car engine rumbled somewhere on the road below.

A dark shape moved stealthily through the gate—Consuela with a black shawl over her head. Something long and white in her hand glistened in the moonlight. She reached through the gap in the gate and pulled out a sleepy Jimmy and then closed the gate carefully. He was wearing a heavy sweater over his pajamas and clutching the Teddy bear. Rubbing his eyes, he looked up at Consuela and she put a warning finger to her lips and shook her head as a car came around the bend in the road with its lights out.

It was an ancient coupe, its engine coughing as it came to a stop in front of the gate. The driver reached across the seat to open the door, and Consuela lifted Jimmy in and sat beside him. The coupe made a U-turn almost going off the road and moved back down the hill. Just before it reached the bend the headlights were turned on.

"What's that all about? Who's the kid?"

"You don't suppose she's kidnapping Jimmy? Harley, let's get your truck and follow them. Hurry." And she started down the road before he could stop her.

"I thought you just wanted to get away."

"Not till I find out where she's taking Jimmy. Hurry!"

"The truck's parked just around the curve. But before I take you anywhere I want to know what's going on."

"Harley, you follow that car and I'll explain, I promise." She couldn't believe Consuela would join in a plot to kidnap Jimmy, but the Devereaux' did have money.

Harley's truck sat on the shoulder, and as he started it down the road, he said, "Okay, talk."

She began with the morning she'd found herself on the desert and told him everything. As she talked the car came into view ahead of them. It wasn't speeding as though escaping the scene of a crime. There was little traffic, and they could keep a safe distance behind it as they wound through the outskirts of the city and came to the downtown area.

This was the first time she had talked it out and she realized how unreal it all sounded. Harley hadn't interrupted her, and when she'd finished, he whistled softly.

"I've been in two wars and been around and met a lot of ding-a-lings in my time, but Doe Eyes, you are it. Wow! You really don't remember anything before last week?"

"No. What am I going to do, Harley?"

"Well, I'm not a doctoring man myself. But I think you need one. In a hurry."

"You think I'm crazy?"

"Let's face it, kid, you're not too right. And from what you told me, I can't see any reason for Devereaux to bring you to Tucson unless you're Laurel. I don't think much of Devereaux' in general but just because a man works out in a gym doesn't mean he's going to hurt you. And he's got a right to be mad. How do I get mixed up in these things, will ya tell me that?"

"Where can she be taking Jimmy?" They were in an older section of Tucson, the streets dark, flat-roofed adobe buildings with their unlighted fronts jutting right to the sidewalks.

"You're walking out on the kid for the second time. What the hell do you care?"

"But what if I'm not Laurel?"

The coupe parked in the next block. Harley pulled over and shut off the lights and motor. "What if you are Laurel?"

A small man in baggy trousers got out of the car, and Consuela lifted her heavy bulk out the other side, reaching in to get Jimmy. She carried him across the street and they disappeared.

The bright desert night seemed darker here. During the day the streets around would be bustling, for they were near the city's core. But there was a ghostly hush about the street at this late hour, the occasional sounds of traffic, distant, a world apart.

"Have we lost them?"

"No, I think I know where they're goin' now." Harley shuffled along beside her, both hands stuffed in his tight pockets.

It wasn't until she glanced through a glassless window frame that she realized there'd been a sudden change in the neighborhood. All that remained of the building was its front, and behind it a giant crane with a wrecking ball on the end of a chain loomed like some monster of the night. The next building wasn't there at all, just piles of brick and rubble.

"What are they doing here?"

"I don't know," he said. "Probably going to build a parking lot or something."

Harley stopped at an open lot between two decaying buildings that were empty but still standing. Toward the back

75

of the lot a mantellike altar was built against an adobe wall, the wall forming a shallow semicircle and topped by a small metal cross. In front of the altar and to each side of it candles burned in metal racks that were encrusted with wax drippings. Patches of the adobe brick behind them had blackened through the years.

A faint breeze fluttered the tiny flames and made dancing lights on Jimmy's blond head as he knelt before the altar, the Teddy bear propped in a sitting position at his side, both looking small and defenseless in this dark place with Consuela's huge black-draped figure kneeling beside them. Another old woman knelt just in front of them, she too wearing a black shawl over her head.

Jimmy, wide awake now, turned to grin over his shoulder at the man in baggy pants who stood a little behind them.

Laurel whispered in Harley's ear, "What is this place?"

"The Wishing Shrine. A Mexican kid was supposed to have been murdered and buried here by his father-in-law because he was making time with his mother-in-law . . . a long time ago. He didn't get the regular Catholic burying. For some reason there's a story that says if you can make a candle burn all night your wish'll come true."

The driver of the ancient coupe turned to look at them. He was Mexican with a shaggy mustache over an uncertain smile.

Jimmy caught sight of them at about the same time. "Hi!" He stood up and the Teddy bear toppled.

For just a second a startled look replaced Consuela's usual stony expression and she rose from her knees to confront Laurel, a protective hand on Jimmy's shoulder.

"Consuela, why did you bring Jimmy here in the middle of the night? He should be in bed," Laurel whispered.

"He has been here many times before, Mrs. Michael."

"But why?"

"To make a wish. I used to come and wish for him, but nothing happened. So I bring him here many times to make the wish. But things happen. The candle must burn to the

76

base, but the wind would blow it out or it would burn too fast or too slow. So many things can happen."

"To wish for what?"

"To wish for the return of his mother. And one night everything goes well and it burns down and the next day you come. Tonight we come for the last time. We come to say thank you, Mrs. Michael, that is all."

It was silly superstition, of course. But in this stillness, with the candles flickering on the weathered adobe, with the reverent figure in the black shawl who had looked up only momentarily from her vigil, where even the breeze seemed hushed and everyone spoke in whispers, it was almost believable.

"We go home now. Come, Jimmy." The old woman took Jimmy's hand and stooped to retrieve the Teddy bear. She gave Harley a searching look as she passed them, and then without turning she said softly, "The little one needs his mother, Mrs. Michael."

Laurel, feeling depressed and defeated, walked slowly back to the truck, a silent Harley beside her. Once in the truck, she looked at the street ahead. The car with Jimmy and Consuela was gone.

"Well, where to?"

"I guess . . . I'm going back, Harley."

And they started back the way they had come, overtaking the old coupe as the road started winding through the low hills outside of town.

"You think I'm Laurel, don't you?"

"It looks that way. If you really don't remember anything, see a doctor, Doe Eyes. Explain it to this Michael. Things'll work out."

"No one will believe it. You don't. I'm sorry you came all this way for nothing. I have some money, Harley. I'll pay you for your wasted time." They pulled up behind the car in front of the wooden gates.

"Keep your money. I'll take this and we'll call it even." He

77

pulled her over against him and kissed her . . . a long smothering kiss that set something in her middle trembling.

"I don't suppose I'll ever see you again," she said.

"You know where to get in touch with me. But no more midnight errands, huh?"

Her last glimpse was of his grinning face through the windshield as he turned the truck around and followed the car down the hill.

Consuela and Jimmy waited for her at the gate and they went in together, Consuela locking it behind them. As they crossed the graveled courtyard a light came on over the front door.

"Take Jimmy and hide by the wall, Consuela, quick."

Consuela and Jimmy had just reached the protective shadow of the wall when Janet appeared. Laurel walked up to her.

"Well, I wondered what was going on out here. Seems to be a lot of traffic out on the road tonight." Janet wore a smudged artist's smock over the dress she'd worn to dinner.

"I couldn't sleep; I was just out for a walk." Laurel could still feel the warmth of Harley's kiss and she was sure she looked as guilty as she felt.

"Of course you were, dear."

She passed Janet and started up the stairs to her room, knowing that Janet would report this to Michael.

As the key turned in the lock behind her it made an echoing click in the quiet entry hall, and Laurel wondered if this is how she would feel if she went to prison.

7

"I do hope now that you're here, Laurel, some of the baby-sitting chores can be taken off Claire's shoulders. It took me two years to train her and I do miss her in my work. Evan is only temporary, you know."

They were in Paul's outdoor laboratory. Laurel leaned against the chain link fence, watching Paul as he poked about the base of a low bush aglow with yellow flowers. There was a clipboard on the ground beside him and he would take the pencil from behind his ear and scribble notes to himself occasionally as he puttered about.

"In fact, I had hoped that when Michael returned from Vietnam he would give up this military nonsense and make a home for Jimmy somewhere. But then I suppose there will always be a need for men like Michael to drop bombs on things and destroy what beauty is left in this world." And he glanced at the sky as if he'd heard the roar of bombers and then back at his garden with a hopeless look as if it were too late to save the things he loved.

Laurel wondered why the soliloquy. Paul had ignored her all week and now this morning had invited her to his retreat. She'd taken little part in the conversation but had let him talk on, waiting for him to reveal his reason for asking her here.

It had been a wild week of sleepless nights and headaches, of days filled with blinding sun and people she could neither understand nor endure for long periods. She'd decided to stay and come to grips with Laurel's world and in a week she hadn't been able to figure out where or how to start.

"*Encelia farinosa.*" He brushed a yellow blossom with the back of his index finger as if he were caressing the cheek of a baby. "Or flowering brittlebush, a hardy plant. But then I suppose you can blame my father."

"For the bush?"

"No, Michael's obsession with the he-man life. That swimming pool was once a reflecting pond. Shortly after Michael was born father had it enlarged and deepened. Later he built a gymnasium."

A bee darted through the chain link of the fence at her shoulder and busied itself about the yellow blossoms of the brittlebush.

"As soon as Michael was big enough to carry a gun father took him hunting. Michael learned to kill at an early age. I suppose he had to make up for his weakling brother." Paul looked up at her through his thick glasses with a resigned half-smile and shrugged.

She felt embarrassed for this quaint, stuffy little man. Was he trying to make friends? Was this an opening for her to make amends with this world of Laurel's?

"What is this thing called?" She walked over to the giant cactus that had impressed her so the night of her ill-fated escape. It seemed less intimidating in the daylight.

"It's pronounced sa-war-o but spelled *s-a-g-u-a-r-o*, the grand old man of the desert. They can grow to fifty feet or more and live to be two hundred years old. This one's over a hundred and fifty." He climbed to the top of the ladder, standing next to it to show her how it still towered above him.

Laurel stuck a tentative finger into the crevice between vertical barbed ridges and was surprised to find the green surface cool and waxy.

"This saguaro was here before that house was built, before you or I were born and it will be here after I am dead and perhaps you. And that is only just. You see, Laurel, you are no more important in the eyes of nature than this cactus or that bush. Not particularly important at all."

He climbed down the ladder and removed his sweater, one side of his salt and pepper mustache quivering slightly as it often did when he was excited or disturbed. "In fact, man was nature's one great error. The most destructive of her predators and a most unnecessary creation. It's as though she created a beautifully ordered world and then as a strange afterthought added a timed, built-in, self-destruct mechanism. A curious thing to do."

"Your philosophy sounds very un-Catholic."

"Oh, yes, the church. I'm a very good Catholic, you know." And again the little half-smile.

"I thought the religious way of thinking was that God created the world for man to enjoy." A breeze stirred her hair and the desert air came alive with the subtle fragrance of desert flowers and a faint smell like that of dried herbs.

"God created nature which created the life forms of the universe, including man, but man created the church, you see. And I am just a man," he said with a sadness she couldn't understand.

Light wisps and then soft puffs of clouds glided over the nearby mountaintops. The sky that had been so empty and washed pale and flat by sunlight seemed to deepen, to gain dimension and color as the little puffs touched and then combined to form larger clouds. More followed them over the ragged brown peaks.

Leaning against the fence again she watched as Paul brought pot after pot of tiny cacti from the laboratory and set them in the sun in long rows against the house. She began to relax in the warmth of the sun. It was peaceful here and lonely. Paul, nursing his plant life with such tenderness while he spoke degradingly of human life, seemed lonely too. It must have been hard for him when his father brought a young bride into the household.

"Paul, tell me about Michael's mother. Did you hate her?"

He looked up from the plant in his hand as though surprised by her question. "Hate Maria? Well, at first I suppose I did. She was very different from Mother. My mother was stern, practical, ugly. She had brought me up to think that Mexicans were dirty and lazy. She and Father never got along that I can remember."

He put down the plant and picked up the clipboard, holding it, gazing out at the desert beyond the fence. "But Maria was everything different—gentle, kind. He married her only a year after Mother died. Maria and I were both nineteen and she was a Mexican. It was all very embarrassing, but we soon became friends. She would come out here often and talk to me while I worked, ask questions. In fact, you remind me of her now, standing there by the fence with the wind blowing your hair."

"Do I look like Maria?"

"Not really. But she did have long dark hair and dark eyes like yours and the same timid, startled expression. I used to get the impression that she was always poised for flight, that if I would frighten her she'd just disappear."

"Did he love her?"

"Father? He had two loves—money and beautiful women. Maria was beautiful, so I suppose he loved her. But he had a way of destroying beautiful things, tearing up the desert for shopping centers, overgrazing it, leaving a scarred earth behind when a mine closed. I have seen him lasso a saguaro from a horse and topple it over just for sport. Do you realize, the chances of one saguaro reproducing itself, let alone a tiny plant ever reaching maturity? They are a priceless and dwindling treasure of the desert." Paul lowered his voice and looked away from her. "And then he killed Maria, too."

"That was an accident."

"When a man crashes through life the way my father did many innocent victims suffer, human and otherwise. And it's always an accident!" He put the pencil back behind his ear

82

and hurried into the laboratory, slamming the screen door behind him.

"Paul, wait." And she followed him. It was dark and cool inside after the desert sun. "Aren't you going to tell me what you asked me here for in the first place?"

"What I asked you here for. . . ? Oh, yes. I'm afraid my conversation, as my life, is a bit disjointed. I did have two things to tell you." He put a lab coat over his short-sleeved shirt and perched on a high stool. "The first is a simple request. Take Jimmy and move to Phoenix with Michael."

"Move to Phoenix? But Michael wouldn't take me with him. Besides I'm afraid."

"Afraid for yourself, Laurel? That isn't a cataclysmic problem. As I told you, you are not all that important. If you can remember that, life will be a great deal easier to get through."

Evan Boucher appeared from the back of the lab and walked past her with a plant in each hand. She avoided his eyes and waited until he'd carried the plants outside.

"I'm important to me!" Paul's insistence on her insignificance as a human being was getting irritating. And the idea of living with this husband she didn't know . . . well, that was out of the question.

"You will never repair your marriage living here, and Michael won't give you a divorce. He'll never do that, Laurel, so what other choice is there?"

Instead of answering him she picked up a book lying on the table by the window. There had to be another way out of this problem. He had to be wrong. The frontispiece read, "The Sonoran Desert; Plant Life, Animal Life, and Nature's Philosophy of Survival and Scarcity, by Dr. Paul Elliot Devereaux II, Ecologist, Philosopher, and Professor of Sonoran Studies. The University of Arizona Press."

"What was the other thing you wanted to tell me?"

"The authorities in Denver have been notified of your casual reappearance and a hearing has been set for June 16."

The book hit the edge of the table and landed on the floor. "Will I go to prison, Paul?"

"I doubt it. You are somebody's mother. And for some reason that holds great weight in the courts." He hunched over a microscope and didn't bother to look up as she left.

By afternoon the puffy clouds had all but filled the sky over the valley, their bottoms growing darker as the day wore on. It was hard for Laurel to believe that it ever rained on the desert, but the smell of rain was in the air.

She went to Jimmy's room and sat in the rocking chair she had carried from the old nursery and watched as he played at her feet. Maria had probably rocked in this very chair, watching Michael. It had taken much persuasion to get Consuela to unlock the old nursery and let her take the chair. But why keep it locked up in that room of shattered, dusty memories when there was a baby in the house?

Tiring of his trucks, Jimmy crawled up on her lap with a high-pitched giggle and snuggled against her, his thumb in his mouth. She felt the bond growing between them, not so much that of mother and child but of two lonely people looking for comfort.

His skin had such a pale, milky tone for a child who lived in so much sun. But then he was seldom allowed out of this room. The house was a prison for him, too. And Paul had offered them an escape, the only one possible. "Take Jimmy and move to Phoenix with Michael."

The room darkened as the storm gathered outside and she rocked harder, holding his warmth close to her. "What other choice is there?" Paul had said.

She sang *Rock-a-Bye Baby* because it was the only lullaby she could remember and because she wanted to shut out the sound of the rising wind. Soon Jimmy slept, his head tilting back and forth with the movement of the chair. And still she sang, repeating the lullaby over and over, the wicker rocker creaking an accompaniment. There had been a storm brewing inside her from the moment she'd entered Laurel's world,

84

and she feared the turmoil would break out now if she stopped singing.

It was getting dark and the wind rushed at the house with rolling gusts that left short breathless spells in between, the great bell in the bell wall clanging hollowly with the stronger gusts. She jumped as lightning tore at the sky and lit the room and sang louder, trying to drown out the answering rumble that seemed to thunder above the house.

And then the door facing her, the door to the balcony, opened and Michael Devereaux was in the room. The lullaby stuck in her throat. It was Friday and she hadn't expected him until Saturday.

The welcoming smile for his son faded, leaving his lips parted, frozen. It was like a dark still life, she sitting motionless in his mother's rocking chair, his son asleep on her lap, and he in uniform with his cap in his hand and his hair mussed by the wind. There was a snap that made her release her breath and again lightning flared, momentarily flooding the room with its cold light and glinting in Michael's eyes.

She watched the play of expression on his mobile face, his eyes widen with surprise and then narrow. Did she bring back some memory of Maria sitting in this chair? There was a tightening in her breasts as excitement mingled with fear. Life with this man could be frightening, chaotic, dangerous, but it would never be dull.

What sounded like enormous drops of rain pelted the tiled roof for a bare minute and the storm was over. It had taken all day to build to nothing.

The tension in the room seemed to ease with the passing of the clouds. As Jimmy stirred in his sleep, replacing the thumb that had slipped from his mouth, she looked down, breaking the current that had sizzled between them when Michael's eyes held hers.

"I thought Jimmy should have the rocking chair. No one was using it."

Michael walked to the dresser and put his cap beside the

portable TV and with his back to her looked up at the ceiling, his shoulders hunched. "What am I going to do with you?"

The hopelessness in his voice made her aware that hers was not the only untenable position in this strange relationship. She could almost feel the agony of this intense man with a wife he could not endure and would not divorce.

In May the days grew so warm that lunch was moved into the coolness of the dining room. The saguaro sprouted creamy little flowers with thick, waxy petals. It looked a bit silly, this giant, with the small circlet of pale flowers on its top and on the top of its arms while tiny cacti that had sat unnoticed behind rocks bloomed with brilliant blossoms that sometimes dwarfed the plant itself.

During the week Laurel settled into a routine, dining with the family and, when Jimmy was alone, spending her time with him. On weekends when Michael could get to Tucson, he and Claire took Jimmy on walks or outings in the car and continued the swimming lessons. Jimmy was not learning to swim, but he was learning in a brave, resigned way to undergo the torture without crying. Weekends were the loneliest for Laurel.

The first time Jimmy called her "Mommy" she realized that she had taught him that. Little slips like, "Mommy will get that for you" or "Come sit on Mommy's lap." It hadn't happened often but he'd picked it up very fast. Their relationship deepened, growing beyond just a friendship into an almost uncomfortable clinging tie that made his wide dark eyes look a little less lost, the only eyes around her that weren't full of reproach. To him she was not an unwanted encumbrance, an embarrassing reminder of family misfortune. He needed her love, her arms as a harbor from Claire's scolding, her reassurance against the coldness of his aunt and uncle, her comforting when he scraped a knee or when

Michael left for the base. His need for her fed her own need for self-respect.

In this time Laurel came to know that she could never give up Jimmy. And she knew that only as Laurel did she have any right to him.

Michael did not come to Tucson for several weekends and she had Jimmy to herself. She slept less as the Denver trip drew nearer. By the time Michael reappeared she was in such a state that she walked the halls and covered walkways until early morning and felt drugged and listless during the day. She would wait in her room until it was late and the house was quiet before starting out on her nightly prowls.

One unusually warm night she left her coat in the wardrobe and threw a peignoir over her nightgown. She descended the stairs to the courtyard and was halfway across it before she noticed Michael standing in the shadow of the walkway on the other side. It was too late to turn around. She would have to confront him sometime; it might as well be now. But she wished she'd worn her coat.

There was a glass in his hand and his coat was unbuttoned. He pretended to study the flagstone of the courtyard. For all she'd learned of his boyhood she couldn't picture him as anything but a grown and bitter man. What would he have been like if he'd never met Laurel? If he'd married some safe and responsible woman like Claire Bently? He didn't bother to look up as she came to stand beside him.

"I see you can't sleep either."

"I'm working on it." He drained half the glass with one swallow.

"Michael, we're going to have to talk sometime." She felt small standing next to him.

"All right. Janet tells me you've taken to sneaking out at night," he said with that menacing softness. "Let's talk about that."

"I went out once, only once. I followed Consuela. Did you

87

know she's been taking Jimmy to the Wishing Shrine? To wish . . . to wish that his mother would come back to him?"

"Poor Consuela. She has delusions about motherhood. Why did you come back anyway?" There were dark hollows around those unnerving eyes.

"That's what I wanted to talk about."

He finished his drink with a second swallow and faced her. "So talk." His voice was almost a whisper.

She was filled with that same breathless sensation, a mixture of fear and fluster she had whenever he looked at her directly. She wanted to run. "I don't know why I came back."

"You're just full of answers tonight." The smell of whiskey was strong on his breath.

"I can't remember why. Michael, I don't remember anything—you—Jimmy—anything. I didn't know my name till I called you from the motel that night. I had your name on a piece of paper and nothing else but the clothes on my back. I can't tell you where I've been because I don't know. Please believe me."

"Oh, yes, I've heard you suffer from amnesia. That explains everything and so conveniently. Christ!" The glass shattered into tinkling fragments on the flagstone and he had her by the arm. "Where'd you get that one, off the TV screen? Well, I'm not the damn fool you married, Laurel."

"Michael!" A voice in her head screamed to her to get away, but he grabbed her other arm and held her against him, his breath hot on her forehead, the buttons of his coat cold through her nightgown.

"Let me tell you why you came back. Things didn't go well with whoever you were living with, did they? Short on money maybe? So you decided a little luxury would be a nice change of pace. Thought you'd look up old Michael and maybe for laughs see what the baby looked like? Or you're in some kind of trouble and you had to get away. Now *that* I could accept, but don't expect me to swallow amnesia."

He let go of her and sat on a stone couch, rubbing his forehead. For just a moment he looked defeated, this man who a second before was in a rage. His bursts of anger seemed to end as abruptly as they began. Everything about him was abrupt, startling.

"This . . . this luxury, as you call it, couldn't have been what I came back for. I don't even like it here."

"Then why the hell don't you go? Leave us in peace. As soon as this mess in Denver is cleared up, you're free as the wind. If it's money you want, I'll give you money. Just get out of my life and Jimmy's."

When he raised his voice, she felt safer with him. It was when he grew so still and tense that she feared him most. "I can't."

"Why? Because of Jimmy?" He was mocking her now.

"Yes. He needs a mother, Michael. Can't you see it?" She sat next to him.

"And just what do you suppose he needed two years ago? You walk out on a newborn baby and now he needs a mother!"

"It was an awful thing to do. I don't know how I could have . . . how anybody could. If you weren't all so sure I'm Laurel, I'd swear it was someone else who deserted Jimmy. I don't remember it . . . I don't feel capable of such a thing. There must have been a reason. I'm sure I'll remember everything soon. Maybe there was a good reason."

"Like what?" He was growing still again, the handsome profile set in concrete.

"I . . . I can't think of any. It was inexcusable, I guess. Whatever the reason it wouldn't excuse what . . . what you say I did."

"No, it wouldn't. So get out now before you do any more damage."

Somewhere in the desert night a bird screeched and fell silent. A breeze rippled the surface of the pool and the water lapped gently against its tile prison.

"I can't do that. I have to make it up to him."

"What is it going to do to him when he starts thinking of you as his mother and you get the wanderlust? You're good at walking in and out of people's lives, not caring what you leave behind. If you've got any soul left in you, Laurel, you won't stay and put him through that."

She saw a boy standing in the wrecked nursery, rage giving way to tears. Michael knew what it was to lose a mother. "I won't let it happen again. Somehow I'll keep it from happening." Laurel realized she was crying. Would she forget again and just wander off? Should she see a doctor?

"You won't go?" He stood up as if to get away from her.

"I can't. Unless they send me to prison." She was looking up at him through tears, as she had that first night in the motel.

"All right, stay. Rot here. But if you hurt my son in any way I'll wrap that hair of yours around your neck and choke you with it."

"I don't want to hurt anyone. I want to make up for what I did." But Michael was gone and she sobbed to an empty courtyard.

8

The next time Laurel prowled late at night around the shadowed arcades of the Devereaux mansion was the last time.

A warm night, in the middle of the week, so she needn't worry about meeting Michael. She left her coat in her room and walked briskly, purposely trying to tire herself. Tonight the moonlight lent a fairy tale softness to the still courtyard. No shadows moved against the walls. Even the leaves on the odd crooked trees seemed to sleep. Blooming flowers in hanging baskets accented the air, their colors dimmed by the strange light of night.

Unable to ignore the beauty around her, she slowed and finally stopped to lean against a column and look down upon the courtyard below.

Moments like this should be enjoyed and remembered. How many such moments had she forgotten? Had there been times in her childhood when something unexpected and beautiful had come to her this way? What were her parents like? Her father must be a cruel tyrant to have turned away a grandson and disowned a daughter. But how could her mother have gone along with it? *How could I have abandoned Jimmy?* Her arguments with herself always ended with this last question.

These thoughts were spoiling the loveliness of the night, and she began pacing back and forth along the balcony. Her parents could not be pleasant people and she wouldn't call them until she'd sorted herself out. Her life needed no more unpleasantness.

Laurel found herself at the top of the stone stairs and stepped down them to the courtyard. Stopping beside a basket of purple petunias, she sniffed their spiciness. *When I do remember, I hope it will be in a peaceful moment like this.* A doctor might help her remember sooner. Would the Devereaux' let her molder in an institution as Evan had implied? She didn't think much of Evan's mentality, but this family clearly did not want her.

"Dear Michael will leave his little problems on our doorstep."

"Take Jimmy and move to Phoenix with Michael."

"I could damn you to hell for coming back."

She stepped quickly onto the flagstone. The problem with not remembering the past was that one remembered the present all too vividly. Perhaps if she jogged, instead of walked. Laurel smiled at the thought of herself doing a clumsy jogging step in a yellow nightgown around a moonlit courtyard fit for a Romeo and Juliet scene.

Directly in front of her, on the wall outside of Paul's study, a shadow moved. Only this shadow moved. The others were still. Her smile went empty.

Moonlight penetrated only the lower half of the arcade and she watched the shadow rise, swing upward in a long . . . slow . . . threatening arch, like an arm rising to strike . . . it disappeared into the solid shadow of the balcony above.

Laurel stood very still and tried to reason with herself. Anyone in her condition could imagine anything. Adrenaline set fire to every nerve ending in her body. It had been too long for an arm. *Get away from here!* Where the shadow had been before moving upward, there was a dark silhouette of what could be a shoe with a leg cut off by some sort of a long coat . . . if someone stood behind that column watching her . . . he might not be aware of his own shadow behind him. . . .

92

Laurel couldn't remember getting to the stone stairs. She was just there, taking two at a time . . . all the other shadows had been still . . . too long for an arm . . . she raced along the balcony. . . .

. . . The moonlight was dimming. Vivid lights shimmered in front of her . . . she fumbled with the knob of the door to her room . . . red and purple lights and green . . . heavenly lightness to her body . . . quieting her nerves . . . slowing her breathing . . . she relaxed against the door. . . .

. . . What . . . what was she doing out here?

A soft padding sounded behind her and she shook the lights away, almost falling into the room as the door opened. She slammed it closed, shot the bolt and listened.

Nothing.

Nothing but her own fear ringing in her ears.

Her skin felt horribly sticky. She'd imagined the shadow and the padding sound. Laurel was breathing too deeply, making herself dizzy.

But the shadow had moved . . . hadn't it? No, it hadn't and that's why they locked people like her away.

She crossed the room and bolted the door to the hallway. It could have been an arm if the hand at the end of the arm held something long and straight . . . like a club . . . or a stick. "Michael learned to kill at an early age," Paul had said. But Michael wasn't home and she was running scared at imagined shadows and losing control of herself and someone stood at one of the long narrow windows to the balcony. A dark figure wearing a loose-fitting coat of some kind, holding a. . . .

Noise, piercing and dreadful, all around her and Laurel put her hands over her ears to shut it away.

"My God, what's happening!"
"Is she hurt?"
"She must have been dreaming."
"Why's she sitting on the floor?"

93

"What time is it anyway?"

"Mommy?"

Legs, slippers, robes, the lights were on . . . her eyes, stinging. . . .

"Claire, get Jimmy back to bed, he shouldn't see this. Laurel, can you stand up?"

"Michael, she hasn't blinked since I came in here."

"Here, see if you can stand up." Michael's voice. Warm hands on each side of her pulled her to her feet. Michael and Paul.

Michael! Laurel drew away from them and sat on the bed.

"Now, why all the hysterics?" Michael put her robe over her shoulders.

"Someone . . . chased me in the courtyard."

"But you were sitting on the floor with all the doors locked, screaming. We had to come through Jimmy's room. Are you sure you didn't dream it?"

"I ran in here and locked the doors and . . . he looked in the window. He carried something . . . something long."

"Who carried something?" Claire came from Jimmy's room.

"I couldn't see . . . someone. . . ." The look of doubt on their faces silenced her.

"Rot! You don't really think there's someone in the house?" Janet, in her grisly night attire was like a butterfly that could continually reenter its cocoon and return as something different.

"I doubt it, but I'll check the locks. Michael, you have a look through the house. You ladies can go back to bed. Lock your doors just in case." There were two Paul's, one fussed about like a little old lady organizing a church bazaar, the other watched from behind his glasses, detached and what . . . reproachful?

Everyone but Janet wore loose-fitting robes resembling what she thought she saw on the silhouette at the window.

Claire rolled her eyes, gave Michael a sympathetic look, and

94

left the room. Paul took Janet's arm and guided her to the door. She could hear them whispering in the hall.

Laurel was left staring back at Michael on the big bed. "I didn't know you were home."

"I work this weekend so I have tomorrow and the next day off. I came in late after you'd gone upstairs and . . . I did *not* chase you around the courtyard." His lips smiled; his eyes looked bored and unamused. "Get under the covers, you're shaking."

"Aren't you supposed to be looking through the house?"

"For what? A phantom carrying something long? Long like what?"

"Like a mallet or . . . an ax." She backed away from him and crawled beneath the covers, putting most of the bed between them.

"First you have amnesia and now someone's chasing you with an ax. Laurel, you used to have a better imagination. You're slipping badly." He moved about the room, turning off lights. He left the one on the bedside table next to her until last. His long graceful fingers coiled around its switch, fine black hairs gleaming in the lamplight. Laurel found she couldn't swallow.

"And believe me, dear wife, if I wanted to do away with you, I wouldn't use anything as messy as an ax."

Michael's low chuckle had barely faded outside on the balcony when she was out of bed and bolting both doors . . . into Jimmy's room and bolting his door . . . back to turn on every light in the enormous bedroom. Laurel came close to not making it into the bathroom in time to vomit again and again.

Clutching her middle, where sore muscles pulled and burned at every movement, she crawled back into bed and waited for the accompanying chills to subside. Michael *wouldn't* use an ax. If he wanted to kill . . . if he were angry enough to kill . . . and he could be . . . Michael would use his

95

bare hands. He'd probably strangle a woman or beat a man to a pulp. He'd taken an ax to the nursery, but that Michael had been only ten. This man Michael just wouldn't. Would he? Unless he . . . or someone wanted to frighten her away . . . had used the ax or whatever it was as a threat. Almost everyone in this house wanted her gone.

From that night on, Laurel walked warily through the Devereaux mansion, kept to her room at night and bolted her doors. If everyone had watched her covertly before, they did so openly now. Janet announced that "poor Laurel" needed something to occupy her mind and Laurel was introduced to Janet's workshop, a small room off the courtyard beneath the old nursery. A workbench sat against one wall, a sheet of pegboard mounted behind it with screwdrivers, hammers, and a saw hanging from nails. Laurel couldn't keep her eyes from searching the room for an ax. Wooden chests, a wardrobe, chairs, and a headboard for a bed . . . no ax or mallet . . . Laurel gave herself a mental shake. The last thing she needed was to become paranoid. A room air-conditioner hummed in the window to the courtyard.

"Surprised at my little workshop?" Janet stood beside the skeleton of a wooden chair sitting on a stained table in the center of the room. She wore a dirty smock and held a paintbrush.

"What do you do here?" Laurel stared at the loose-fitting smock.

"Refinish antiques . . . well, some are antique and some are merely authentic. I make foraging raids into Mexico now and again. Here. . . ." She handed Laurel a square of sandpaper and pointed to an oblong chest on the floor. "You can start anywhere you like. I just want the varnish and stain removed, not the deep scars and gouges. I think I'll restain over those and linseed it."

"Why don't you use an electric sander?"

"For the same reason I don't brush my teeth with a wire scrub brush!"

Laurel knelt beside the chest and started on the lid where she'd have a smoother surface to work with. The sandpaper was of a coarse grade that left the surface roughened but made inroads on the many coats of varnish amateurishly daubed over the chest. They worked in silence for only a few minutes.

"Have you thought of a good story for the judge yet?"

The sandpaper stopped. Laurel didn't look up. "No."

"Still don't remember?"

"No, I don't!"

"You could always say you got cold feet about being a mother and went to live with friends in the mountains or something. That sanding works better if you do a small patch at a time, dear."

Leave it to Janet to come up with a story. It was flimsy but better than anything she'd thought of herself. But coming from Janet it was suspect; Laurel didn't trust her.

They both went back to work and Janet changed the subject. "You should have seen this place when I first came here. You wouldn't believe the valuable pieces that were stored away and the junk they used for furniture. Maria must have shopped the Goodwill. She was certainly no house-keeper, had no eye for quality."

"Did you know her well?"

"She'd been dead for two years when I married Paul. Surely Michael told you something about us? But then I suppose you would have forgotten that, wouldn't you?"

There was another silence and Laurel began to relax. Sanding was hard but soothing work. She didn't have to think about what she was doing and thought instead of this sophisticated woman who was the last person in the world she would have expected to enjoy the messy work of refinishing furniture. She thought how quick she was to judge others, that she understood them no better than she did herself.

"As I was saying, you wouldn't have believed the place

when I came here. They actually ate in the kitchen with Consuela. The front of the house was closed up except for the study and all the really nice things were covered or stored away. Well, you don't throw a Boston girl into a situation like that without a major upheaval. When I insisted we dress for dinner and use the dining rooms, I thought Father Devereaux would have apoplexy. But he dressed and he came. He said it was just to see if 'poor Paul could tame his little filly.' That man was a horror. We all breathe easier now that he's gone."

"When did he die?" It almost seemed that Michael's father, Paul I, was still alive the way everyone talked of him.

"Eight years ago, just before Michael went abroad. But I'd had ten years of the old man and, believe me, I didn't cry at the funeral. And the way he treated Paul was criminal. There, that's done. What do you think?"

Laurel nodded approval of what still looked like the skeleton of a chair to her and marveled at how Janet kept the mess on her smock while whatever showed above and below it was the meticulous butterfly. Laurel felt grimy from the roots of her hair to her shoes and had sanding dust between her teeth. "I'd heard Paul and his father didn't get along well."

"Didn't get along? There was hatred there, my dear. And if there was ever doubt about that when Father Devereaux was alive he proved it in his will when he died." Janet dabbed at her fingers with a rag and turpentine.

"What about the will?"

"Really, Laurel, if you remember anything, you remember that." Her husky voice developed a purr. "That's why you came back, isn't it?"

"Your father-in-law never knew me, Janet. How could his will affect me?"

"You know, sometimes I could almost believe you. You're one of the most practiced liars I've ever met. That will was Father Devereaux's last joke on Paul . . . and me. The fair

98

way would have been for him to divide the inheritance between Paul and Michael."

"Didn't he?"

"Some of it. But the bulk of it was left in trust for the first child born to either of them. So you see, once I stopped to think about it, your coming back wasn't such a surprise after all."

"Jimmy."

"Yes, when dear sweet little James Michael Devereaux comes of age he's going to be a very wealthy young man. And I'm sure he'll take good care of his mother. You'll see to that, won't you?"

"How could he have known you wouldn't have the first child? I mean . . . you're Catholic and. . . ."

"No. Paul is Catholic, I'm not. I didn't care to go through that loathsome business of childbearing and rearing. I made it pretty plain to the old man when he kept making snide remarks about my not getting pregnant or about Paul being impotent. The leering old . . . oh well, he got the last leer I'm afraid."

"What if Michael hadn't had a child?"

"If no heir was born within ten years of the old man's death or if that heir did not live to legal age the money would revert to Paul and Michael. But he knew Michael. Michael showed his womanizing talents early. It would only be a matter of time before some woman got a ring out of him. And knowing Michael, she'd be pregnant before she could get the rice out of her hair."

"Poor Jimmy, it's a wonder no one's strangled him in his bed." And Laurel bit her lip; she hadn't meant to say it aloud.

"Or hit him over the head with an ax?" Janet's voice hardened. "Really, Laurel, don't let your imagination run away with you. You have enough to worry about without that. I hear you want to move to Phoenix."

"That was your husband's idea, not mine."

99

"Well, I wouldn't advise it. Our Michael can be difficult when he's angry. It's soon time for lunch. Let's get cleaned up. You can come back and work on that chest any time you want something to do." Janet removed her smock and hung it on a nail by the door as they left.

"Whatever you do, Laurel, don't cross him. Michael. Don't ever cross him."

Janet had a way of lingering over Michael's name, her voice caressing it, drawing it out as if it were the name of a food she relished.

The sandstone of the courtyard seemed to soak up the heat and throw it back at them as they walked toward the stone stairs. Claire didn't see them as she carried Jimmy along the shaded walkway to the kitchen.

"Poor Claire. You really threw a monkey wrench into her plans. And she's been trying so hard, reading all those baby books, trying to show off to Michael. Do you know she actually pleaded with me to stop getting nurses and let her take over with Jimmy? She'd like Paul to think I drafted her. But I thought why not? She might as well be earning her salary for a change doing something useful. Come to my door a minute, will you? I have something for you." Laurel waited outside and Janet returned with a letter. "Here, you answer it. Maybe she'll stop pestering me."

It was from Laurel's mother, Lisa Ann Lawrence, to Janet, a touching letter pleading for news of Jimmy and pictures of him with a warning to please send them to the address given, the neighbor's house, so that Mr. Lawrence wouldn't know his wife had written. Laurel could almost see the tears shed over this letter.

It came from Charles City, Iowa. She tried to marshal her memory into giving her some recollection of Iowa but got instead the familiar block. It would be inhuman not to answer this letter, but what would she say? Somehow her parents didn't seem quite human to her either.

June came and she hadn't answered it. Other things occu-

100

pied her mind. The hearing in Denver. The need to be careful, watchful, to put her trust in no one. Nothing had happened since the night she'd been chased to her room and that part of her that reasoned thought she'd imagined the whole thing. But another instinctive part of her told her that the members of this household were more than just unpleasant. One of them, at least, was deadly. This instinctive side of her insisted she get up repeatedly during the night to check the locks, and it forced her to keep closer track of Jimmy. Since discovering his part in his grandfather's will, she feared for his safety too. Then, of course, if anyone wanted to harm Jimmy, they could have done so long ago. But still. . . .

The family kept her busy now, constant little jobs in the workshop, filing for Paul, watering potted plants in the courtyard. One Friday Janet decided to set up the large dining room for dinner. She and Laurel were polishing silver when Michael arrived from the base.

"One of your famous late dinner parties, Janet?" For some reason he reminded Laurel of a patrolman in his tan uniform.

"I'm afraid anyone worth inviting to a party has left this hot hole by now."

"When do you plan to make your yearly flight from the heat? Little late, aren't you?"

"I've decided to stay in Tucson this summer." Janet smiled across the table at Laurel. "I wouldn't want to miss out on any of the drama here."

"You still haven't explained what the occasion is."

"I thought it about time we celebrated . . . Laurel's homecoming. Oh, and I've asked Evan Boucher to stay for dinner. I thought it might be amusing."

By anyone's standards but Janet's, the dinner was a flop. Six people couldn't converse comfortably around a table meant for at least twice that many. Not that one couldn't hear. Acoustically, the cavernous room was a wonder. Everyone could hear whispered conversations intended to be private. But with the distance between chairs, each diner became his own little island in his own sea of tableware and any sense of a convivial party atmosphere was lost.

Laurel overheard Claire complaining to Michael that she couldn't get into Jimmy's room in the mornings until Laurel unbolted the door. She heard Janet explaining to Evan that "poor Laurel thinks she's being chased by an ax murderer." She noticed everyone grinning when Evan, sitting next to her and looking very pale, whispered that she should call him if she ever felt threatened again. He even surreptitiously wrote his phone number on a cloth napkin and slipped it to her. Laurel found this embarrassing and at the same time touching. Evan was a stranger in this house, too. And he was the only one who believed her or really cared about what happened to her.

Course followed course, too much wine passing with each. A weary Consuela shuffled from sideboard to table, perspiration on her dark face shining in the candlelight. Evan, who was clumsy enough at lunch, was at a total loss with the extra silver, the surfeit of delicate crystal. He must have dashed home for the ill-fitting coat and tie before dinner. Michael watched every move Laurel made. She sat directly across from him and met the intensity of his stare each time she looked up. Conversation became stiff and finally ended altogether.

Just the clinking of silver on china, the gurgle of wine pouring from bottle to glass, an occasional throat being cleared, the click of Consuela's shoes on tile. Laurel, her lips numb from the wine, prayed the dinner would end soon so she could hide away in her locked room, be near Jimmy. He was alone up there. If he awoke, no one would hear him.

When Janet's low voice rasped from the far end of the table, Laurel jumped and stained the white lace tablecloth with blood-red wine. "And how was the grand lecture this afternoon, Paul dear?"

"I did not deliver it." Paul didn't even look up from his

102

plate. He'd treated the whole dinner as if he were not a part of it.

"Why ever not?"

"Because Evan's hero delivered an address on my platform."

"John the Baptist? He's here?" Evan's face flushed with wine and excitement. "In Tucson?"

"I believe his real name is Sidney Blackman and, yes, he is very much here. Just took over the hall."

"John the Baptist? The one with all the robes and hair?" Janet peered around the brass candelabra.

"The same. Considers himself a new prophet. He reminds me more of Adolf Hitler with a beard." Paul's mustache quivered and a tiny dot of cream sauce trembled at one end.

"What did he say?" Evan Boucher came to life, straightening, leaning forward with his elbows on the table, placing any number of side dishes in danger.

"The title of his address was 'Peaceful Revolution—the Great Wool Blanket of the Establishment.'" Paul's sigh suggested weary but amused contempt.

Michael finally looked away from Laurel to his brother. "What's that supposed to mean?"

"Oh, he's trying to incite the students again. Things have been too quiet on the campuses lately. Ask young Evan there; he seems to know the current dogma by heart." Reflections of candle flames danced on the lenses of Paul's glasses, all but hiding the eyes behind them.

Laurel watched Evan's unbelievable necktie approach and then dangle in the contents of his plate. "Well, really all he's saying is that the youth of the country is a minority group in society . . . as much as the blacks or Chicanos or the poor and just as powerless at the polls and the only thing they can do is join other minorities in a revolution to unseat the powers that be at political, economic, and academic levels and to bring relevancy to these institutions in a. . . ."

103

"Isn't he the one who caused the riots at Boulder a year or two ago?" Michael interrupted quietly, leveling the full power of his half-lidded gaze upon Evan.

"Well, yes. But . . . society leaves no other course but to revolt. . . ." Evan lost the staring contest and looked down at his plate. "There's no other way. What with Presidential candidates chosen by corrupt political machines and all." He turned suddenly to Laurel. "What do you think of John the Baptist, Mrs. Devereaux?"

"What?" She'd been so engrossed in the reactions of the participants she had only half-listened to the conversation.

Janet laughed. "I don't think Laurel has picked up a newspaper since she's been here. Her own world is such an exciting one . . . shadows in the courtyard and what not. Which reminds me, we're celebrating Laurel's return to her family. Fill up the glasses, Consuela." Candlelight was kind to Janet, softening the lines on her face, bringing out the sheen of her copper hair. "I propose a toast to"—and she raised her glass—"to Michael's wife."

Claire set her glass down, hiccuped, and left the room.

Michael raised his slowly . . . and carefully poured the wine into his water goblet.

9

The night before the Denver trip, Laurel's sleep was disturbed by a confusion of nightmares. John the Baptist in flowing robes, Michael wielding an ax, Paul leading her through a prison door. . . .

The fitful night did not leave her rested for the flight to Denver. She sat next to Michael, her eyes dry and burning, the depressing headache barely controlled by the aspirin she'd swallowed before getting on the plane that afternoon.

Jimmy perched on Michael's lap at first excited at the prospect of a plane ride, but soon bored as the sleek jet refused to do anything exciting. Paul sat across the aisle.

They were in the air only a short while when a stewardess offered drinks. Laurel ordered a Martini and watched the interest in the girl's face as she leaned toward Michael for his order. She was plump and blond and managed to look fresh despite the artful eye makeup. Laurel wondered what she had looked like at that age.

The Martini made her feel better and strangely braver.

"Mommy?" Jimmy stretched out his arms toward her. She handed the drink to Michael so Jimmy could crawl onto her lap and at the same time met her husband's glance.

"You don't like him to call me Mommy, do you?"

"Why shouldn't he?" Michael turned away to study the seat in front of them.

"What am I going to do when we get to Denver? I don't know what to tell them."

"I'm sure you'll think of something. You're very persuasive. Paul has hired a Denver lawyer for you."

The plane soon dipped below the clouds and circled wide over mountains that were green with trees and valleys, their tops a jagged gray. She could imagine the rich scent of pine, the shadowy forests. Did Colorado put its prisons in the mountains?

Laurel cuddled the sleeping child closer to her breast and tried not to think as the plane swooped to meet the rising runway.

The dining room at the Denver Hilton was crowded that evening and Laurel kept busy trying to keep Jimmy in the highchair until his dinner came. It was closer to his bedtime than his dinner hour.

Paul introduced her to Mr. Leon Hawley, her lawyer, who joined them shortly after they were seated. He was young and brisk, and she studied him in the dim light, certain that he would only add to her depression. Mr. Hawley appeared businesslike and unemotional and totally incapable of sympathetic understanding of her problem, much like a doctor who understands your illness but not your fear of it.

The men talked of general topics and she concentrated on picking Jimmy's food off the floor while her own dinner grew cold. When the table had been cleared and coffee served, Mr. Hawley finally turned his attention to her.

"I think your best bet tomorrow, Mrs. Devereaux, would be to waive the jury, plead guilty, and let me do the talking. We just might be able to get out of the trial altogether. The court dockets are full and Judge Gillan is very busy right now. It would be months before a trial date could be set. If we can convince him that the child is in good hands and that you've mended your ways, we might get away with a fine and a probationary period without a formal trial."

"You mean I won't go to prison?"

"Under the law you could get three months, but desertion

is a misdemeanor. If we can keep this at the hearing level we might get off with probation, and you wouldn't even have to come back for a trial. There is also the problem of jurisdiction. The boy was removed almost immediately from Denver and has been living with his legal family in another state so. . . ."

"Misdemeanor?" Laurel looked at Paul, and he offered only a smug wink as if they shared some secret plan.

The lawyer talked on. Michael brooded into his coffee as though he couldn't really care what was said. Paul gazed politely at the lawyer, a thin smile under the mustache.

"Now, we must have some statement from you about how you spent those two years and why you left the baby." Mr. Hawley took pencil and paper from his briefcase and looked at her expectantly.

Michael looked up from his coffee.

"I went up into the mountains to stay with friends."

"Why?"

"Because . . . I was afraid. Afraid of being a mother."

"Just exactly what made you afraid?"

Laurel lifted Jimmy from the highchair. "That's all I can tell you, Mr. Hawley," she said and carried her son from the room, leaving the lawyer with his mouth open, his pencil suspended in midair.

Judge Gillan was a heavy man with sagging cheeks and great tired eyes. He listened to Mr. Hawley without interruption, often glancing at his watch. He stared at the ceiling most of the time but occasionally his eyes would rest on Jimmy who bounced from Michael's lap to Laurel's. They had about exhausted their supply of diversions—Michael's keys, a pencil, Laurel's handkerchief, a mirror.

Laurel knew they couldn't keep him happy much longer and still Mr. Hawley talked on.

It wasn't until the lawyer got to Laurel's reason for abandoning her baby that the judge's eyes met hers directly.

107

Mr. Hawley went on quickly to the question of the court's jurisdiction, but Judge Gillan's glance stayed on her—penetrating. Laurel squirmed and looked away.

The lawyer finished at last and a long silence followed. Judge Gillan leaned forward, resting his elbows on the table and rubbing his eyes. Finally he looked at Michael.

"Mr. Devereaux, have you decided to take this runaway wife of yours back into your home?"

Michael had the proud but hopeless look of a doomed man. "I'm Catholic, Your Honor."

"That does not exactly answer the question, does it? Your affiliation with that particular church poses a problem if you should desire to remarry. But I asked if you are accepting this woman back into your home as a mother to your child?"

Michael stared back at the judge, started to speak, then closed his mouth tightly. Laurel could see the flexing of his jaw muscle as he pondered his answer. The sound of her own heartbeat filled the silent room.

"Well, Mr. Devereaux?"

"She has been living in my home since April."

Judge Gillan did not seem satisfied with Michael's answer. The two men studied each other a few seconds and then the judge turned to Laurel. "Your lawyer has given a rather scanty explanation of your reason for deserting the child, Mrs. Devereaux, but no reason for your sudden return to your family. Perhaps you could enlighten us?"

"My nephew is heir to a rather impressive fortune, Your Honor." Paul's voice came from behind her. She had almost forgotten his presence in the room.

"She didn't know that, Paul." Michael turned to face his brother. "I didn't tell her."

"I didn't know it until after I came back. I just want to make up to Jimmy for what I did."

"This is a frightening world into which to bring a child, Mrs. Devereaux. But then it always was. To allow him to be brought up motherless is hardly a solution." Judge Gillan studied some papers Mr. Hawley had set before him.

"It is the general procedure in this court to set a fine and a prison sentence not longer than ninety days in cases of desertion. This is an unusual case, however. A fine would probably have to be paid by Mr. Devereaux, and he is not on trial here and has suffered enough through Mrs. Devereaux's actions.

"The child has been neither neglected nor abused and the family is resident of another state. Although the welfare of the child is always paramount to other considerations of the court, the question here is the conduct of the mother in deserting her child.

"Should the question of legal separation of the parents arise, I am sure, Mr. Devereaux, that you would have little trouble in gaining custody of the child should you wish to present the facts of the mother's desertion to any court in the country.

"It is therefore the decision of this court to sentence you to the full penalty under the law of ninety days imprisonment. . . ."

Laurel drew in her breath with an audible hiss and pressed Jimmy's head against her breast so hard that he cried out.

". . . and to suspend that sentence, placing you, Laurel Jean Devereaux, in the custody of your husband, Michael Devereaux, for a period of ninety days. In which time Mr. Devereaux may decide whether or not you are capable of providing a normal home for his son and whether or not it is possible to continue the marriage."

Judge Gillan reminded her of the right of appeal, stared at her for a moment as though wondering if he had done the right thing, and then adjourned the hearing.

Mr. Hawley beamed and shook hands all around. "That was even easier than I thought. I don't think the judge was too sure about jurisdiction here either."

Michael threw her a glance that sent a shiver through her, turned abruptly, and left the room. The lawyer's proud smile began to waver.

"Excuse my brother, Mr. Hawley. You did a fine job and the family is grateful." Paul turned to Laurel. "Aren't we, Laurel? You and I won, didn't we?"

"What do you mean?"

"You are in Michael's custody now."

Laurel sat back down on the hard chair. She was not going to prison. She did not have to give up Jimmy—yet. But it had just dawned on her what her reprieve meant. What Paul had been working toward all along. A swift image of that shadow rising on the courtyard wall floated through her mind.

"Don't you see, Laurel? Michael will have to take you to Phoenix now."

10

After the colorful bloom of spring, summer lay on the vast landscape like the aftermath of war. The flowers and patches of green were gone from the roadsides and the desert vegetation looked more twisted and barren than ever. The giant saguaro and its smaller cousins alone appeared undaunted by the ravages of summer sun.

They rode in air-conditioned comfort, a world apart from that outside the metallic blue car. Jimmy sat on her lap, the back seat as well as the trunk piled high with boxes and luggage.

Laurel grew very conscious of the man beside her, although he seldom spoke. There was something suffocating about his presence in the crowded closed car. This was the second time she'd ridden toward Phoenix, dreading the thought of reaching it. The first time she'd relaxed next to Harley McBride. There was no relaxing with Michael Devereaux. In Harley's truck she'd felt that panic followed her, somewhere behind the truck. On this trip, it traveled in the car with her.

The judge had thrown her together with a stranger. A man she feared more than just a little.

It had taken Michael a week to find them a place to stay. During that week Laurel vacillated between relief at leaving the house in Tucson and terror of living with her husband. And, added to it all, a certain unreasonable, unexplainable excitement.

Claire hadn't bothered to hide her reddened eyes. She'd sat silent at meals and often didn't come down for them. She spoke only of her heartbreak at parting with Jimmy. But Laurel knew, and so did everyone else, that her heart was breaking at the thought of losing Michael. Laurel didn't know how much there was between Claire and Michael. It was hard to imagine that he'd had no romantic interests for those two years. Perhaps there was a woman or more than one in Phoenix.

Evan Boucher took her aside one day and whispered that he'd call her when he knew where he'd be. He looked very worried and that didn't make her feel any better. He too would be leaving Tucson now that Claire could go back to the lab and his plans were to enter summer school in Phoenix.

Paul was obviously pleased at getting her and Jimmy out of the house. Laurel expected her sister-in-law to be relieved at the new arrangement too, but Janet had been irritable and short-tempered this last week. She took every occasion to warn Laurel of Michael's "awful temper," to commiserate with her on the judge's "unfortunate decision," to deepen Laurel's anxiety over the impending move.

Her last morning in Tucson, she'd knelt on the parquet floor of her room beside Consuela, packing linens, towels, and toys into cardboard boxes. Jimmy bounced on the big bed while they worked. The room was already growing hot under the red tiled roof. Consuela stopped often in her packing to watch Jimmy.

"You're sad to see him go, aren't you, Consuela?"

"I shall miss him, Mrs. Michael. But he is going where he belongs. Someday this house will be his, but now it is not safe for him here."

"Not safe? Why?"

But the old woman rose from her knees and went to Jimmy's room. When she returned with another armload of toys Laurel confided, "I think it will be good for Jimmy, but I'm afraid of moving to Phoenix with Michael."

"You have reason to be afraid." Consuela knelt across the box from her and dumped the toys into it and then laid her hand on Laurel's arm, the hand hot and a little damp. "You made him love you once. . . ." Consuela's face came close to hers, her breath smelling faintly of stale onion. "When you are together, away from this place, you must make him love you again, Mrs. Michael. You must do this for Jimmy."

Laurel pulled her arm away from the old woman's grasp. "How can I, Consuela? He hates me."

"You are the same woman he loved. It is what you have done that he hates."

"But how can he ever forgive that? I can't even forgive myself."

"It is good that you fear his anger so that you can be careful of it. But Michael is not so hard and unforgiving a man as he seems. When Maria was killed, I thought that his hurt and anger would grow and would poison him. But once he had cried and broken things it was over. When Mrs. Devereaux first came here and tried to change everything Michael would get so angry he would kick or break things. But he did not hold his anger against her. He would let it out before it could grow worse."

"I could get my head bashed in while being forgiven."

Consuela gave her a long searching look and said quietly, "I have never seen him take out anger on people, Mrs. Michael, only on things."

She should have been in that motel room with me. Laurel slid a careful sideways glance at the man beside her in the speeding car. Had he been the shadow in the courtyard? Consuela would never believe any wrong of Michael. Did she really know him?

The car raced through the desert and Laurel's mind raced with it. If nothing happened in her new home, she would

113

know that it had not been Michael in the courtyard or that she'd imagined everything. But if he was the danger she feared, there would be no locks between them now. Nothing to stop him.

She shivered and snuggled Jimmy closer. He was all she had and she couldn't have Jimmy without Michael. If she couldn't make a success of the next three months she'd lose them both. Michael's hatred for his wife was understandable. And Laurel had given up the hope that she might not be the woman who had deserted him and his newborn son.

They'd driven about an hour when Laurel found her white summer dress soaked where Jimmy had wet through the plastic pants. She reached for the diaper bag on the floor at her feet and tried to lay Jimmy out on the seat between them. With his head on Michael's lap and legs on hers, it was just possible. Laurel felt nervous performing this motherly task in front of Michael. She wasn't very good at it.

He looked disgusted and said, "He should be trained to use the bathroom by now." He glanced away from the road to her, a hint of sarcasm in his eyes. "You can start on that immediately, little mother."

Mother or no mother, she had no idea how to toilet train a child, but she'd never admit it to Michael.

Luke Air Force Base was on the outskirts of Glendale, a suburb of Phoenix. Through the chain link fence that bordered the base she could see a golf course, its thick grass a deep green with sprinkler heads throwing away rainbow water under the thirsty sun.

Across the road from the base were the backyards of brightly colored homes and then a series of blinding white townhouse apartments in pseudo-Spanish style with black wrought-iron casements and gates. She wondered if they would be living in one of the bright houses where young palm trees provided shade. There had been a swing set in one of the yards. Or would a captain live in a townhouse?

As if he knew her thoughts, Michael said, "We won't be

114

living in base housing but just across the street from the base, farther down."

And almost immediately he turned the car onto a dusty side road and then in the front yard of a house. He might as well have described it, "just across the tracks."

Three squat one-story houses of peeling stucco sat close together, one pink, one beige, one green. No trees, shrubs, or driveways. There was little need for a driveway because what grass remained of the lawns sat in sparse dry clumps a foot apart.

The car parked in front of the middle beige house, facing the door, and to her right she could see the green of the air base across the main road. That green ended with the fence. On this side, all was arid and dusty.

"Perhaps military life doesn't look so appealing after all? Something of a comedown after Tucson?"

Laurel didn't answer, but opened the car door. She could take anything he could hand out—she hoped. Stepping out of the air-conditioned car, she could almost feel the weight of the sunlight on the top of her head. The heat took her breath away.

Inside was even worse. The house was a choking stucco oven draining life from anything that moved in it. The front door opened into a small living room furnished with a Danish modern couch and two chairs—the wood scuffed, the dark brown upholstery worn and pilled. Cheap identical lamps sat on end tables. A coffee table, its blond finish out of place, stood in front of the couch.

Along one wall between a bedroom door and a small hallway sat a long low stereo console, too large for the room, too expensive for the house, obviously moved from Michael's bachelor quarters. Faded blue drapes, bare brown tiles, no bars to protect the windows, no massive bolted doors. The house seemed open, vulnerable.

Michael began carrying boxes and luggage in from the car and she followed Jimmy around the partition that made up

115

one wall of the living room. One could walk around either end of this partition to enter the kitchen.

An ancient refrigerator banged instead of hummed. It and the white steel cabinets, apartment-size gas stove, dinette set, and a new clothes washer with the tags still on it crowded the kitchen to overflowing. She explored and found food in the refrigerator, plastic dishes and odd pots and pans in the cupboards.

Sliding glass doors led into the backyard, their undraped panes reflecting the sun's dazzle off the white concrete patio. A wire fence enclosed the backyards of all three houses making a good-sized play area and Laurel was relieved to see a swing set, sandbox, and tricycle. Jimmy would at last have playmates. Separate sets of clothesline were strung out behind each patio. The one on the left held a lonely bra.

A bath and two tiny bedrooms completed the house. Michael had set up Jimmy's crib and one twin bed in the back bedroom. In the front bedroom was the mate to the twin bed and Michael's belongings.

So that was how it was to be.

Laurel dragged back to the kitchen and sank into a chair. Jimmy followed with a little truck he had retrieved from one of the boxes and lay on the floor at her feet sucking his thumb, pushing the truck back and forth languidly with his free hand.

It was too hot and close to move. Laurel couldn't help but compare this with the shaded walkways and huge cool rooms of the house in Tucson.

It started with a giggle. But soon she was laughing so hard she doubled up, her head on the table. She didn't know why she laughed, she didn't have the energy, she shouldn't use up what little air remained in the stifling kitchen. Jimmy perched on one elbow and grinned at her.

Michael came to lean against the partition, his shirt front soaked with sweat, his tie loosened. "You are sane, I hope," he said, his forehead and dark brows set in quizzical lines.

The comment sent her into another fit and Jimmy squealed delightedly.

Michael almost hid the amusement in his eyes. He caught himself and opened the refrigerator to find a can of pop and two cans of beer. Jimmy soon made a sticky mess of himself and the floor with the pop. She gulped at the icy beer between giggles.

"Welcome to Castle Devereaux, appointments by Cheap Rental," Michael said, raising his can in a mock toast. "I'm glad you find it so amusing." His eyes were half-lidded, secretive as he leaned against the refrigerator, looking down at her. He dwarfed the kitchen, looking even bigger than he had in the house in Tucson.

"Amusing? It's pathetic. We'll fry in this place. Isn't there any way to cool it?"

"We don't run to refrigeration, but there is a swamp cooler on the roof. If I can figure out how to turn it on."

She jumped and Jimmy ran to clutch at her leg as a grating, clanging noise like that of a car with a loose radiator fan filled the house. A musky odor soon seeped into the room.

"Pe-u, now I know why they call it a swamp cooler."

"It hasn't been used for a while. The smell should go away soon. The switch is here by the bathroom door," he yelled above the racket. The cooler settled to a roaring hum, drowning out even the ancient refrigerator.

Michael didn't join them for lunch but showered and dressed in his tan uniform. He stopped in the kitchen to get a peanut butter kiss from Jimmy and turned to leave, saying over his shoulder, "Have fun, little mother." He was gone before she could ask when he would be home for dinner.

She bathed Jimmy, put him down for a nap, showered and dressed in yellow slacks and overblouse, sandals, and a yellow scarf to tie back her thick, hot hair. Jimmy had adjusted to the cooler noise and slept untroubled as she moved about the room unpacking their clothes.

At the bottom of the last suitcase she found the battered

117

orange slacks and thought of Harley and of her meeting with Michael in Raymond McBride's motel. She held them for a moment, running her finger over the tear in the pant leg, wondering how it got there, then put the slacks back into the suitcase.

Her future was the main worry now, but the orange slacks fed her nagging anxiety over the past. When would it catch up with her?

The house felt cooler, especially in the hall as she moved through it to the kitchen. But heat still filtered through the exposed glass of the sliding doors. Those doors would have to be draped; the glare was almost worse than the heat.

Opening the refrigerator to find another beer, she heard a rapping behind her and turned to see a woman in shorts standing on the patio. Laurel slid the door back.

The woman was short and plump and wore her shorts a little self-consciously. "Hi, I just came home and heard your cooler going so I figured my new neighbors had moved in." Her smile was friendly, her eyes curious.

"Come in. I was about to open a beer; will you have one with me?" It was a relief to get the woman inside and slide the doors closed against the heat.

"I could use one. I never really appreciated beer until we transferred to the desert. I'm Myra Patrick." She spoke all in a rush as though nervous or excited. "I live in the pink dump next door." Myra slid into a chair by the table and looked around the kitchen. With brown hair cut short and deep dimples in each cheek, she looked like a slightly overweight pixy.

"Laurel . . . Devereaux," she said, handing Myra her untasted beer and finding herself another in the refrigerator.

"Devereaux? You don't know a Mike Devereaux, do you?"

"My husband's name is Michael." Laurel sat at the table and opened her beer.

"No, this one isn't married . . . or he wasn't." Myra sat up in her chair. "Captain? Mike J. Tall, dark . . . blue eyes?"

118

"That does sound like Michael."

Myra was in the process of lighting a cigarette, but she gaped at Laurel and the match burned down to her fingers. She jumped, blew it out, and lit another.

"You mean you landed Mike Devereaux? Wait till this gets out." She rolled her eyes in amused wonder. "When did all this happen?"

Laurel got her a saucer for an ashtray and turned to find Myra looking at the highchair.

"No, still wrong one. You are not newly wed. This Mike came from Tucson. He and Pat, my husband, served in Vietnam together. Mike's got darkish skin and funny blue eyes. He's pretty fast but not that fast," and she grinned at the high chair. "Tell me about your Michael and kids."

Laurel was embarrassed. She'd better straighten things out before Myra said anymore. "We have one son—Jimmy. Jimmy and I have been living in Tucson with Michael's family and Michael has darkish skin and funny blue eyes. We were married before he went to Vietnam. Jimmy is two. I think we're talking about the same man."

The cooler roared into the silence between them. Myra's cigarette halted halfway to her mouth and stayed there. It was the first time she'd sat still since she came in.

Michael could have warned her that he was moving them in next to friends of his.

Her visitor didn't look quite convinced. "He's been stationed here for months. Why did he wait till now to bring you here? I guess I . . . we just assumed he was single. He always had plenty of money, and married men don't. He never mentioned you or the baby. And he seemed free to . . . ." She caught herself and looked at the refrigerator to avoid Laurel's eyes. "I'm sorry. I didn't come over here to drink your beer and then spread tales."

"I think I know what you were going to say. But it's all right . . . I. . . ."

"All right!" Myra's friendly expression hardened as she

dashed the cigarette into the saucer. "Look, I'm sorry I said as much as I did. But if we're talking about the same man my opinion of Mike Devereaux has just fallen to dead zero."

"Don't be too hard on him. You see we've been separated for a long time. He. . . ." Laurel caught herself with surprise; she was actually defending Michael.

"Well, that explains a few things. I guess I'd better let you get to your moving in." She rose quickly as if eager to get away.

"Myra? You will come back?" Laurel said, suddenly realizing how lonely she was without friends.

"Oh, sure. Tell you what. I'll round up Colleen. She lives on the other side of you and we'll have coffee at my house tomorrow morning. Nine-thirty? Bring Jimmy. My Sherrie is three and they can get to know each other. Okay?"

"Tomorrow morning."

But Myra still shook her head as she stepped off the patio and headed home.

Laurel stood Jimmy in front of the toilet in the bathroom when he woke up from his nap. She tried to explain what she wanted of him, but he just looked blank. When she finally gave up, he hosed down the floor, one wall, and her slacks.

That afternoon she scrubbed the bathroom. Motherhood wasn't as easy as it looked.

She waited dinner until six thirty and then fixed eggs and bacon for the two of them, turning on the radio that sat on the kitchen counter, to relieve the loneliness of their dinner.

". . . of the rioting at the University of Arizona in Tucson. Officials at the University in Tempe say that they will be ready for any such student disorders on their own campus but don't look for any trouble during the hot summer months.

"Newsmen report that summer has forced the hippies from their winter encampments on the desert and that even the largest colony, near Florence, has been evacuated.

"Officials report that the incidents of hepatitis have decreased in the southern part of the state as the hippies have moved north.

"On the weather scene, tomorrow will be clear with temperatures ranging over 100 degrees in the Valley of the Sun and. . . ."

Laurel switched off the radio. The mention of hippies always reminded her of Harley and his mistaking her for one. Where was Harley now? What was he doing?

Michael didn't come home until after they were in bed. When she got up the next morning, he had dressed and was going out the door. He paused only to say good-bye to Jimmy.

Laurel finished the breakfast dishes by seven thirty and decided to try out the new washer. Lifting the lid of the plastic diaper pail she choked on the acrid smell of ammonia. Picking up the pail, she closed her eyes and dumped the whole grim mess into the machine. Then she worked on the sticky spot on the kitchen floor where Jimmy had spilled his pop. Finally she gave up and scrubbed the whole floor. It was barely eight thirty in the morning and already her back ached.

At first it sounded like an explosion. The floor trembled beneath her, the windows rattled, and there was an answering tinkle from the cupboards, a roaring noise from outside the house.

"Jet, Mommy!" Jimmy, jumping in his excitement, tried to open the sliding doors and point all at the same time.

They both rushed out onto the patio and watched as one jet after another, sun glinting off their silvery sides, rose from the base, crossed the road, and screamed over the house.

Laurel dashed back into the kitchen, her hands clamped over her ears. Her body trembled, her heart raced. The noise . . . something about that noise sent her into near panic. She didn't know why.

Some time after the last plane had soared above them she finally stopped the trembling in her legs. Tears smeared her cheeks as she stood gripping the cool edge of the sink, trying to understand her reaction. Just as she turned from the sink, a picture floated before her inner vision.

A picture of gently swaying tall-tipped pines encircling a patch of sky . . . a contrail drifting diagonally across it . . . the white streak in the intense clean blue outlined in moving jagged green-black . . . as if she were lying on the ground looking up at the sky.

Suddenly she began to tremble again.

11

A sleepy-looking blonde sat at the table drinking coffee with Myra. Laurel tapped on the glass.

"Come on in!" Myra filled a third cup from the percolator. "Laurel, this is Colleen Houghton."

The blonde was beautiful, small and already made up over a glorious suntan. "Welcome to the ghetto." Colleen Houghton gave her a dreamy smile and then looked at Jimmy. "So this is Mike Devereaux's little boy."

"Do you know Michael, too?"

"No, but I've heard a lot about him." And in a languid drawl that had to be Texan: "You're going to be something of a shock around here."

Myra's house was identical with her own, less shabby, with more color to the walls. A little girl in a sundress and ponytail peeked around the partition wall. Jimmy leaped onto Laurel's lap and glowered back at her.

"Sherrie, come meet Jimmy," Myra said. "He's going to live next door and you'll finally have someone to play with."

Sherrie moved timidly toward Jimmy, reaching out to touch his leg as if she couldn't believe he really existed. It took some persuasion to get them out the door, but before long the children sat in the sandbox throwing sand at each other.

"Are you Air Force, too?" Laurel asked Colleen.

"Well, sort of. I'm what you call a hanger-on."

"Don't be silly," Myra said matter-of-factly. "Colleen lost her husband last year in Vietnam." Neither woman even blinked.

Colleen shrugged. "I've just never got up the gumption to leave. My friends are here and it's cheaper living near a base with the BX and all. More eligible men, too." She gave Myra a knowing look and said, "You might as well tell her."

Myra bit her lip and looked away. "I'd just gotten Colleen around to saying I could fix her up with your husband. I honestly didn't know he had a family, Laurel, and it's the same Mike. I saw him leave this morning."

"Oh," Laurel said a little lamely. She could see Colleen's blonde next to Michael's dark; they'd make a stunning pair.

"No harm done, I guess. I hadn't said anything to him about it. Don't tell, huh?" Myra refilled the cups. "I feel pretty silly."

The conversation promised to last until noon, settling into woman talk, Myra's recipes, Colleen's golf, gossip of the base that Laurel couldn't follow, dull nothing chatter to pass the time. Laurel was soon bored and disturbed. She felt no more at home here than she had in Tucson. Using the excuse that she still had some unpacking to do, she left.

Taking Michael's Polaroid camera outside, she snapped pictures of Jimmy in the sandbox and on the swing. When Colleen left Myra's, she asked her to take a picture of the two of them.

All afternoon the jets returned home. Michael didn't.

Another late lonely dinner, and when she'd put Jimmy to bed, she sat on the lumpy couch with pen and paper. She'd had an uneasy feeling that time was running out for her since morning when the roar of jet fighters had sent that strange vision bubbling up from the shadows of her mind. Laurel couldn't explain why; she didn't know if it was a memory. It could have been a picture she'd seen on a postcard or something irrelevant her subconscious had let surface at random as it might in a dream. But it had made her resolve early in the day to write that long overdue letter to Lisa Lawrence. Pride would not let her go to the phone to talk to this remote mother who could give her up so easily. But fear drove her to at least write her plea for help.

Her first inclination was to start the letter with "Dear Mrs. Lawrence." But she wrote instead, "Dear Lisa," looked at it and started again on a fresh piece of paper, "Dear Mother." She began her letter in a breezy style, explaining that she was back with her family, living near the air base, much of Jimmy, little of Michael. And then she moved abruptly to a detailed list of what she had learned about herself, pleading with Lisa to fill in the gaps.

"This will sound strange, I know, but I can't remember anything before last April. No one here will believe that. I want to know about you, my father, my home, myself—anything you can tell me may help me to remember. I am so afraid, not knowing about myself and what I have done in my life. But worst of all, I don't know what I might do. How I will react to things. It is like living a nightmare, watching myself and others but unable to change anything or control my life at all. And this will sound the strangest yet, but I sense that I'm in some kind of danger and I don't know what it is. I must remember before it closes in on me. The one thing that keeps me going is Jimmy. I am trying hard to make up to him for what I did. I love him so." Laurel asked that her letter be answered at once, enclosed the pictures, and sealed the envelope.

Then she sat back and considered all the things she hadn't said, couldn't say. The threatening shadow in the courtyard. The hearing in Denver. The probationary sentence. The fact that her husband didn't want her. That everyone loathed her and she didn't remember one good thing about herself.

If Claire could have convinced Jimmy he really was a "bad boy," would he have grown into one? If she could see herself only as she was mirrored in the eyes of others would she become what they thought she was?

With Jimmy asleep and the cooler off the house lay in prickly silence. An occasional car would go by on the road running between Myra's and the base. Her nerves jumped when the old refrigerator clicked on. During the day it was easier to forget the fears that haunted her nights.

Saturday morning she awakened before Jimmy, dressed, and walked to the kitchen only to stop in the doorway and stare.

Michael stood in front of the sink in pajama bottoms, filling the coffee pot.

There was something incongruous about this large half-naked man in the tiny kitchen. He looked now more like the "Mike" Myra spoke of than the sophisticated reserved Michael she had known in the elegance of Tucson.

But when he turned to face her, she was looking at the old Michael with the cold pale eyes and steel set to his jaw. Michael could look arrogant even in pajama bottoms.

Laurel felt the answering sullen pout forming on her lips as she moved into the kitchen to prepare breakfast for three.

Jimmy did most of the talking at the table, regaling his father with his activities of the week. Since he'd been playing with Sherrie his vocabulary had at least quadrupled.

Michael watched him with interest. "So you like living here?"

"Yeah. It's good. Sherrie pays wis me and Mommy tell me story and. . . ."

"Don't you miss Claire?"

"Claire's a bad boy!" When he'd finished his breakfast, Laurel turned Jimmy out to run through the sprinkler with Sherrie, and she and Michael sat over a second cup of coffee.

He looked tired, the worry lines on his forehead too deep for his age, his movements slower, less abrupt. She wasn't surprised. If he'd slept much that week, it hadn't been at home.

"What do you do? On the base, I mean."

126

"Train pilots."

"Do you fly?"

"Some."

"Shouldn't you get more sleep?"

"Are you worried about me, Laurel?" His eyebrows lifted in mock surprise as he rested both elbows on the table and held the cup to his lips.

"It just seems dangerous, is all." She met the coldness in his eyes above the coffee cup and looked away. He seemed to be able to go forever without blinking.

It was unreal sitting in this room with him. To an outsider they would look like a normal couple talking idly over the breakfast table. She tried hard to remember a time when they might have done this before. She couldn't even imagine it. "What was I like . . . before you went to Vietnam?"

"Oh, for God's sake."

"No . . . please . . . just pretend I know but I want you to tell me anyway."

"What do you want now, Laurel, compliments?" He took a long time stacking his dishes and then rose, holding them in one hand, and stood by his chair for a moment looking down, not at her but through her. "You were . . . just like you are now." And then his eyes focused on hers. "But all that's in between hadn't happened." He took his dishes to the sink, effectively closing the subject.

Laurel thought that anyone changes in two years surely. It was as if she'd stepped into some kind of suspended time when she walked out of that hospital. As if she had skipped those two years while everyone else lived, grew, changed. . . .

A brief rap and Myra slid the screen back and stepped into the kitchen. She stopped as she noticed Michael, her dimples fading uncertainly. "Oh . . . hi, Mike."

"Myra."

"Excuse me for barging in. But I wanted to know if you all would come over tonight for a barbecue? Colleen's bringing

127

the beer, and you could bring a salad and bread. I'll have the rest. Kind of late when it gets cool?" she blurted out nervously, one hand still on the screen.

"Do we dress?" Michael looked amused at her discomfort over finding him home.

"Well, you could put on your pajama top and a tie. Can you come?"

"We'll be there," he answered for both of them, as if he did it always.

Laurel was surprised that he hadn't already made plans of his own for a Saturday night.

With Michael home, her day was confused. The heat drove them inside with the cooler, which did at least move the air around, but the three of them seemed to stumble over each other in the tiny house. Laurel felt self-conscious with Michael ever-present and strangely unable to find anything to do.

Jimmy watched television. Michael settled with a book at the kitchen table while she set yeast dough to rise for the patio party. Although she felt Michael's critical eyes on her back, whenever she turned to glance at him he seemed engrossed in his reading. She started nervously every time he turned a page. When the sunlight began to fade and she could prepare the greens for the salad, she sighed with relief.

A distant roar and then a fighter screamed overhead. She cut her finger instead of the onion she was chopping.

Just as she felt the now familiar panic rise in her throat at the sound of the plane, an image literally exploded into her mind.

Laurel stood transfixed, letting her finger bleed into the sink, her eyes closed . . . five mounded graves stretched side by side on the desert with little wooden crosses . . . tall cacti standing guard over them. . . .

"What are you going to do? Stand there and bleed to death?" Michael's curt voice cut through her thoughts, forcing her eyes open, driving the image away.

Stinging sweat ran into her eyes. Laurel sat down on the kitchen floor before her knees could buckle beneath her.

Dusk was just turning to night as they congregated on the Patricks' patio for barbecued ribs. A soft pink lingered in the sky to the west. Heat still rose from the concrete under them, but the air moved a little now, balmy, cooler.

Colleen arrived last with a tub of ice and beer and a young man in tow. She introduced him as Gary but he knew the men. Sitting at the picnic table with Jimmy on her lap, Laurel braced herself for Gary's wide-eyed start as she was introduced to him as Michael's wife. Michael merely stared him down as if daring him to comment.

Pat enlisted Gary to help pass out beer before the situation could grow uncomfortable and smoothly hurried the dinner and the conversation. Pat was short, stocky, relaxed, with squint lines at the corners of his eyes like Harley's. A comfortably good-natured man with a raft of ribald stories and the confidence to pull them off. Laurel envied Myra the peaceful life she must have with him.

Michael sat beside her and helped her fill Jimmy's plate, solemnly playing the role of family man. Laurel knew without looking that the others watched them closely.

She winced visibly as Michael leaned across her to hand Jimmy a roll he'd buttered and looked up in time to meet Colleen's curious glance. The Devereaux' must appear a very strange couple to these people. But there was no help for it; they were a strange couple.

Later she helped Myra clear the table and bring out chairs while Colleen regaled the men with a story of her own. The sweating tub yielded another round of beer. Sherrie and Jimmy raced the length of the yard. And it was night. . . .

They sat, beer in hand, in a rough semicircle around the light of the kitchen that streamed through the sliding glass doors. No porch light was needed, for the Arizona night was not dark, just soft, mellow. Laurel and Myra sat together at one end of the semicircle facing Colleen, who'd placed herself between Gary and Michael. And Pat, the perfect host, sat between the two groups, joining them together.

Myra was quieter with men around, turning often to watch the children at play. But Colleen in her short white dress and deep tan listened attentively, tossing her blond head and laughing on cue as the men talked of German pilots they were training. She managed to flirt mildly with all three of them.

Pat held his beer between his legs and put both hands behind his head, leaning the kitchen chair back on two legs. "Hell, those Krauts go at it like they're planning World War III. Had one up yesterday—he got so excited I thought he was going to eat the stick."

And Laurel felt disembodied, as though she were outside the semicircle, watching but not a part of it, only half-conscious of the conversation, half sleepy from the heavy meal and the beer, hearing again her husband's laughter as Colleen had finished her story.

She'd been in the kitchen with Myra and the laugh had mingled with that of the other men, but still distinct, deep, abrupt. She'd singled it out, known it at once and yet was hearing it for the first time. He didn't laugh like that even when he played with his son. Something in her responded to that laugh, and it lingered in his eyes as she walked onto the patio.

Then his eyes had met hers and the laughter died. She'd killed it by just coming into view, by just being Laurel.

A car drove past on the road, its lights tunneling into the night ahead. Stars winked above mountains dark on the horizon, reminding her of Tucson. Slow-dying coals glared with red undersides in the barbecue, and the smell of charcoal and spicy ribs still hung about the patio. A muffled giggling erupted from the sandbox.

Light from the kitchen fell on one half of Michael's face, leaving the other half in a satanic gloom, reflecting the sheen

130

of his black head, glinting in his eyes—more gray than blue tonight, the color of weathered aluminum.

He relaxed with his legs outstretched, crossed at the ankles, his arms folded, cradling the beer can with one hand in the crook of his elbow. The curve of muscle rolled out under the short sleeves of his white knit shirt.

". . . when the hippies come back in the fall."

"Think they'll be back?" Gary was talking to Pat but grinning at Laurel's knees. She crossed her legs.

"Sure. The world's getting lousy with them. They've got to go where the weather's nice so they can commune with nature. Myra and I went to Florence last winter just to stare. What a mess. Made the desert look like a city dump. They lived in tents and old cars. Just get rid of the wetbacks and now hippies."

Laurel watched Michael's jaw muscle constrict, his lips tighten to a thin line at Pat's mention of wetbacks. No one else seemed to notice that a social *faux pas* had been committed.

"Well, I feel sorry for them," Myra said it almost apologetically, as if she had no right to an opinion of her own but couldn't keep still. "Some of them looked ill. And there were two small kids—dirty, listless. Those hippies can live like that if they think it proves anything, but they don't have the right to treat children that way."

"At least they don't drop bombs on *other* people's children." It came to Laurel's lips and was said before she had time to consider it. It was the wrong place to say it.

They stared at her in silence, probably as startled by the sound of her voice as anything. She'd barely spoken all evening. But if it surprised the others, it left Laurel dumbfounded. She had voiced an opinion. Not well thought out or well expressed, but an opinion. Backed by conviction.

Pat finally spoke. "Hey, Mike, you brought a dove into our midst?"

131

"I'm sure I would be the last to know." Michael had gone still, watchful. An immense ugly beetle flew into the side of his shoe and flopped onto the concrete on its back, helpless threadlike legs flaying the air, making a horrid buzzing sound.

Michael brought his heel down on the bug's middle, squashing it.

Laurel looked away, fighting the beer back down her throat.

"I saw that John the Baptist when I was in Colorado a couple of months ago visiting my folks in Boulder. He was the weirdest-looking creature," Gary said, finally pulling his eyes off the mess at Michael's foot and reaching into the tub behind him for another beer. "All robes and hair."

"What's his problem anyway?" Colleen asked.

"Oh, he's trying to set a fire under the hippies. I saw him in the city park speaking to a bunch of them. They gather there and lay around on the grass. He's quite a speaker, I'll say that for him, but I didn't notice anybody getting stirred up. They just smiled and rolled over."

"He's got the students rioting in Tucson now."

"No, that's fizzled—too hot. But he'll be back in the fall. If anybody can organize that bunch it's him. He almost made you want to stand up and say—*heil!*" Gary shot his arm forward in the Nazi salute.

Michael listened quietly to the conversation. He leaned back to empty his beer, and when he brought his head down, his eyes, half-lidded, seeing but not revealing, met Laurel's and held them. To her his stare carried the illusion of weight like the desert sun at noon. Her throat was suddenly so dry it hurt to swallow.

Colleen finally came to her rescue. "Hey! None of that, you two. You've been married too long."

Pat hooted and got up, grinning, to replace Michael's empty can with a fresh one. "It's the beer. Always works on the quiet ones first."

When Myra left the semicircle to collect Sherrie for bed,

Laurel followed her lead. Just as she was fighting a dirty, reluctant Jimmy into the house she heard Pat saying from next door . . . "Won't be long before we're calling you Major Devereaux, will it, Mike?"

She didn't wait to hear an answer but heard voices and Colleen's tinkling laughter long after she'd gone to bed. She didn't know when Michael came in.

Sunday morning he took Jimmy and they were gone until late afternoon. Michael was determined to be a weekend father if not a weekend husband.

She watched the Patricks go off as a family. Laurel was miserable—the feeling of being left out, of not belonging, overwhelmed her. After fixing herself a lunch she couldn't eat, she stretched out on the lumpy couch and tried to nap. Her thoughts turned to the patio party, the people, the conversation . . . and then that haunting little graveyard with the five wooden crosses flashed across her mind's eye and was gone. That must be something she'd seen . . . a faint twinge of nausea, the beginning of a headache. . . .

Laurel sat up on the couch. Why should that memory, if that's what it was, affect her so violently?

A car pulled up and she went to the door expecting to see Michael and Jimmy. But Evan Boucher crawled out of a Volkswagen.

The shy smile that moved the thin, drooping mustache out at the corners, the soft hazel eyes. She'd almost forgotten he existed.

"Hi," she said before he could, and opened the screen door for him.

"You look surprised to see me, Mrs. Devereaux. I told you I'd keep in touch."

"How did you find us?"

"I called your sister-in-law." He followed her into the kitchen where she mixed two tall glasses of iced tea. "Is everything all right . . . I mean . . . well, you know?"

"Everything's fine," she lied. "I'm glad you stopped by,

Evan. Michael and Jimmy are at the zoo and I was looking for something to do."

He stayed nearly two hours, chatting, drinking several glasses of tea in the little living room. She was grateful for the visit; it relieved the loneliness of her day. They discussed the weather, Paul's research, and Evan's summer courses in Tempe. She let him ramble about John the Baptist.

Evan seemed more relaxed and less clumsy here than in the more intimidating atmosphere in Tucson. He was letting his hair grow longer and had added cowboy boots to his regular jeans and work shirt. He still blushed if she stared at him too intently.

Finally they sat quiet for a few minutes and then Evan said, "Are you happy here?"

"I feel lost wherever I am."

"But nothing's happened? No one's tried to hurt you or anything?" He blushed and looked away. "That's really why I came. I was worried. . . ."

"You think I'm in danger from my husband, don't you, Evan?"

He shrugged and shook his head. "I don't know the man . . . but I don't like the way he looks at you, Mrs. Devereaux. What do you think?"

"I think he's had plenty of time to do something . . . if he wanted to. We're pretty much alone here. Sometimes I think I imagined that someone chased me in the courtyard in Tucson . . . and sometimes I worry that I'm not quite sane." She walked about the room restlessly and then sat next to him on the couch. "Evan . . . those people who . . . where you worked . . . *some* of them remembered? Didn't they?"

"Sure. Most of them did." He put a warm hand over her cold one. "And you will, too. Nothing's come back yet?"

"No," she lied again because she didn't want to discuss those two brief flashes of memory, didn't like her reaction to

134

them. "Maybe I *should* be in an institution, but I don't want to leave Jimmy. I can't stand to be away from him."

He patted her hand absently and looked off into space. "That kind of institution is a pretty rough place to be in." Evan Boucher's hand trembled. "I almost went crazy just working in one. . . ."

12

The heat in Phoenix and Glendale was worse than that in Tucson because of the humidity. Canals, irrigation ditches, and irrigated fields that made the Valley of the Sun a unique green oasis of the desert also made it a sticky, choking hotbox with the air so thick one almost had to chew it to breathe it. This situation was relieved only when dry winds hurled off the desert, breaking tree limbs and driving sandy grit into homes and cars and mouths.

July brought rain, violent electrical storms that promised coolness but left behind a humid unbreathable heat worse than before. After a gentle flowering spring the desert summer seemed intent upon forcing out its human intruders.

The cooler clanged away day and night doing a little more than just moving the air around but adding to the clamminess within the house until clothes, sheets, towels, and skin were constantly sticky. It depended upon evaporation for cooling and could do little with the humid heat. The Patricks gave up and bought a refrigeration unit. The Devereaux' endured.

Laurel, Jimmy, and the Patricks gathered on their front steps the night of the Fourth to watch public fireworks displays in the sky over Phoenix. But they were soon forced inside as nature crashed down at them, drowning out the fireworks and putting on a breathtaking display of her own.

Laurel stood at the doors to the patio holding Jimmy in her arms and watched as the lightning creased down from the dark cloud bank etching the sky like lighted rivers with their

136

tributaries on a black map. Jimmy hid his face against her shoulder, holding himself rigid, his arms almost choking around her neck.

Lightning cracked close and the lights went out. They waited in a tense, dark silence for the next crack followed at once by floor-jarring thunder and, when it was over, for the next. Each seemed incredibly closer and raindrops turned to sheets of water as the lightning stalked them.

Laurel's hands were sweating as she carried Jimmy into the little hallway as if to hide them from the violence outside. "Jimmy, we're safe in our snug little house. The lightning and thunder can't get us here." *I hope.* "There's nothing to be afraid of."

His answer was one long shuddering sob choked off at the end and no release of the tension in his body. And the storm moved past them, on to terrorize other small children, other childish women.

The next storm arrived a week later but it came during the day, and this one left a rainbow as if in apology. It was naptime and Jimmy had slept through the thunderous racket. Laurel sat at the kitchen table with a glass of his Kool-Aid and a magazine. But the colorful cover could not compete with the proud rainbow sky. Bold red, a lighter green, and faint lavender feathering at the edges—the rainbow arching up out of her sight.

A banging on the front door filtered through the noise of the cooler, and when she faced Claire Bently through the screen, Laurel could only stare dumbly at her visitor. It was the same Claire with the full-skirted shirtwaist and light brown hair. But the hair which was usually straight now hung in limp curls, those close to her neck stringy from perspiration. Dark red lips and spots of rouge on each cheek highlighted her sallow skin and some of the jet-black mascara was smudged under her eyes. A strangely pathetic Claire.

Postrain heat seeped through the screen.

"Can I come in?"

"I'm sorry, Claire, come in. I was just surprised to see you."

"I thought I'd look in and find out how you and Jimmy were getting along. We sort of looked for you the Fourth." Claire giggled unnecessarily and stared about the room as if she were thinking of buying it.

That war paint isn't for Jimmy or me. "We're fine. Jimmy's asleep now. Want some Kool-Aid?" Laurel started for the kitchen.

"Have you got anything stronger?" Claire didn't follow her but stopped at the door of Michael's room. When she turned to Laurel the pathetic look had changed to one of triumph. "You can't both sleep in that little bed."

"No. How about a Martini?" *How about some rat poison?*

"I'd love one. The house is so quiet now you've all left. Professor Devereaux has finally got a start on his new book. He's kept me busy doing research." Claire settled at the kitchen table fussing with her hair while Laurel fixed the drink. "Mrs. Devereaux is sweltering in the heat. Whatever possessed her to stay this summer, I don't know. Especially now that Michael won't be coming home much."

"Why should that matter? I thought she didn't like him."

Claire took a gulp of the drink, which was meant to be sipped, and shuddered. Her eyes filled with tears as the stinging liquid burned down her throat. Laurel grinned. "The only thing she doesn't like about him is that Michael refuses to notice her sexy ways. She just doesn't realize that he's above that kind of thing."

This time it was Laurel's turn to choke over her drink even if it was only Kool-Aid. "Come now, Claire. You haven't built Michael into some kind of saint, have you? Or a monk?"

Claire lifted her head proudly. "Michael would never be tempted by a woman he didn't love. Especially not by his brother's wife. I feel sorry for Professor Devereaux. You can't imagine what he's had to put up with."

"The Devereaux brothers seem unlucky in love," Laurel

138

said more to herself than to her visitor, and a little bitterly.

"Oh, he never loved her; he just felt sorry for her. Before he knew what had happened he was married." Claire finished her drink with defiance as if she'd taken it on a dare. "Her father killed himself because he'd gambled away the family fortune. Her fine old Boston family was broke. Old Mr. Devereaux was always throwing it up to her that she was too good for the Devereaux' but not for their money."

The Martini had caused Claire's pupils to dilate. The attempt at sophistication was giving way to the more natural sullenness. She looked about her with obvious contempt. "This place is awfully small. Do you like it here?"

"I don't mind it." Laurel busied herself putting a leg of lamb and some potatoes in the oven, hoping to heat Claire right out of the house.

"I've always wished I could learn to cook. But Mother did most of it until she got sick, and when she died I came to Tucson. So I've always had it done for me. Did you know I was born in China?" Claire went into a lengthy tale of her parents, who were missionaries in China, being forced out by the revolution, of their parish in San Diego, her father's death, and the struggle for survival of his wife and daughter.

It was a bleak story. Claire nursed a sick mother, worked long hours in a drugstore, and went to night school to get secretarial training. They lived in one cheap apartment after another, each cheaper than the last. Laurel could picture her walking into the grand existence of the Devereaux house with a room of her own, dining with the family, someone to wait on her and a handsome Michael about her own age. No wonder the Devereaux' were so important to her.

Claire's eyes kept slipping to the electric clock over the refrigerator. "When does Michael get home? I'd like to see him before I go."

Laurel sighed and put an extra potato in the oven. "I don't know. He doesn't come home at any particular time." *Not till he thinks I'm in bed.* The pilot light in the oven had gone

139

out and it whumped as she relit it. She put the salad in the crisper and fixed them both a drink.

"You know, you've changed, Laurel. You look . . . oh . . . harder. More like I expected you would look." Claire giggled nervously and went on to talk of Janet's irritability.

But Laurel had stopped back at the first statement, barely listening to the chatter about Janet. She *was* changing. They were making her into the Laurel they expected her to be.

Claire stopped in midsentence, a slow Martini smile lighting her face, looking beyond Laurel. And Laurel turned to find Jimmy just inside the kitchen, his hair rumpled from sleep, the Teddy bear dangling from one hand. He stood stiffly tense, as he had when she'd held him during the storm, staring at Claire with round mesmerized eyes. She expected him to bolt as their visitor suddenly got to her feet and gushed toward him.

"Hello, little fellow. Claire's missed her little boy so much." But he didn't run and Claire picked him up. Jimmy gave a long shuddering sob and dropped the Teddy bear.

"Claire, you're frightening him."

"Don't be silly. I raised him, remember? You're not afraid of your old Claire, are you?"

Jimmy placed a hand on each of her shoulders and pushed back, his feet kicking her in the midsection and below. Claire gasped and released him, and he fell to the floor next to the Teddy bear.

"Jimmy! Are you all right?"

"Is *he* all right? What have you done to him?"

Jimmy peered at Claire from the safety of his mother's arms. "My house!"

"Honey, Claire just came to visit you in your house. She isn't going to take you away. He's just afraid you've come to take him back to Tucson."

"What does he have here he didn't have in Tucson?"

"Freedom, the run of the house, the backyard, a playmate, and he gets to see more of his father."

140

"Humph! His skin is too fair to be out in the sun much. And look at the scratches on his legs." But her eyes were saying something else. *You've done this. You've turned him against me.*

Claire's lips pressed in so tight a line they almost inverted. Hurt and hate bulged in her eyes, outlined by the crimson flush. And Laurel felt the other woman's hate engulf her, felt her own body stiffen as Jimmy's had. For a moment she too was afraid of Claire Bently.

"Go see Sherrie?" The plea in Jimmy's voice drove her to change him and take him over to Myra's.

While Laurel set the table, Claire swirled the olive around in her drink. They both had wilted some in the sweltering kitchen. "Aren't you going to wait for Michael?"

"Sometimes when he's late he eats on the base." She set a place for him anyway, knowing he probably wouldn't be there to use it. "Won't you stay for dinner, Claire?" *Please don't.*

"Oh, I wouldn't miss it for anything. Somehow I can't see Michael sitting in this room eating." Claire's smile hardened and she said quietly, "He'd have married me if you hadn't come back, you know."

"Paul says he wouldn't divorce."

"He couldn't. You weren't there to divorce. But in five more years you would have been declared legally dead, and then he would have remarried and it would have been me."

"Had your plans all made, didn't you? Well, Michael wasn't exactly unoccupied here while you so self-sacrificingly took care of his child in Tucson." Laurel leaned across the table and put her face as close to Claire's as she could get it. "Claire, has Michael ever asked you to wait for him, told you he loved you? Has he?"

"Yes. No. Well, he didn't have to. It was understood." Her giggle gave her away. "He doesn't have to tell me anything, because I know him." Her angry flush deepened the color of her rouge.

141

"Okay. You know him. I didn't mean to upset you, Claire, don't cry."

"I'm not crying!" Smudgy mascara tears ran down her cheeks. "And I don't believe Michael has been seeing women here. You're just saying that because you're jealous of me. Things aren't going so well for you, are they? He isn't coming home for dinner. He never does, I'll bet. And he sleeps in a separate room. And do you know why? It's because of me, Laurel. Me." Laurel started to rise, but Claire grabbed her arm and forced her to sit.

"And you know what else? I'm glad you came back. Because now he'll see every day what kind of a person you are and his loathing for you will grow to the point that he'll get rid of you no matter what any church says."

Laurel broke away and went to the oven. "You'll feel better after some food, Claire." But when she'd put the dinner on and returned with Jimmy, Claire was fixing herself another drink. "If you don't eat instead of drink, you'll never get back to Tucson tonight."

Claire got through a few bites of lamb and the entire third Martini before she fell apart. She was in the middle of her one date with Michael. It had been his last year in college and they'd gone out to dinner with several other couples and then to a dance. Finally Laurel forced a swinging, swaying Claire to dance into the bedroom, and took her dress off.

"The bedshpinning round, round, round. . . ."

"I'll call Janet and tell her you're spending the night." But Claire already slept. She'd just returned to her dinner when Michael came home.

"Claire sick, Daddy."

"More like crocked," Laurel said between her teeth as she sliced off some roast and put it on Michael's plate.

He looked at the empty place, the empty gin bottle on the counter, and arched an eyebrow. "I'm sorry I missed the party. Where is she?"

"In my bed—if the spinning hasn't thrown her out by now. You get the floor tonight."

"She really hung one on?" That marvelous laugh filled the kitchen. "Good old Claire. What I don't learn about women in my old age." Michael explained that he'd eaten, and then decimated the roast anyway. He was still chuckling as he crawled into his makeshift bed on the living room floor where he managed to block all movement within the room.

Laurel went to sleep thinking how unwittingly cruel men were. She dreamed that the beige bungalow was burning and that Claire Bently was outside the door swinging an ax at her whenever she tried to escape and Michael stood on the patio laughing and laughing and. . . .

The next morning a subdued pale-greenish Claire left before breakfast, explaining that she must get back to her work, pausing long enough to blush a good-bye to Michael.

He was in rare good humor, so Laurel got up the courage to ask him for money. When he handed it to her, he grabbed her wrist and held it so tightly her hand went cold. She couldn't look at him.

"If you're going to use this to skip out on me, don't take Jimmy with you. I'll have the law on you if you do." Then he laughed at her and left, looking like an astronaut in his silver-gray flight suit.

She, Myra, and the children spent the afternoon shopping at the Base Exchange and then went on to a nearby shopping center. Among other things she returned with a round avocado area rug and matching drapes for the living room, yellow drapery material for the patio doors, twelve pairs of training pants, and a red tricycle.

Pat sat in the kitchen with a can of beer when they hauled their purchases into Myra's house to separate them. He helped them carry Laurel's packages to her patio door.

"I forgot, this is locked. We can't get in this way. I'll go around. . . ."

"No it isn't, see?" Pat slid open the screen and then the door.

"That's funny. I'm sure I locked. . . ."

The odor seemed to gush out the door and into their faces—heavy, nauseating, unmistakable. . . .

"Get back." Pat dropped the packages and ran across the kitchen floor to the stove, turned, and ran back out to take a deep breath. "It's not the jets on the stove." He pulled the patio door shut.

"Shouldn't you open the house up?"

"I don't want to move it around. Gas rises. Where's my toolbox?"

"Under the barbecue where you left it. Pat, you're supposed to open windows. . . ."

He rummaged in the toolbox. "Myra, this is no time to argue. And will you two get away from that door?"

"But. . . ."

"If that gas gets stirred up and seeps down to those pilot lights, that place will—where the hell's the wrench?—that place will explode. I'm going to try to turn it off at the meter."

He pulled a wrench from the jumble of tools. "If I can figure out how to do it . . . God almighty, will you get away from that door!"

Laurel and Myra moved off the patio.

"Myra, call the fire department and the utilities company. Tell them there's a massive gas leak in that house. Laurel, get Colleen and the kids together. Then everybody out of here. Go over by the base fence . . . Laurel! Laurel!"

Pat shook her roughly and then slapped her. "Move. Both of you!" He roared it at them. His face had turned ashen. He ran off around the side of the house.

Myra looked shocked at her husband's actions but did as

144

she was told. Laurel moved in a half-daze to Colleen's door. Colleen was gone.

She gathered the children from the swings and took them across the road to the chain link fence. *My God! Who? Why?*

Michael came home just as the firemen were wrapping up the cords on the big explosion-proof fans. Only a hint of the nauseous, deadly fumes remained.

Laurel stood backed up against the sink, her hands holding onto the counter behind her. A repairman, a fireman, and Pat Patrick knelt around the back of the stove, shaking their heads. The stove had been pulled away from the wall.

Michael literally ran around the partition. "What's happened? Where's Jim?"

"Gas leak. He's at our house; he's okay." Pat stood up. "This is Mr. Devereaux."

"Had a close call here, Mr. Devereaux." The fireman pointed behind the stove. "These old rentals aren't kept up like they should be. You're lucky Mr. Patrick was around and knew what to do."

Michael looked from Laurel to Pat to the repairman. "The stove?"

"No. The compression nut between the service pipe here and the flexible connector on the stove." The repairman was short and wiry and obviously puzzled. "That nut was almost completely off."

Michael knelt with the others to look. "How could that happen?"

"Well"—he scratched his chin—"the best way is to take a wrench and loosen it."

"You think someone did this purposely?"

"I didn't say that but. . . ." He shook his head for the hundredth time. "I've only seen this happen once before. Usually if there's a leak, it's because the stove's been moved around too much and the flexible connector gets a crack in it. But just last month, a suicide case decided turning on the

145

jets wasn't fast enough and he loosened the compression nut. If you want it fast . . . that's a good bet."

Suddenly everyone was looking at Laurel.

"I wouldn't decide to commit suicide, loosen the connection to the stove, and then go shopping for the afternoon." Her voice sounded far away, as if she were hearing herself from the next room.

The fireman busily wrote his report as they talked and just as busily crossed it out. "Look, I've got to put something down here. Did you move the stove at all today, Mrs. Devereaux?"

"I haven't moved it since we've lived here."

"Have you been working around the back of the stove? Or tried to retrieve anything that had fallen behind it?"

"Jimmy's truck rolled back there."

"How'd you get it out?"

"With a broom handle, but I'm sure I didn't touch anything. It was just after lunch. Before we left. . . ."

The fireman brightened and turned to the repairman. "Could that do it?"

"I suppose . . . if it was loose and she hit it. . . ."

Everyone looked satisfied and relieved. Everyone but Laurel and the repairman.

"You're lucky you and your family weren't home. If you'd been awake you would have smelled it, but if you'd all been asleep . . . it could have been bad . . . real bad." He was still eyeing the faulty connection. "Oh, and Mr. Devereaux, I suggest you have your landlord replace this stove; it's in very poor condition."

Michael nodded and walked over to Laurel. "Are you all right?"

"No."

He put his arms around her and held her gently, his warmth making her realize how chilled she was. "Come on. We'll treat the Patricks to dinner out and then go buy our own stove."

13

Laurel sat at the kitchen table trying to adjust the tension on Myra's portable sewing machine to handle the heavy yellow drapery material. She wished she had a mechanism to adjust the tension inside her.

In five months the blackout in her mind had lifted only slightly, giving her a peek at two meaningless images. And it was obvious where her life was heading. She'd soon be without a family as well as a memory. If she could even hold onto her sanity and her life long enough to see the end of her probation.

The new electric stove jutted out beyond the partition wall, creating a menace to the traffic pattern. It had enough dials to fill the control panel of a rocket ship.

Anyone could have loosened that compression nut. Claire Bently and Evan Boucher had been in the kitchen recently. The patio door was unlocked, so even Janet or Paul could have come to the house, found her gone and seen their chance. Had she left it unlocked? Even Colleen or the Patricks could have loosened it at any time, waiting for her to jiggle it or bump it. For all she knew, any of them could have a motive that she didn't know about or couldn't remember. It could possibly be someone else from her unknown past. It didn't *have* to be Michael. He had the obvious motive and the most access to the stove. A man trained as a mechanical engineer and a pilot might well think of such a strange yet

147

logical weapon. But he wouldn't jeopardize Jimmy's life as well. *Please don't let it be Michael.*

Michael's attitude had softened some since the gas incident. When he took Jimmy for an outing now, he included Laurel. He was very patient, trying to teach her how to use the new stove. But this gentleness could change to the old hardness in an instant and often did.

Out on the patio Jimmy squealed as he raced his tricycle around Sherrie's. Laurel turned to watch them. Each day he grew bigger, browner, more scratched and bruised. His face and body grew leaner, his coordination astounding. All little boy now, he showed every sign of becoming a giant of a man. But when he came fresh from his bath with his hair still damp, smelling of soap and powder, to snuggle against her for his nightly bedtime story—he was her baby. The thought of losing him was so agonizing that she would sometimes cry while she read and his eyes would turn sober, the thumb he was fast outgrowing once more seek his mouth.

Michael would have to have her jailed to keep her away from her son. Or killed. . . .

She turned back to the sewing machine. The gas leak had heightened that sense of urgency, of time racing her toward some unknown end. It *could* have been an accident; she *could* have imagined being threatened that night in the courtyard. But her nerves told her that the two incidents were connected and that she'd need all her memory and her wits to face what was coming.

What if she went back to that double track in the desert, followed it to the spot where she'd awakened to a new existence on that morning in April? Would that jog her memory? How would she get there?

Laurel went into a flurry of decorating, and all the beige rooms gained a little sparkle. New drapes and curtains at every window, new bedspreads and bright throw rugs, flower arrangements and wall hangings.

No amount of genius could make the little house a

148

showpiece, but its character had changed. From a neglected cheap rental it seemed to settle with a sigh into a home that someone cared for. Laurel wondered how much longer she'd be there to care for it.

One evening she stepped out onto the patio on her way to the clothesline to take in the clothes and stopped to enjoy the relative coolness of approaching night.

It was a quiet evening and the clothes hung still on the line. Water splashed from the revolving sprinkler head. Sherrie and Jimmy played contentedly on the swing set.

Voices came to her from Colleen's kitchen. Her cooler must be off and her patio door open. Colleen's voice was followed by Myra's, and Laurel heard her own name mentioned.

". . . they're married? Not just living together?"

"That's silly, Colleen. Why shouldn't they be married?"

"I don't know. They're such a weird couple. And Jimmy doesn't look like him. She doesn't wear any rings. Maybe he just moved them in to keep women like me away."

"Are you serious?"

"Okay, laugh. But how many couples that age do you know who sleep in separate rooms?"

Myra giggled. "Maybe he snores. Oh, don't get mad. She told me they'd been separated. Maybe things aren't going too well between them. Although he did seem very considerate and worried about her that night they took us out to dinner after the gas leaked into their house. But I do think she's a little afraid of him."

"I don't blame her, the way he looks at her."

"Like how does he look at her, lady detective?"

"Like he wants to commit murder . . . or rape. Like he doesn't know which. Like. . . ."

Myra cut her off with a burst of laughter that made the kids look up from their play.

"Colleen, your life must be exciting with that imagination. Tell you what. If I find any bodies or ladies in distress lying around, I'll call you in on the case."

149

Laurel crept back into the kitchen, squirming inside, the wash forgotten. She closed the screen, then the glass door, and then the drapes.

The last Friday in August Michael announced that he was taking Jimmy to Tucson for the weekend. She was welcome to come along if she liked. Laurel had no intention of being separated from her son, even for a weekend. So they locked up the beige house on Saturday morning and raced across miles of beige desert.

The temperature had climbed to 102 degrees when they left Glendale. The car radio announced that it was 105 degrees when they reached Tucson. Leaving the desert floor, so baked it had cracked in places, they wound along the low foothills, where only the saguaro seemed really alive, and finally rounded the bend in the road where the great white house stood above them on the hill.

The stolid saguaro still stood sentinel duty in its fenced enclosure; palm fronds peeked over the wall of the outer courtyard. And above it all the bell wall, its two empty niches staring sightlessly into the noonday sky. Sun glinted off the great bell in the center niche and the house seemed whiter, less mellowed in the summer sun.

To Laurel this was not a coming home. The house seemed to remind her that there were less than three weeks left of her probation and then Michael would be free to hand her her hat. If something worse didn't happen before that.

"Come on, Jimmy. We're here." Laurel pushed the seat forward and reached in to help him out. But Jimmy crouched against the back seat, sucking his thumb, staring at the giant front door of his inheritance. One of his eyes was blackened from a fall off the new tricycle. He looked slimmer now that he didn't wear bulky diapers under his shorts.

"What's the matter with him?" Michael came around the car.

"I can't get him out. Don't you want to see Consayla?"

Jimmy stared back at them—unblinking, not moving.

When Michael snapped his fingers Laurel jumped, but their reluctant son hit the floor and scrambled out of the car. He grabbed Laurel's hand and she had to drag him into the house.

The entry hall was empty and as unreal as ever. It looked cool and dark with its high ceiling, and the sunburst on the red tiled floor lay in shadow. A quiet house greeted them.

Michael looked into the library and then closed the door. He came back to the doors of the main salon. Laurel followed, Jimmy still tugging at her hand.

The heavy green drapes were open and light streamed through the two-story windows, brightening the rich upholstery and deepening the luster of the wooden tables.

"Well, here you are. And just in time." At the far end of the room Janet stood halfway up a ladder to the side of the fireplace.

Consuela, looking monstrous and dark against the white wall, held the ladder for her.

Michael walked across to them, his feet making no sound on the thick carpets. His deep voice echoed in the high-raftered room. "Just in time for lunch, I hope."

"Lunch right after my surprise. Consuela, get the others in here."

The housekeeper didn't move. Janet climbed down the ladder and confronted her. "I said get the others."

"Please, Mrs. Devereaux. . . ."

"Now listen, old woman. . . ."

Michael put an arm around the housekeeper's shoulders and said softly, "What's wrong, *Abuelita?*"

"Mr. Michael, it is awful. . . ."

"I'm afraid Consuela doesn't like my surprise. Do you want me to get them?" Janet's low voice had developed an unpleasant rasp.

"I will go." But before she left, Consuela knelt in front of

151

Jimmy and kissed him lightly on the cheek. He grinned shyly but didn't release Laurel's hand. The housekeeper disappeared through the door under the balcony.

"Well, Laurel. How are you? Not *too* many bruises, I hope?"

"What the hell kind of remark is that?" Michael towered over his sister-in-law.

"Really, Michael, your military career has done nothing for your vocabulary. Must you swear?" Janet wore her working smock; her once-molded copper curls had frizzled in the heat, the lines on her damp face no longer softened by makeup. Lines that Laurel hadn't noticed before pulled down on the corners of Janet's mouth.

Michael moved to stand in front of the fireplace where the bulky outline of a picture frame showed through the green velvet draped on a copper rod above the mantel. "Is this the surprise? Have you turned artist now?"

"You'll see," Janet said, flopping down on a nearby couch. "Fix us a drink, Michael. Something cold."

If Michael noticed her commanding tone, he didn't show it. But Laurel could feel tension rising in the room as he moved to a bar under the balcony.

Janet turned to her and Jimmy. "Well, sit down, you two. Don't stand there like beggars. After all, you practically own the place."

Laurel sat across from her, Jimmy close beside her. She wished they hadn't come, too.

"You haven't said a word since you came into this room. Does he beat you to keep you silent?"

Laurel felt anger rise up her throat, and she managed through clenched teeth, "Only on Sundays." She caught Michael's startled glance as he bent over her to offer a tall glass on a tray and his deep-throated chuckle as he passed the tray to Janet.

Paul entered through the door under the balcony, Claire and Consuela behind him. "What is it now? You know we can't be dis . . . oh, Michael, Laurel. I forgot you were coming. Forgive me."

"Deep in another book, Paul?" Michael asked, handing the tray around.

"Yes, well into the research anyway." Paul and Claire were still in their lab jackets, and both sides of Paul's mustache quivered impatiently. He looked drawn and tired and somehow older, like a sad old bird peeking out through the magnified cages of his glasses.

"They've been locked up in that smelly laboratory for months, don't even come up for meals. They actually locked me out."

"Janet, you made that necessary—barging in at the worst possible times. Interrupting everything." Paul's expression was one of irritation almost to the point of desperation.

"You can at least forgo meals in the laboratory while Michael and Laurel are here."

Claire moved to Michael's side. She'd reverted to her plain Jane role and had even forgotten the brown-rimmed reading glasses that perched halfway down her nose, forcing her to look over the top of them.

"Well, get on with it. Whatever it is." Paul sighed and sat beside Laurel.

"I just hope the light is good enough to do it justice," Janet said, pulling a cord at the corner of the green velvet and uncovering a portrait in oil of a woman seated with a young boy on her lap.

With Janet's present mood and Consuela's swollen eyes, Laurel was ready for anything, expected something nasty. But the portrait seemed innocent enough. The woman was pretty in a dark, slender way. She sat at an angle, her black hair pulled back in a French roll, her white suit with too much padding on the shoulders setting off the pale olive of her skin. Her head was turned so that she looked directly into the eyes of the observer over the dark head of the child on her lap.

It wasn't until she felt a cold wetness on her sandaled foot that Laurel realized Paul had let his glass slip through his fingers. His hand was still cupped as though he held it. He made no attempt to retrieve the glass, no move at all, his eyes riveted to the picture above the mantel.

Laurel looked around for Consuela to come and wipe up the mess, but the housekeeper hid in the shadow of the little stairway that led to the balcony, her breath coming in sobs.

Claire peered with interest at the picture over her glasses.

Michael had gone pale. A muscle twitched in his cheek. His lips parted but he didn't speak.

And Janet gloated, watching each face for its reaction. She certainly got plenty of that. But why?

It was obviously a portrait of Maria and a young Michael. They must have seen it before. And it was good, fitting its place on the wall and in the room as though it belonged, much better than the hunting scene it replaced.

Maria watched them, too, unsmiling, sitting very straight as if she would clutch her child and dart from the picture if anyone moved suddenly. Her dark eyes, almost too large for her face, opened too wide as though the artist had just startled her with something slightly bewildering or frightening. Maria had doe eyes, too.

"I found the portrait in an old wardrobe, and the frame is one of my finds. The combination turned out well, don't you think?" Janet, satisfied that the bomb she'd dropped had had its effect, sat down on the couch and picked up her drink. "You don't like it, Michael?"

But Michael was almost to the door of the entry hall, and even from that distance Laurel could hear him swearing under his breath. Consuela hurried after him.

"Why, Janet?" Paul finally tore his eyes from the picture. "You've tried to stir up trouble all summer. And now this. Just tell me why?"

"Why not? It's the only family portrait I could find. Surely

154

you're not ashamed of your precious Maria? Besides, it belongs here. It's much too good to be moldering in a drawer."

Paul removed his glasses and rubbed his eyes "I'm going back to the lab. You don't need to come in until after lunch, Claire," he said as he left the way he'd come.

"I heard nothing but Maria when I married Paul and came here to live. I wondered why there was no picture of her anywhere. She'd been dead two years and they were still in mourning. Father Devereaux would speak of her and then quietly sit and stare at the wall. Paul would get positively misty-eyed. And Michael would take on a hangdog look and go off and kick something." Janet stood in front of the fireplace, gazing back at Maria. "I still can't see why they. . . . She's been something of a mystery in my life, I can tell you."

"You could have looked at her and put her back in the wardrobe," Claire said quietly and Janet turned to face her. "But you brought her down here so that you could watch Professor Devereaux and Michael hurt. Just because you're bored and everyone else is busy and because you're jealous of a woman who's been dead for twenty years."

"There's something in what you say, *Miss* Bently. I was curious to see if Paul still had this infatuation for his father's dead wife. I'd thought Michael over his mother complex until I saw this portrait. But I wanted you two to see it especially."

"Why should *we* be so interested in it?" Claire asked.

"Because you both want Michael. And you saw him just now." Janet pointed dramatically to the portrait. "There's the only woman he'll ever love."

"Most everyone loves his mother, Janet. This whole melodramatic scene is disgusting." Laurel set her glass down and rose from the couch.

"Laurel, dear. I'm only trying to tell you what you have a right to know. You're trying to get him back, but you never had him. He didn't marry you for love but because you look like her." Janet clutched her arm. "Look at the eyes, Laurel, the shape of her head, her expression."

"Are you through?" Laurel pulled away and turned to leave, but Janet took Jimmy's hand. He tried to wiggle loose but she held him, talking rapidly now so as not to lose her victim audience.

"No. There's one more thing. Look at Jimmy and then at Maria and Michael." She grinned almost haglike. "There's proof there."

"Proof of what? Janet, you're hurting him." Laurel rescued Jimmy and picked him up, wanting only to get them both out of the room.

But Janet's next words stopped her.

"Proof that Jimmy is not Michael's child." Sure again of her audience, Janet turned back to the portrait. Even Claire's interest was revived.

"Maria was Mexican, but most of her family came from Spain. Consuela told me there were some blue eyes in the family. Father Devereaux had eyes like Michael's and Paul's, hence Michael's eyes are possible. But how could he with his background and you with your darkness have a blond child? This is hardly probable."

Claire moved closer to the fireplace and looked from the portrait to Jimmy. "We've always known of Michael's background. Why is this suddenly proof?"

"Because with her out in plain sight, Michael will have to admit to himself what the rest of us have known for a long time. That Jimmy must have had a blond father. The heir is a fake."

Laurel hugged her son tighter, old questions that she'd refused to let surface rising in her mind. She'd wondered too when she first saw Jimmy how he could be Michael's. Even Colleen had noticed it.

"I think you've outsmarted yourself this time, Mrs. Devereaux. This is the first I've noticed any resemblance between

156

Michael and Jimmy." Claire looked squarely at Laurel and shrugged. "It was a good try though."

Laurel took a closer look at the young Michael. He nestled against his mother in a way that gave an impression of security, possession, his expression seeming to dare anyone to come between them.

She guessed him to be about Jimmy's age when the portrait was painted. Only in the incongruous metallic eyes did he resemble the powerful, self-sufficient man he would become. The plumpness of his cheeks did not suggest Michael's rugged cheekbones. His size, the shape of his head and nose were Jimmy. Change the color of the eyes and hair and that would be Jimmy sitting in the portrait.

They left Janet alone in the immense salon peering at her brittle victory, her shoulders hunched.

"Jimmy wants go home." He didn't even remove his thumb to speak.

"I'm with you there, big boy. Let's hunt up your father and persuade him, too." They were just starting up the staircase in the entry hall.

Claire, a little ahead of them, turned with her embarrassing giggle. "Consuela has put you and Michael together in your old room. I'm interested to see how you work that out."

The wild horses still romped over the spread on the king-sized bed. Dark wooden furniture stood as massive as ever. The light spilling through the windows onto the parquet floor was still cut into patterns by the bars of iron grillwork. This room looked enormous after the cubbyholes in the beige bungalow.

But all was not the same. The lamp that once sat on the dresser between the double mirrors now lay in several pieces across the red rug. And Michael stood at a window overlooking the desert outside. He turned to glare at her with such an intensity that her request wavered on her lips.

"Jimmy and I . . . would like to go back home."

"This is Jimmy's house and mine."

157

"I don't think this is a good time to visit, do you?"

"I won't be forced from my home by that bitch." It was the kind of a statement that should be shouted but it wasn't. It was delivered in a quiet, emphatic manner that made it useless to argue.

"But what are we going to do? Consuela has put us both in here."

He didn't answer but continued to stare at her. Drops of moisture glistened on his upper lip.

"What's wrong?"

"I guess I'd forgotten what my mother looked like. I didn't realize how much you resembled her."

"Is that why you married me?"

"I was a grown man when I met you, Laurel, looking for a wife, not a mother."

"Grown men don't break lamps."

"Would you rather I broke heads?"

"I don't think anyone would be too upset if you went down and bopped Janet a good one right now."

"Did she explain her little performance after I left?" he asked, turning back to the window.

"She wanted to get everyone's reaction. She thinks that Paul still loves Maria and you married me because I look like her. That you'll never love anyone but Maria and that Jimmy is not your son because he has blond hair."

"That's all nonsense." He picked up Jimmy and held him against his shoulder.

"Then why all the reaction, Michael? It's a good picture and belongs in that room. Why was it put away? No one's ashamed of Maria. Why wouldn't you all want to remember her?"

"My father had her things put away because we didn't want to be reminded of our loss."

"But. . . ."

"Do you know what I remember—what that portrait downstairs brings back to me? Screams. Screaming tires and a screaming woman. Blood all over everything and a form covered by a sheet that wouldn't answer when I called to it. Blood soaking into it, pieces of flesh and hair sticking to it. Arms that held me back so that I couldn't touch it, go to it." His voice was so low yet so powerful that it forced the ugly, pathetic picture from his mind to hers. But his hand, so gentle, so protective, stroked his son's hair.

"We can't all block out what we don't like to remember as conveniently as you, Laurel."

"Then you do believe that I can't remember?" A tenuous hope flared within her.

He considered her a moment but didn't answer her question. Instead he carried Jimmy to the connecting door. "You can sleep in here tonight. I'll sleep with Jimmy."

But Jimmy didn't sleep with Michael that night. He crawled out of the crib and crept into Laurel's bed. He barely spoke all weekend, refused to let his mother out of his sight, to take a nap. They had to set him a place in the dining room where he could eat with Laurel, perched on a stack of books.

Neither Janet nor Paul appeared for lunch or dinner Saturday, so they ate with Claire and spent most of the afternoon and evening at the pool. Jimmy trailed Laurel like a shadow, screaming and kicking if she even tried to close the bathroom door on him.

That evening at the poolside Michael lounged in a deck chair after a rigorous, monotonous, exhausting swim that had taken him from one end of the pool to the other so many times that Laurel lost count. He was still breathing heavily, watching Laurel with half-opened eyes that frightened her a little, embarrassed her a little more. She wondered how Colleen would interpret that look.

Her pink bikini seemed to weigh a ton but covered nothing as she dragged herself out of the pool and stretched out on a beach towel. Jimmy sat close beside her. He'd refused to get into the water but had walked beside it, keeping pace with her.

"What have you done to him?" Michael's voice startled her, coming out of the quiet, darkening night—the moon not yet up.

"Bathed him, fed him, comforted him, read to him, spanked him, loved him, been at his beck and call twenty-four hours a day, seven days a week. The same thing any mother does."

"Sounds exhausting."

A bat swished close over head, dived toward the pool for a drink and flew off. Laurel felt the goose bumps rise.

"It's no more than your mother did for you." She sat up and put her arms around Jimmy, drawing him close. He was fighting to stay awake.

"I lost my mother at an early age."

"Jimmy isn't going to lose me . . . not again." She laid him back on the towel and he didn't move.

"You sound sure of yourself," Michael said in a warning whisper.

Laurel returned his stare, surprised at the determination in her voice. "I'll fight for him, Michael. I don't know how, but I'll fight."

"And you think I won't? That I'll just give him to you?"

"No." She looked away, unable to stare him down. "I think it would break his heart to lose either of us."

"He's young." And then a low rumbling chuckle and that infuriating lift of his eyebrow. "Are you suggesting we continue to live as we have been? Just how long do you think that can last?"

"I don't know. You're leading a full life, out almost every night. You seem to be enjoying yourself." She hated the shrewish tone in her voice.

"Do I?"

Suddenly angry, she rose and stood over him—her nails cutting into her flesh as she balled her hands into fists. "I'm sorry I messed up your life. I can't go on apologizing forever. I don't know how or why I left or why I came back. I just

160

know I'm here. I exist. I have no excuse for it, but I exist. And you're going to have to face it, Michael."

"And then what? Take you back as my loving wife because you're Jimmy's mother? And because you'll condescend to take me, too, to get Jimmy?" he said, a shadow of a smile on thin lips. "It won't wash, Laurel. There was never a flimsier excuse for a marriage."

"We could try." It came out as a choked whisper. She wasn't sure she'd really said it until his pale eyes widened and the smile vanished. Somehow she'd caught him by surprise and herself as well.

"Hey! Can I join the family swim?" Claire came up beside them in her pear-shaped tank suit. She looked from one to the other. "Oops! Didn't mean to interrupt a *domestic* squabble." Getting no answer, she climbed down the ladder into the pool.

Laurel returned to her place beside a sleeping Jimmy, tears of embarrassment in her eyes. *Why did I say that?* She looked over her shoulder to find Michael's eyes still on her. She'd shaken him, too. No. She was imagining things. No one ever shook Michael.

Claire stayed in the pool only long enough to get wet and then took the chair next to Michael's. Laurel sat with her back to them, making a pretense of toweling her hair.

"I really am sorry if I interrupted anything." Claire didn't sound sorry.

"We'd just finished a very interesting conversation," Michael answered.

Laurel felt her cheeks burning. Was he laughing at her? He proposed nightcaps and left the courtyard to get them.

"Why isn't Jimmy in bed?" Claire said behind her.

"He's afraid to have me leave him. He doesn't like it here."

"He liked it all right before you came along. And he never got his eye blackened around here either."

"That was an accident, Claire. He fell off his tricycle."

"My, you're just tearing into everybody tonight."

161

When Michael returned, it was to an atmosphere of cold silence. But he and Claire were soon reminiscing, with long silent spells in between. They had little to reminisce over, Laurel noted with satisfaction.

"Is Paul overworking you?"

"Oh, you know how he gets when he's this close to something. But it's exciting. We think he's figured a way to transplant saguaro. He's been trying to for years. And that big one in the lab garden has been diseased. Well, he's about cured that; it'll be another year before we can be sure. It's really our test case. But it could be the end of the decline in the saguaro population."

"What's he going to do, run around and doctor every saguaro on the Sonora?"

"No, but this book might get the state and conservationists interested in a mass transplanting and disease-control program. You can't save them all, just stop 'this race toward extinction' as he calls it."

Michael was silent for a long while, the ice tinkling in his glass as he swirled his drink, and then in a hesitant manner that was unusual for him he asked, "Is it just me or . . . has Paul aged this summer? This work seems to be affecting him strangely. I don't suppose Janet's making it any easier for him."

"They argue more, at least she does," Claire said. "She likes to be the center of attention and right now that cactus is more important to him than any human being could be. Do you know he talks to it? He feels so responsible for saving them . . . if this experiment fails. . . ."

Laurel gathered up Jimmy and as many towels as she could manage and left them without saying good night.

She was still awake when Jimmy crawled into her bed. She snuggled close to him. Somehow, unintentionally, in her blundering way, she had won a small victory that night. She'd given Michael something to think about.

162

14

Laurel was sure of it the next morning when Michael invited her to go to mass.

They seemed like a family for the first time, sitting in church with Jimmy between them, other families around them. And Laurel waited for something familiar to happen, to stir an old memory. But everything seemed wrong. The service was in English, the rest of the congregation stumbling as much as she through their responses, having to read out of little books provided in each pew.

The congregational singing was off-key, a robed choir leader trying to lead them through it. She seemed only a little more lost than everyone else.

No memories came back to her that morning, but she knew a certain happiness as unfamiliar as the church service. She was a part of something—a group, a family. This happiness lasted until dinner. For Janet had yet another bomb in her arsenal.

Sunday dinner, with the red and gold brocaded tablecloth that looked like a drapery, the brass candlesticks, and everyone present, even Jimmy propped on his books beside Laurel. It was the first they'd seen of either Janet or Paul since the previous morning.

The atmosphere was strained, but Michael was more relaxed, more talkative than she'd ever seen him. He drew Paul out of his sullen silence and soon had his brother talking animatedly of his hopes for the saguaro, the work he'd done on the big cactus in his fenced laboratory. When he could talk of his work, Paul seemed less detached. Claire joined in and Laurel asked questions. The tension eased.

Even Janet listened attentively. She'd groomed hard to bring back the butterfly illusion, but the summer's toll still showed on her face.

It wasn't until Consuela had cleared the table and begun to serve the iced dessert that there was a lull in the conversation and Janet spoke up. "Did Evan Boucher get ahold of you, Laurel?"

"Yes, he stopped by one afternoon."

"When was this?" Michael asked curtly.

"One Sunday when you and Jimmy were at the zoo."

"That reminds me." Her sister-in-law had a triumphant expression that didn't seem in keeping with the shambles she'd made of the weekend. She placed her spoon on the plate under the sherbet glass as a signal for everyone to begin. "Someone else has been calling for you here."

"For me? Who?" Laurel felt the tension seep back into the room.

"I didn't know exactly how to handle it until I'd talked to you." She tasted her dessert, looking around the table to be sure she had everyone's attention.

She did.

"And so I told him you were out and I didn't know when you'd be back."

"Him?" Laurel felt her face growing hot.

"Yes. He's called several times. I didn't know if you wanted me to give him your new address. He sounded . . . oh, rather uneducated. He wouldn't leave a number."

"Who was it?" But she knew. There was only one person it could be. And she knew what Michael would think. She could feel his stiffness next to her without even looking at him.

"Well, let's see if I can remember." Janet made a pretense of concentrating. "Ummm . . . McBride, yes, that's it,

164

McBride. Harlow McBride . . . no . . . Harley. Harley McBride! Do you know him?"

"Yes."

"Any relation to the Florence McBrides?" Paul asked, and when she didn't answer, he turned to Michael. "You know, the old man who hung himself on the Milner ranch when Father closed the place? No, maybe you weren't home then. It's been some time ago. Had six children, I think."

"Harley is his son," Laurel volunteered. It didn't matter anyway. Nothing did. She was sunk. She wished she'd told Michael about Harley, but he'd always cut off any discussion about anything that had happened before the night he'd found her in Raymond McBride's motel.

They left immediately after dinner, a cold dangerous Michael driving as if the car were a jet with no traffic to skirt. Laurel had visions of herself under a sheet like poor Maria, pieces of hair and flesh. . . . She was too frightened and defeated to explain anything, knew it would be useless to try. She hoped that Jimmy, asleep in the back seat, would be spared as Michael had been on that fateful ride so long ago.

When the state patrol car pulled them over to the side of the road, Michael got out to talk to the patrolman. Laurel waited for him to take a swing at the officer. He was in that mood she didn't trust. But after a long and seemingly polite conference Michael returned without a ticket.

"Just a warning?" She couldn't believe it.

"Yes." It was the only word he spoke to her on the long drive home.

In fact, he said little more than "yes" or "no" to Laurel for the next week. He came home before dinner, played with Jimmy, showered, and left carrying a light sport coat over his arm. Laurel and Jimmy ate alone, the faint smell of Michael's after-shave lingering to remind them of him, to remind Laurel that he was probably not dining alone. Her small victory had been short.

Saturday morning she woke with a headache so intense it

made her dizzy. She'd lain awake until Michael came home, trying to cry, to release the leaden pressure that had built up all week.

Michael and Pat had driven off together that morning in Michael's car, wearing twin flight suits. His working hours kept her in constant confusion. He worked some weekends and then was off a day or two during the week. Sometimes he flew at night. Her only clue to whether he left for the base or just to get away from her was the clothes he wore.

Through the kitchen window over the sink, Laurel watched Jimmy and Sherrie splash in her new wading pool as she washed the breakfast dishes. Myra walked across the yard, bent and splashed water on them. She turned and came to Laurel's door.

"Hey, you wouldn't have some iced tea, would you?"

"Bring the jar in." Laurel dried her hands and pointed to the glass jar on the patio where the desert sun had brewed tea for her, a trick she'd learned from Myra.

"We're going to have to bring those kids in early. It hasn't cooled off since yesterday." Myra sugared her tea and lit a cigarette. "You don't look so hot."

"I woke up with a headache."

"Mike doesn't look so good either."

"No." And then to change the subject because she didn't want to discuss Michael, she said a little lamely, "They're enjoying the new wading pool. I wish I'd thought of it, keeps them cool."

"Yeah," Myra said, turning to look at them. "Sherrie hates to take a bath, but I can't get her out of that pool. Kids."

"I wonder if they'll become hippies someday. We're always scrubbing them, making them mind, thwarting them. I wonder if they'll rebel."

"Probably. But they won't be hippies. Hippies will be establishment by then, another generation that made this awful mess of the world. They'll have some new kick of their

166

own—God help us all!" Myra giggled and then turned serious. "But that's not what I came to talk about."

"I thought you had a reason."

"Laurel, Pat asked me to talk to you. I told him it was none of our business. But he's honestly worried about Mike. They've been friends for a long time."

"What did he say?"

"Oh . . . I'm not very good at this . . . but Mike has. . . ." She brushed imaginary ashes off her shorts. "We don't know anything, you understand. We don't want to pry. Mike has never discussed his personal life with us, not even with Pat." Myra talked rapidly, to get it over with.

"Pat told me after you moved in that he'd gotten the idea that your husband had once had an unlucky love affair or something. Mike seemed down on women. But Pat didn't know about you or Jimmy. This was overseas. And then when Mike got back here, he seemed to be getting over it, enjoying himself more." Myra had to relight her cigarette. Her hand shook.

"And then I showed up?"

"Yeah. The base grapevine has been sizzling ever since; he was getting pretty popular. But he's changed since you came here, Laurel—crabby and moody at the base and not getting enough sleep, drinking. He's tied into student pilots for no reason. It's not like him. And this last week he's pulled a couple of boners in the air himself that could have piled him up."

"And Pat thinks it's my fault?"

"Well, things aren't right around here. But I told him that lots of men have family trouble . . . I wish I didn't get myself into these things."

"You've gotten this far; you might as well finish it."

"Do you realize he's been out with a different woman every night this week? The strange part of it is, you don't seem to care. That's a lot of man you've got there, Laurel. I could

167

name a number of gals who'd love to be in your shoes. If you don't patch things up pretty soon, you're going to lose him one way or another."

"If I told you what the problem is, you wouldn't believe it."

"I don't want to know. I just want you to do something fast before you ruin a good man. He's up for major, you know. And if he keeps on like this . . . well. . . ."

"Thanks for telling me, Myra."

"It wasn't easy. But look at you. What I've just told you . . . and there you sit in that cold, detached world of yours. Don't you care?"

"Yes, I care. I don't want to ruin Michael. Tell Pat I'll try to think of something."

"I'm going to say one more thing and get out of here as fast as I can." Myra leaned against the glass door, her hand on the handle. "You're a looker, Laurel. A gal like you ought to be able to get around a man. If you'd just warm up a little."

That night Laurel fixed tacos for dinner. She always made enough dinner for Michael, too, and she and Jimmy often ate his portion for lunch the next day. But Michael ate his own tacos that night.

He came home with a paper sack full of liquor bottles, mixed them each a drink and then went in to watch television with Jimmy. He looked exhausted.

It wasn't until they sat down to dinner that she spoke to him. "Myra came over today for a heart-to-heart. She thinks I'm ruining you."

"A man doesn't get credit for doing anything for himself anymore."

"She says you've been seeing other women."

"*Other* women?"

"Michael, I want to explain about Harley."

"Let's just eat. At least, you haven't forgotten how to make tacos."

"Just listen to me." And she told him everything from

waking up in the desert to ending up in Raymond's motel. And then she told him of her attempt to run away, of Harley's coming to get her, their following Jimmy and Consuela to the Wishing Shrine, her decision to stay. She didn't tell Michael that Harley had kissed her.

". . . and that's the last I've seen of him. He thought . . . I was crazy. I don't think so; I just seem to stop thinking when things get painful. I avoid things." She listened to her own monotone. It did sound cold, detached.

"Since then I've tried off and on to remember. I've come up with . . . almost nothing. I've written to my mother, hoping she can tell me something that will jar things loose, but I've had no answer."

He scooped chorizo into the curved tortilla and looked at her for the first time. "What do you want of me?"

"I want help. I want you to help me remember."

"Do you want a doctor?" His impersonal tone matched hers.

"No. I want to go back to this place on the desert."

"What makes you think you can find it?"

"It's on the road to Florence. Off on a side road that leads to the ranch where Harley's father committed suicide."

"The Milner homestead, Paul's mother's old place. That's where my father got his start."

"Will you take me there?"

He met her plea with a cold stare. "Why not ask your friend Harley or Evan Boucher?"

Either he didn't believe her or he was inhuman.

Laurel felt something inside her click off. It didn't click on again until September 12, the day her probation ended, the day of the plane crash.

15

Friday, September 12, dawned hot, the two-month record-breaking heat wave still unbroken. Laurel fixed breakfast as if this were any other day, and Michael said nothing about the end of her probation before he left for the base.

She'd spent the last two weeks in a slow dream, living from moment to moment, enjoying her son. She'd taken the time to notice the gleam of sunlight on his pale yellow hair next to the golden brown of his skin, the way he wrinkled his baby nose when he looked up at the sun—one eye screwed tight shut. The exciting rhythm of morning coffee hitting the glass dome of the percolator. Her own image in Michael's sunglasses when she could imagine his expression was not the one she knew was there. She'd lived the last two weeks as if this day would be her last on earth.

Laurel had no plans for the days to follow. Once it had occurred to her to take Jimmy and run off, but that was just a fleeting thought. She hadn't tried to remember anything. It no longer seemed important. She sensed that the danger she feared still lurked somewhere waiting for her. Let it wait. Life would be over for her when she lost Jimmy anyway.

She left the breakfast dishes half done and stepped out into the backyard. Funny how the coarse, stubby grass remained brown no matter how much water Myra put on it. Funny how this could be doomsday and she should feel so little. Just mildly lazy and peaceful under a sun so hot that her hair felt fiery to her fingertips when she brushed back a stray strand.

A roaring across the road told her that all the planes hadn't left yet. Even planes overhead hadn't panicked her these last weeks, and she shielded her eyes to watch the long gleaming jet thunder above her, its wings swept back like a dog's ears in a race. Still-spinning wheels retracted behind silver doors, a white star on a circle of blue with red and white bars on either side, and deadly slender tubes were visible on the underside of each wing. The pointed nose seemed to head straight up and then the jet circled back over the base toward the mountain range on the skyline.

"Boy, that one was loaded. Must be headed for Gila Bend." Colleen walked across the yard toward her.

"That's not a town, I hope."

"Well, I'm talking about a target range out in the desert where the boys pulverize everything in sight. Doesn't Mike tell you anything?"

But Laurel didn't answer. The jet seemed to be losing altitude, its nose heading downward. No, it must be the distance. But she found herself pointing it out to Colleen.

"Oh-oh!" was all Colleen had time to say before the distant rumble.

Smoke billowed into the sky just this side of the mountains. There must have been a lot of fire, but she couldn't see it . . . only the smoke . . . dirty black smoke that trailed away at the edges only to be replaced by more and more . . . and two figures struggled on the packed desert floor, rolling over and over, jabbing each other anywhere they could . . . one reached for the other's throat and. . . .

"Laurel! I'm going to throw water on her if she doesn't come out of it pretty soon."

"No, Myra, her eyes are open and she's sitting up. She's not unconscious."

"Mommy?"

"What do you suggest then?"

"I don't know, maybe she's in shock. She hasn't blinked for ten minutes."

"Mommy!"

"Think I should call a doctor?"

"She didn't pass out or anything. Could she be in some kind of trance? She doesn't take drugs, does she?"

Jimmy's red shorts and plump legs wavered in front of her . . . many feet and legs . . . her eyes stinging. She closed them.

"Hey, I think she's back with us. Laurel, you all right?" Myra looked silly on her hands and knees.

Laurel giggled. "What are you doing?"

"I'm trying to see if you've come back to the world. Where've you been?"

"The plane."

"Take it easy. See if you can stand up. Poor little Jimmy's been scared to death."

"The plane?" She stood up with Myra's help, feeling nauseated.

"It crashed. Look, Laurel, with all the jets in the air around here and student pilots, that's going to happen."

"Who was in it?"

"We don't know yet." Myra sounded angry, or was it worried? "It could have been any one of hundreds of men or a couple of them and they might have ejected anyway. You don't know that it was Mike—odds are it wasn't. Now, let's get you out of the sun."

It was a student pilot who went down. They heard it on the radio about half an hour later. He hadn't ejected.

It couldn't have been ten minutes after Myra and Colleen left her that a knock brought her to the door to find Evan Boucher blushing on the step.

He took one look at Laurel and opened the door for himself. "What's happened? You look awful."

Laurel explained about the plane crash. ". . . And, Evan, I just . . . just blanked out . . . and my probation is up today."

172

She shuddered and turned to the wall next to the door of Michael's bedroom, leaning her forehead against it.

"Has he told you to get out?"

"No, but I expect he will."

"Well, if that's all he does. . . ."

"If that's all! Evan, I can't live without Jimmy."

"Don't cry. I didn't mean it that way." He turned her gently to face him, and then he just looked into her eyes, willing her to truly see him. She'd always dismissed Evan as ineffectual, but there was a sensitivity and strength in his face she'd never noticed before. "If he kicks you out, call me and I'll help you find a place to stay near Jimmy and he'll have to let you see him some, even if he gets custody. Just promise you'll call me."

"Why are you helping me?"

"I always jump headfirst into a fight where the little guy's getting stepped on." Those two vertical furrows formed on his forehead and then relaxed as he grinned. "But I'm warning you, I often get massacred."

"Is that why you went to work in a mental institution?" Laurel studied him; he couldn't be much over twenty.

"Yeah, I was really going to help those poor people and I didn't last six months. Hey, you're still shaking." And he drew her close, letting her relax against him. She'd known so little kindness, so little sympathy. . . .

"Sometimes I wish I'd never met you. I wake up at night and see those big troubled eyes of yours and wonder if he's hurting you."

But Laurel had stopped listening to him. They stood near the front door. With one side of her head resting against Evan, she looked through the screen directly into Michael's eyes. He stood frozen on the step, his hand on the door latch. His lips were white. He turned suddenly and walked to his car.

Michael didn't come home for three days.

Laurel's lazy peacefulness was gone and she dragged

173

through the endless routine. Even the extension on her probation brought little comfort as her nervousness grew. When it became too much, she'd probably blank out.

It frightened her not to know when it would happen.

On Monday, the third day of Michael's absence, the cooler broke down. By that evening she'd opened the windows and sliding doors to entice some of the evening air into the house. But the air lay still inside and out. Jimmy slept in nothing but night diapers and rubber pants. Laurel lay across her bed, trying to will herself into the hot kitchen and the eternal dishes. What did they matter anyway? . . . Two men rolled over and over on the desert floor, jabbing each other. . . .

She soon stood over the sink, the steamy heat of the dishwater floating up to her face, sweat trickling into her eyebrows, her own bedraggled image staring back from the window in front of her.

Without the racket of the cooler the house lay silent; even the old refrigerator was still for once. The only sound the buzzing and thumping of bugs as they dashed themselves against the screens.

Laurel paused as a car pulled in. A door slammed. She rinsed a glass with trembling hands. The front screen door opened and closed.

The empty quiet had fled.

When she looked up, Michael stood in front of the patio doors, gazing out at a night he couldn't see, filling the room as he always did. She'd expected him to be different—unshaven, tousled, perhaps drunk. But he looked much the same.

"Jimmy's been asking for you." She could smell whiskey in the close room now. The stoop in his shoulders seemed slightly exaggerated.

"The cooler broke down."

Michael turned to face her and she could see the darkness around his eyes, the deepened lines running from the edges of his nostrils to the corners of his mouth.

He moved abruptly to the refrigerator, took out a tray of ice and mixed two drinks in plastic juice glasses.

His silence made her uneasy and she moved away from him. "Say something."

"You're a mess." He leaned against the counter, cocking his head to one side, looking arrogant, dangerous.

"It's been hot in here."

"Homemaking is hard work, isn't it, little Mother?" Tonight his eyes were almost colorless, seeming larger because of the shadows that surrounded them.

"It's not the work. It's the tension."

"Your probation is up."

"Are you going to kick me out?"

"I thought you'd have run by now. Back to your friends in the mountains . . . when life didn't turn out as luxurious as you'd expected."

"That was just a story I made up for the hearing. I got it from Janet."

"I even thought you might try to take Jimmy."

"I thought of it."

"You'd have been very sorry," he whispered.

The way he watched her, with his eyelids half-lowered . . . something in his stance—a relaxed readiness . . . the twitching just above his jawline. The time for a showdown had come. She drained her glass, hoping for courage, but the sting in her throat just brought tears to her eyes.

"Tell me something, Laurel. Is there anything behind that blank stare of yours?"

He was baiting her now. She must stay calm. But it was then that she started backing away from him.

"Who was the man, Laurel?" The silken warning in his voice. "Was it Evan Boucher or this Harley?"

"I don't know. I don't know where I was." Her back came up against the refrigerator.

"Who was the man?" Michael repeated, closing in on her so that she had to look up at him.

175

"How do you know there was a man?" Sound filled the room now—the rumbling of the refrigerator, their breathing, the roaring in her ears. "Damn you. You could try to help me remember if you're so curious. But you don't want to help, you want to drive me crazy, drive me away. . . ."

Trapped between the refrigerator and Michael, Laurel darted sideways, but he grabbed her wrist and jerked her back, hard.

"You're afraid of me."

"Yes, I'm afraid of you. All you've done is threaten me. I don't know you . . . what you might do. Don't you see? I don't remember you at all."

He reached above her to set his glass on the refrigerator, bringing his hand down across her cheek, her throat. It was not a caress. "You don't remember anything."

"No."

"Are you still here because Jimmy is going to inherit money?"

"No. I want Jimmy. He's mine, too."

"You want Jimmy. Is that all you want, Laurel?"

She wanted to beat on his chest with her fists, to force him to really listen to her, to make him understand that he was a stranger, to make him feel her terror of mind and memory slipping away with no warning, to convince him of her desperate fear that time was closing in on her.

But it was like judgment day after a life of guilt and from which there is no appeal. Whatever was coming to her she'd brought upon herself. Part of Laurel wanted to make a plea on her behalf; the other told her it was too late—would be glad to have it over at last.

Just when she thought she'd be crushed between the hardness of his body and that of the refrigerator he released her arms and grabbed a handful of hair, propelling her toward his room.

"Let's see if we can help you remember."

Laurel yielded to him one moment and struggled against

176

him the next. His smothering weight brought a silent screaming to her mind, an answering desire to her body.

There was no romance, no magic, no barriers between
them. Just a silent, sweaty struggle in a hot darkened room
on a bed meant for one. When his knee forced her knees to
part she bit him. Michael slapped her.

Now, now I'll blank out. But her arms curled around his
neck and the back of his head pulling his face down to hers,
her lips finding his and holding them. Her body pulling him
inside her and holding him.

It wasn't until she'd released him that she felt the various
aches, the soreness brought on by the struggle. Even then she
lay calmly by his side until his comment brought an angry
flush to her face.

"If you think that waited three years for you, you're a
damn fool."

"I hate you." And her feet were on the floor.

But his arm encircled her waist and drew her back to him,
to wait until he was ready for her again. She was ashamed at
how quickly her body answered his demands.

It was Jimmy's muttering in his sleep that woke her. She
was hot and one arm prickled where it lay under Michael, his
bare shoulder and arm heavy but relaxed across her chest. He
slept on his stomach, his face turned away from her.

There was no moonlight, but enough light filtered through
the bedroom doorway from the kitchen to make them
visible. Jimmy mustn't find them like this. She slid gently
from under Michael's arm and off the bed. He didn't stir. She
gathered up her clothes and then turned to look back at him
from the doorway.

She should hate him for tonight, but she didn't really.
Instead she felt just a little less alone. *Don't, Laurel, he didn't
make love to you. It was more like rape.* And she had fought
him, but not too hard, just enough to make it exciting. *You
knew what you were doing and it won't mean anything to
him tomorrow.*

177

Cloudy, greasy dishwater still half-filled the sink and as she let it out her image confronted her again in the kitchen window, more bedraggled than before, a dark swelling under one eye. Would she get pregnant?

Laurel turned out the light, took three aspirins, and crawled into her own bed.

16

Dear Laurel Jean,

This letter is so late because it is the second one. Daddy caught me writing the first one and tore it up. I tried to tell him that you were back with your family, but he said he didn't want to hear about it and walked off. I think he is relieved though, but you know him—he won't show it. It is also late because I couldn't think what to tell you. I've thought and thought where we went wrong to make you do such a thing. I was awfully worried that something had happened to you. But Daddy said you were all right.

Honey, about your Dad. Well, you were always such a good girl—nice, quiet, thoughtful. We were so proud of you. And when we didn't have a boy, well, he pinned all his hopes on you. Fathers do that and you were all he had. He was disappointed that you went so far away to teach, but when you married a Catholic it just about broke his heart. And then running out on the baby—it was just the last straw. I think he would have gotten over Michael if it hadn't been for that. I saw him looking at the pictures of Jimmy and he didn't say anything but he didn't tear them up.

Your cousin Kenny is taking over the implement business as Dad is close to retiring. He has left it all to Kenny and I think this wrong. But after seeing Michael's house in Tucson I guess you won't need it anyway. Aunt Bertha sends you her love.

I keep looking at the pictures you sent. You look so thin, but Jimmy is a darling and so big for his age. I pray to God every night that Daddy will give in and at least let me come out and see him (Jimmy and you, too).

My flowers are about gone now. They were so nice this summer. I have repainted the kitchen pink and made new curtains—a flowery design. I just put up pickles, preserves, and peaches this year. Guess I'm growing old.

I don't know if you know it, but Daddy hired a detective when we went to Denver after you left the hospital. He wrote Daddy about two months later and he (Daddy) wouldn't let me see the letter. He just said that the detective said that you were all right and not in any trouble and knew what you were doing. I told Daddy that Michael should know where you were, but he just swore at me. I almost wrote Michael myself, but I didn't know what to say to him since I didn't see the letter.

Well, I must get dinner on. Please write me again and don't wait two years this time (but don't send it here). I'm so glad you're back with your family.

Love,
Mom

P.S. If you have trouble remembering things, see a doctor right away. Have you been to the dentist lately?

Laurel didn't know whether to laugh or cry. So she did both, sitting on the lumpy couch, the letter in one hand, an ice pack in the other hand propped against the swelling on her cheek.

Casual clues like Kenny, Bertha, implement business, flower garden meant nothing to her. But much worse was the longing inside her for these two people who were her parents. *Mom and Daddy.* Oh, how she needed them now. And yet they were two unapproachable strangers.

Her father knew where she'd been for those two years. And she'd been doing something so terrible that he couldn't tell her own mother about it. What could be that awful? Prison? No, she wouldn't be lost then. Prostitution? *Oh God, not that.*

If she picked up the phone and called him would he tell her what the detective had learned? No. He wouldn't believe she didn't know. It was obvious in Lisa's postscript that she hadn't believed it.

Of course, all he could do was hang up; he couldn't hurt her. Not like Michael had last night. But that was physical. Her father's rejection would hurt another way, a deeper way. She curled up on the couch, tucking the ice pack under her cheek, and considered the telephone on the floor next to the stereo console.

It rang.

At first she couldn't believe it. When it rang the second time, she jumped to answer it before it awakened Jimmy from his nap. Could she have willed her father to. . . . No, probably someone selling patio covers or swimming pools.

"Devereaux's."

"Doe Eyes?"

"Harley?" Even his voice gave her a lift. "Oh, Harley."

"Hey, all I said was 'Doe Eyes.' " Laughter in his voice—how long since she'd heard laughter?

"It's just so good to hear you. How did you get my number?"

"You're in the phone book now. Didn't you know?"

"No. But I'm glad you called. Where are you?"

"In a filling station in Glendale. I just closed a big deal and I was going through and I thought to myself . . . I wonder if there are any ladies in distress who need a dragon slayed or something. And I happened to think of you. Don't have any ol' dragons around, do ya?"

Wonderful, preposterous Harley. "The word is 'slain' and I don't see any at the moment. But I do need some help, if you're not tired of doing me favors."

"Just name it. I feel real helpful today."

"I want to go back to that road where you picked me up, the one that leads to the ranch where . . . you lived."

"When?"

"Right now. Can you find my house?"

"I got the address right here. Be there in fifteen minutes."

She raced to the bathroom, put on lipstick, brushed her hair, and examined her cheek. The swelling was down, but the bruise had progressed to an even uglier purple. What was Michael doing now? Did he feel badly about last night? He'd left before she'd awakened that morning.

She woke Jimmy and dressed him, smiling to herself. It would be very good to see Harley again. When the old blue truck rattled to a stop in front of the house Laurel was out the door to meet it, Jimmy in tow, before Harley could get out. "Hi, dragon slayer."

Harley looked a little surprised to see Jimmy.

"Do you mind if he goes, too? I can't leave him alone."

"Don't look like I got much choice. Well, get in and we'll go find a dragon."

The dusty cab, the familiar gasoline smell, and she sat next to Harley again. Just like that morning in April. But now she held a son on her lap.

"Why're we going back to this place? Not that I have to know. Somehow when I'm around you, life is one big mystery." That fatal grin under the gristly curly hair, the long sideburns, a badly stretched T-shirt and faded Levi's . . . oh, it was good to see grinning, uncomplicated Harley again.

He caught her eyes devouring him, and the grin slowly spread into a smile as he reached over to touch her bruised cheek. "Looks like things are gettin' rough at your house."

"I don't suppose you'd believe it if I said I ran into a door?"

"I don't suppose I would."

"Why are men so violent, Harley?"

"Because they're honest."

"Honest!"

"A man hits you and you know you've pushed him too far. You know where you stand. But I don't hold with hittin' women. Not that I haven't wanted to. But you take a woman, they're sly and secret—deadly dangerous, every one of them."

"Even me?"

Harley lit a cigarette and squinted as the smoke curled past his eyelashes. "Lady, you're walking dynamite."

She had to laugh, partly at what he said and partly because she felt so good to be there. She hugged Jimmy and he turned to smile up at her. "To show you that I'm not secretive, I'll tell you why I want to go back. I want to see if I can remember how I got there. Harley, I'm sure I'll remember things in time. But I can't sit around and wait for it to happen."

"Why not?"

"Because I've got to explain a two-year absence to my husband pretty soon or I'll lose Jimmy. And because I think someone is either trying to scare me to death or kill me and I. . . ."

"Wait a minute. Hold it right there. Who is trying to kill you?"

"I don't know. It could be anybody." She told him of that night in the courtyard and of the gas leak. "It could even be you, Harley."

He shook his head slowly. "In the *real* world that shadow with the ax, or whatever, could have been imagination or a dream, and the second is something that could happen to

183

anybody, but in *your* world. . . ." Harley shrugged and then chuckled. "And if you thought I was going to kill you, you wouldn't be sittin' in this truck."

"If I can trust anyone, I guess it's you. I don't know when I've felt so relaxed."

They skirted Phoenix to the south and were soon rumbling down the highway to Florence, the windows open, her hair flying about her face, the dry herby smell of the desert prickling her nostrils. Although it was not cool, the summer heat had broken. It was a drier, more breathable heat.

Jimmy excitedly called out the colors of the cars they met, and Laurel settled back to enjoy the ride. They'd both needed to get away from the beige bungalow.

"You in love with this husband of yours?" The absence of the grin told her that Harley wasn't all that uncomplicated.

She paused to think before answering him; he deserved an honest answer. "No, I don't think so, Harley. I don't even know him."

"What's he like?"

"Big, attractive, dark. He has a nasty temper—very hard to get to know. I don't see much of him."

"And you don't know how you feel about him?"

"Sometimes I hate him, sometimes I'm afraid of him. Sometimes . . . I feel beautiful just standing next to him."

"You don't need a man to make you beautiful, Mrs. Devereaux."

"Don't call me that."

"Don't you like your name?"

"It's not the name. It's the way you say Devereaux."

"I've got no call to love Devereaux'." And with an unnecessarily sudden swerve he turned the truck onto a side road and stopped in front of a cattle guard. "Well, here's your dragon, Doe Eyes. Ready?"

Now that they weren't moving and the air didn't swirl through the cab of the truck, the heat was more impressive. Laurel's face felt sweaty, gritty, with tiny hard particles of

dirt between her teeth. Jimmy's weight was suddenly unbearable, and she transferred him to the seat between them. "Are
you sure this is the place?"

"I'm sure." Harley watched her curiously.

The flowers were gone from the ditches on either side of
the truck. And so was her gay mood. The double track still
meandered off into cacti and low trees, but where there had
been green there was now gray and dirty brown . . . no grass
. . . the trees barren of leaves. . . . "Harley . . . I don't think I
want. . . ."

"Huh-uh." They coasted over the cattle guard. "You
wanted to come out here; you're goin' through with it. How
far in were you?"

"There was a dry stream bed not far from the road."

"That wash follows the road most of the way. How long
did it take you to walk out?"

"Not more than ten minutes."

It wasn't long before he stopped the truck, got out, and
stood looking around him with his hands on his hips, his
T-shirt soaked where he'd leaned against the back of the seat.
Laurel sat still, staring at the dirty windshield.

"Mommy, I hot."

Harley came to open her door. "Come on." When she
didn't move, he took her arm and pulled her out. Jimmy
scrambled after her.

"I shouldn't have come here."

He shrugged, his grin growing thin. "You have got to be the
most screwed-up dame ever born. I'm beginnin' to see why
your old man slugged you."

He placed a hand on each of her shoulders and pushed her
in front of him around the truck across a few feet of desert
to the wash. She couldn't see the highway.

"Hey, kid. Stay away from that cholla," Harley yelled.

Jimmy's enraged screams changed to a whimpering as he
limped toward Laurel with one tennis shoe full of lime-green
bristles. "Ouchy! Mommy! Ouchy!"

185

"Oh, hell." Harley bent to grab an ankle and began pulling out short bristles and hooked barbs. Jimmy returned to his screaming and Harley said, "Jesus, what a family."

Laurel knelt to help and then drew Jimmy to her. "Hush, baby, they're out now. Harley, he's only two." They were kneeling close together so that they could look directly into each other's eyes over Jimmy's shoulder. Harley's forehead wrinkled and a questioning expression came over his face.

"What?" Laurel said and then she heard it, too. The rumble of an engine. . . .

"Car, Mommy." Jimmy's sobs turned off instantly. "Blue car."

"Oh, God, no."

Harley's eyes were fixed behind her now, one hand shielding out the sun. She turned in time to see the long gleaming car come to a stop behind the truck, sunlight flashing back off the deep metallic finish.

"Daddy's car."

Jimmy shot forward, but she and Harley were fixed in their kneeling positions as Michael stepped from the car and slammed the door.

Green buglike sunglasses in gold wire frames hid his eyes, the familiar tan uniform—short-sleeved, navy blue belt, multi-colored strips of ribbon above the left pocket of the shirt, silver wings above the ribbons. He would have looked even more official if Jimmy hadn't been attached to one leg. His hand ruffled his son's hair, but the sunglasses were directed at the pair on the ground. And with the sun behind him, Michael cast a formidable shadow.

Harley rose slowly to his feet. "Well, what d'ya know, a real live Devereaux."

The sunglasses followed Harley's rise and then, still silent, Michael removed them and laid them on top of the car. For an instant his chilling, unblinking glance rested on Laurel and then moved back to Harley.

"You wouldn't bring me here, so I asked Harley. . . ." she said.

But both men seemed to have lost all interest in her. Harley squinted back at Michael and the grin slowly returned. "Well, I never . . . a blue-eyed Mexican."

"Harley, don't. . . ."

Michael carefully guided Jimmy over to Laurel, and as he straightened, he jerked his fist into Harley's face with a horrid cracking sound and Harley lay at his feet.

"Get Jimmy back." Michael's command was thrown at her over his shoulder.

"No. Please." But she moved a few feet away with Jimmy.

Harley raised up on one elbow, shaking his head, and when he looked up at Michael, Laurel shuddered. It wasn't the teasing grin she'd become so fond of but something different, something cunning, naked on Harley's face . . . *he's enjoying this!*

Harley got to his feet with surprising quickness, dodged Michael's next blow, and, with head lowered, rammed into Michael's middle. And now Michael sprawled on the desert floor.

"Daddy."

"Get out of here." He fought to regain his breath between clenched teeth and to push Jimmy away before Harley was on top of him.

Laurel snatched a kicking Jimmy to safety and covered his eyes with her hand, watching, fascinated, as the two men rolled over and over jabbing each other anywhere they could. Harley a little stockier, Michael longer and quicker . . . rolling down the slight incline to the bottom of the wash . . . Michael's hand finding Harley's throat . . . screams rising in her own throat. . . .

She sat in a depression in the earth, a miniature stream bed without water that twisted among small trees and clumped

187

bushes until out of sight. Cacti, weird and distorted, rose above the bushes, some taller than the trees, with spiny green arms reaching upward . . . the sun scorching her eyes, her face . . . voices behind her.

She tried to turn her head but it made her dizzy, so she turned her body around on her hands and knees until she faced the other way. Two men ran toward her, one fair, the the other dark, both soaked with sweat. They were too big, too close. She felt too weak to run. Slowly, she sank facedown onto the sandy pebbly earth, so hot and tired she didn't care.

Rough hands forced her to roll over, and the blinding sun was on her face again. Splotches of violent moving red and green almost blotted out their shapes as they knelt above her.

"Laurel?"

"Maybe now you'll see she gets a doctor."

"She's none of your business, Mr. McBride!"

Her eyes focused on a third shape, a small boy. He looked terrified as he held a hand out to her. What did he want? She wanted to reassure him, but the two men were lifting her to her feet. When she wobbled, the dark one picked her up and carried her.

The streak of blood at the corner of his mouth confused her. "Was there an accident?" she asked.

He gave her a strange look but didn't stop walking.

17

Laurel was up and dressed when Dr. Gilcrest made his "visit" that morning. She wanted to convince him that she was ready to go home. After a month of counting the tiny holes in the ceiling tile she felt she'd suffocate in the crowded room if she had to spend another day in it. A couch and two easy chairs had been packed into an already furnished hospital room to make it look less like what it was.

She waited as the young doctor stood in the doorway briefing himself from the papers in a manila folder on who she was and why she was there. Then he would beam his personal "And how are you this morning, Mrs. Devereaux?" as though they'd known each other for years, while impersonal eyes studied her closely. And she would answer, "Fine." Because he expected it, so he could start her talking, so he could prove to her she wasn't fine.

"And how are you this morning, Mrs. Devereaux?"

"Fine."

"Good. Good. All dressed I see. Good. Good." He sat in a chair and motioned her into the other, scratching his crew cut with the end of the pencil. "Still no luck in locating your parents. Their vacation seems pretty extended."

"Dr. Gilcrest, I don't want my parents. I just want to go home to my son."

"And your husband?" His eyes were quick to search hers.

"Yes."

"You really think you're able to handle the world this

time? And I don't mean the world the way you want it to be, but the way it is?"

"I have to face it sometime. Why put it off?"

"You're not afraid you'll forget again?"

"It didn't last long this time." After the first night here she'd awakened, remembering everything. Everything since last April.

Dr. Gilcrest leaned back in the chair, crossed his legs, and chewed on the eraser end of his pencil, his eyes under sandy lashes never leaving her face. "We can be fairly confident that your memory will return. All of it. Some of it is likely to be unpleasant or you wouldn't have locked it away to begin with. Wouldn't you rather be here when that happens?"

"How soon do you think. . . ."

"Your recent trouble might well be an indication that it will be quite soon. Then again. . . ." He shrugged.

"I can't stay here. I have a child to think of."

"Which is quite a responsibility for someone who can just walk away from life when there's a crisis," he said, smiling his open, frank smile.

He'd done it again. Every morning he kicked away the props that she would spend the rest of the day and most of the night rebuilding. "You think I'm insane?"

"There are many levels of mental illness, Mrs. Devereaux. What we know of your behavior in the last few years is at least peculiar. But no, I don't consider you insane, dangerous, or even incompetent. Neither do I consider you entirely healthy. Amnesia is an illness of the mind as pneumonia is an illness of the body.

"As I've said before, there are no bars on the windows. You have not been legally committed. You are here on a voluntary basis because you need help, but I cannot help you if you won't let me."

"I've told you everything I know." And she had, over and over until she had her story memorized in the same words, used them in the same order.

190

And it hadn't been as bad as Evan had led her to believe. Dr. Gilcrest had patiently plumbed her fears, held them up for her to examine. He had shown her how her nervous state could have produced that shadow in the courtyard. How, after hearing the story of Michael's wrecking the nursery, she was ready to see the figure standing at the window with an ax. How, given this line of thought, she was able to construe a dangerous but accidental gas leak as a personal threat, imagine even the look of doubt on the repairman's face.

He could not explain how she could have foreseen Michael and Harley fighting on the desert. It was a relief to talk to someone and her reasoning side could not dispute his logic. But her instinctive self was not convinced. It had learned since April to trust no one.

The fear that now took precedence over all the others was the fear that she might not be allowed to leave. That the interrogation would go on and on, driving her to real madness. It wouldn't take long in a place like this.

Dr. Gilcrest leaned forward, tapping the pencil on his knee. "There is a garden here, a lounge where other patients meet; you have a television, and newspapers are delivered daily. But you stay in your room, seldom watch TV, the newspapers leave this room unopened, and the nurses report that whenever they look in you are either sleeping or sitting by the window. You have a great deal of free time here. Now, how would you interpret this behavior?"

"I needed rest and the other patients make me uncomfortable."

"They frighten you?"

"Yes." Hollow eyes, sad eyes, crafty eyes . . . eyes filled with hopelessness, terror . . . empty eyes. . . .

Dr. Gilcrest narrowed his probing eyes and pointed the pencil at her. "And the newspapers—do they frighten you?"

Laurel stared at the end of the pencil and tried to swallow. She was trapped again. She had avoided newspapers and news in general because it depressed her. He would note it as

191

another example of her inability to face the world. A lot of people didn't read newspapers for the same reason. She'd be willing to bet that Myra read nothing but the women's pages. But Myra wasn't in the hospital.

"Newspapers, Doctor, concentrate the hysteria and horror of the world. Then they're thrown on your doorstep like a hand grenade. With just a few pages of newsprint you can keep daily tallies on war, super weapons, crime, riots, revolution, starvation, poverty . . . when I read that my very way of life is destroying the air I breathe and water and wildlife and vegetation, when I read of whole generations of people who can't even talk to each other . . . yes . . . I'm afraid. And I don't think that's crazy."

She'd been sitting straight, her hands folded in her lap, trying to impress him with her calm control. But now she had to get up and move to the window. "When I see a picture of an injured child in the newspaper, I see Jimmy and how I'd feel if . . . or read of a young man killed in battle, I see Jimmy fifteen years from now and I hurt. I almost bleed myself. I. . . ."

The pencil scribbled furiously in the manila folder. "Oh, I give up." She flopped down on the couch.

"Go on. Don't stop."

"What's the use?" Five holes on one side of the square tile and five on the other makes twenty-five. *No, count them out. One, two, three. . . .*

"Mrs. Devereaux, this personal involvement with life's terrors and the consequent avoidance of the news media, which refuses to concern itself with much else, this is more common than you might think and surprisingly frequent among young mothers. But few resort to amnesia. Some have nervous breakdowns." He rearranged the folder, put it under his arm, and rose. "The amnesia is an overreaction. But I think you are going to work this out for yourself. In fact, I think you are doing so already."

192

"Then why am I here? When can I leave?"

"I'll stop by this afternoon. We'll talk about it then." With a glance at his watch, Dr. Gilcrest left her.

That evening Michael made his nightly duty visit. He usually stayed no more than a half hour, uncomfortable half hours in which he assured her that Jimmy was getting along "fine" with Myra and Sherrie, and then he'd fidget in the cramped room until his time was up and he could escape. She didn't help him much, felt relieved when he left. When they'd exhausted the subject of Jimmy, they had little to say to each other. Or maybe they had a lot to say—but Jimmy was the only safe topic.

Once he'd started to explain that he was on his way home early that day a month ago to apologize for the night before, only to see her in Harley's truck. He'd thought she was running off with Jimmy and had followed them. But she became upset and he stopped explaining.

Michael was the only visitor they allowed her and she always knew of his arrival because the blond nurse with the bad teeth would stick her head around the door, her face covered with blushing smiles and utter some inanity like, "That *gorgeous* man is here again. Ready?"

But this time Laurel was at the door to meet him and Michael was visibly startled as she took his hand and drew him into the room.

"Guess what?"

"I can't imagine," he said, trying to smile.

"I'm getting out."

"Making a break for it?"

"No. Dr. Gilcrest said I can leave in three days. I'm to see him once a week at his office and call him if I feel myself slipping again."

Michael sat on the couch, the haunted look he'd worn the last month unrelieved by her news.

"You will let me come home . . . won't you?" She'd ridden

193

high on relief since her talk with the doctor that afternoon. Now first doubts assailed her. She sank down on the floor in front of him. "Please say I can come home."

The pale mesmerizing eyes studied her intently down the long slender bridge of his nose. Then he leaned forward and said quietly, "You don't know me."

"I don't know anyone else either. Please?"

He drew a pack of cigarettes from his pocket and lit one, the first time she'd seen him smoke. "Do you want to take Jimmy and go back to Tucson?" he asked.

"No."

"You'd be more comfortable."

And more easily watched? "I want to go home to the beige bungalow. I'll try not to interfere with your life . . . I promise. Just let me. . . ."

"You can come home. Now get up off the floor and tell me what the doctor said."

She repeated what she could remember from her afternoon session with Dr. Gilcrest, but she'd found it hard to concentrate, waiting for him to set a time when she could leave. Something about fear and guilt and an exaggerated aversion to violence, the problem being the fear rather than the things she feared, a tendency to avoid reality (even Michael grimaced at that understatement). "He said he wanted to speak to you."

"Sounds like I'd better see him. I'll make an appointment." He rose and picked up his cap with the silver wings. He wore his dark Air Force blue that she didn't see often in the desert clime.

"Wait. Don't go."

"What do you want now?"

"I want to thank you for coming to see me so often. You didn't have to."

Michael just shrugged and stood waiting.

"And I want you to tell me about before . . . how we met and everything."

"That's a long time ago."

"You're the only one who can tell me, Michael."

He sighed, threw his hat down impatiently, and sat beside her. A big man in a crowded room with an unwanted wife he could legally get rid of but under a moral obligation to take care of a nut. It wasn't the first time Laurel had felt sorry for him.

"We met in a little tourist trap in the mountains of Colorado called Estes Park. I'd been hiking with some friends and you were there with some female teachers in front of a sidewalk stand that sold hot, buttered sweet corn."

Michael rubbed the creases in his forehead, leaning his head on the back of the couch. "You were rather appealing with melted butter running down your chin. Your friends were the lumpy, giggly types that fluster when a man talks to them, but you were relaxed, natural, soft-spoken.

"Eventually, after a lot of silly chatter, both our groups ended up in the park down the street with sweet corn and hot dogs and that night in Denver with beer and pizza. Rather naturally we paired off and you ended up with me."

"What was I like?"

"Your hair was shorter, your skirts longer. Quiet, dreamy. I didn't analyze you. Perhaps I should have."

"How did we . . . come to marry?"

"That I don't know. These things just happen. I was stationed near Denver. We dated fairly often for a few months, enjoyed each other's company. I decided I wanted you all to myself, so I married you. We rented an apartment near your school and. . . ."

"Wait . . . were we in love?"

Michael lit another cigarette and then stared at it instead of smoking it. " 'In love,' Laurel, is a silly phrase people use to cover for strong emotions or the lack of them. I personally don't know what it means. I remember feeling proud of you, responsible for you—in some ways you seemed a little . . . vulnerable . . . like you needed caring for. I felt comfortable

195

with you, different from what I'd felt around anyone else. I don't know, perhaps it was the beginning of something that might have grown."

"Did I love you?"

"You seemed to." He turned his eyes from the cigarette to the ceiling. Was he counting the holes in the tile to retain his patience? She could sense his desire to get away from her, from the dredging up of things she needed to remember and he wanted to forget.

"I think at first you had a kind of schoolgirl crush on me—you were more of a girl than a woman at twenty-four. This is just the way I remember it now. I don't know what I thought then."

"Did I seem . . . unstable?" Laurel watched the twitching muscle above his jaw. He wouldn't take much more of this.

"You'd get very depressed at times over hard luck cases at school; you'd get involved with your students and their family problems. I thought it was because you were a good teacher, a sensitive person. You were upset when I left for Vietnam, but that seemed natural. We'd known it was coming. I'd barely arrived there and you discovered you were pregnant; your letters didn't sound happy about it . . . You had this crazy idea about not wanting children, not wanting them to have to live in this world or starve or whatever . . . but you seemed to be adjusting to it. Until the last letter. . . ."

"Did you keep it?"

"No." Michael picked up his hat and stood by the door. "I've explained all this to the doctor, Laurel."

"Don't go before you've told me what that letter said."

He wiped his forehead with a handkerchief and continued, his voice low, controlled, and resonant but restrained, his consonants clipped but precise. "Mail delivery wasn't always the best over there. The letter was garbled—but you wanted me to come home. You were afraid. I'd written you to get your mother out for when the baby came, but in this last letter you wrote that you hadn't even told her about it. You just went to pieces on paper.

"The next day I was contacted by the Red Cross wanting to know what to do with Jimmy. I gave them your parents' address and then wrote the hospital. They said a nurse had seen you walking out under your own steam. Two years later I get a phone call from a motel in Phoenix. It's my long lost wife. And now . . . I have to leave, Laurel." He made his escape before she could ask any more questions.

Laurel sat just where he'd left her, trying to assimilate all he'd said and hadn't said, until the nurse came to remind her it was bedtime. It began to sound as if she'd told the truth at the hearing after all.

"My, he certainly stayed a long time tonight, didn't he?" The nurse bustled in, holding the tiny white paper cup with Laurel's pills—yellow for sleep, pink for happy. Or was it the other way around?

"However did you meet a man like that?"

Why did people with bad teeth have such broad smiles, Laurel wondered as she watched the nurse turn her bed down—a gentle hint.

"With butter on my chin," she said and closed the bathroom door.

Once in bed, she swallowed the pills and decided to shake up the staff by watching the ten o'clock news. Students fought police at the university in Tempe. (Actually, the police watched while students cavorted for the TV camera.)

There was a giant crackdown along the border called Operation Intercept to slow down the drug traffic from Mexico. It also slowed down auto traffic—long lines of cars were stopped at Nogales, one of the crossing points to Arizona, as officials searched for marijuana, heroin, amphetamines, and barbiturates.

Tourists and hippies were flocking back to the desert now that the hot summer was over. It was rumored that John the Baptist was back in Arizona, hoping to organize students and

197

hippies for a demonstration at Luke Air Force Base to protest the training of "murderers and assassins of the air" and the fact that the President's troop pullout of Vietnam was only a "token appeasement of the dissatisfied elements of society" and not really meant as an end to United States involvement there.

The still photo on the screen showed a tall, gangly youth in beard, shoulder-length curly hair, and enormous wire-rimmed glasses that looked ridiculous with his drab monkishlike robes. He didn't appear capable of organizing anyone.

Inflation still soared and babies in Vietnam with swollen tummies and hollow eyes still starved.

Laurel yawned and then giggled. She wished she could give the dour-faced newsman a happy pill. He had trouble rolling out the pompous words and overlong sentences while taking time to breathe and still hold onto his "this-world-is-no-laughing-matter" expression.

But the weatherman was all smiles, congratulating Arizonans on their marvelous winter season as though the blistering summer had never been.

She rolled over and slept. Toward morning her dreams turned to Jimmy's swollen tummy, blank eyes, his bony arms held out to her in a plea for food and she looking around the bombed-out shell of the beige bungalow for something to feed him, feeling an agony too real for a dream because there was no food and he didn't understand. Dawn filled the room when she woke, and she muffled her sobs in the pillow so that they wouldn't hear, make her stay longer because of depression.

On the morning of her release Laurel dressed carefully, wondering what that long-ago Laurel, with the butter on her chin, had worn the day she met Michael.

It wasn't Michael who came to get her, and the disappointment must have shown on her face when Myra bustled in.

"The boys are flying today—guess you'll have to settle for me," Myra said. And the dimples returned to her plump face, the familiar warmth to her voice. "How are you, Laurel? I've missed you and so has Jimmy."

"Is he with you?" Laurel bent to pick up her suitcases and hide the tears in her eyes.

"No, I left the kids with Colleen. Are you all checked out or . . . whatever you do?"

"I'm ready."

Early October and the sun a soft benign warm, the air sweet and delicious with freedom, the streets and sidewalks crowded. Moving slices of shade cut strange patterns on people's faces as they passed her under the arcade of palm fronds stirring gently overhead.

"This way. I'm parked way down the street. I had quite a time even getting here with all the barricades up."

"Barricades?"

"Haven't you heard the news? The governor called in the National Guard this morning."

"Because of the student riots?"

"Yeah, you can't get anywhere near Tempe."

Myra stopped in front of a red sports car with its top down. "Well, here it is. Like it?"

"Did you get a new car? It's beautiful."

"Huh-uh. You did. Came yesterday. But you can't drive it till you get a license."

"It's mine?"

"Present from your husband. Rather much for grocery shopping, and how we'll fit all this baggage in, I don't know, but I wouldn't mind a surprise like this someday." She did manage to stuff the suitcases into the little trunk and then turned to laugh at Laurel. "Well, you *can* touch it."

"Did he say why?"

"A man gives you a brand-new Jaguar and you have to ask why?" Myra rolled her eyes and climbed in behind the wheel. "My advice to you is to take it and shut up."

Black upholstery hot from the sun stung her bare legs. The car had a smell of new paint and real leather, its engine a powerful rumble as they pulled out into traffic. Laurel couldn't believe it. What had gotten into Michael?

An embarrassed silence fell between them on the way home. Laurel had to hold back her flying hair with both hands as they roared through city traffic, past sloping concrete irrigation canals and then through Glendale—every mile and every minute bringing her closer to Jimmy.

"Laurel, I want to apologize." Myra had to shout over the rumble of the Jaguar. "If I'd known you . . . had problems . . . I mean . . . well, I wouldn't have hit you like I did with that little talk about Mike. I hope that I didn't . . . cause . . . Oh, Laurel, I've felt like a rat ever since you went to the . . . hospital."

"Myra, don't blame yourself. This is something that started a long time ago." And she found herself explaining almost against her will, maybe because of the crack in Myra's voice, the paleness of her round cheeks; they sat in the car after they'd parked in front of the beige house, Myra leaning the side of her head on the steering wheel and staring at Laurel without interrupting.

"You don't know what it's like, not having a childhood, feeling guilty every time you look at your own son or his father, knowing your parents have disowned you—even if you can't remember them, it hurts. And living with the fear that this can happen again any time and there's nothing you can do, your whole life wiped out because something in you decides to forget about it."

Myra looked so astounded already that Laurel didn't say she had suspected her life was in danger, that part of her still did. Having just come from a mental hospital, she would sound hysterical at best.

"God, Laurel, I don't believe it. Things like that don't happen. Can't the doctor help?"

"Oh, sure. I get to repeat what little I know about myself once a week and take happy pills four times a day. Haven't you noticed how tranquil I am?"

200

"You always did seem tranquil on the outside—but what you must have been going through inside. Let's go get Jimmy. He'll do you more good than ten doctors."

Jimmy had grown at least an inch and his hair needed cutting. He sat on the floor of Colleen's living room with one knee propped up to support his elbow and keep his thumb in his mouth, listlessly pushing a plastic dump truck over Sherrie's leg with his other hand.

"Jimmy?"

He looked up at the sound of her voice as she stood in the doorway between Colleen and Myra, but he didn't move. And Laurel's heart ached as she read the expression on his face. He knew her. He just didn't trust her anymore. This was not the reunion she'd expected, and it was a hurt deeper than any she had known.

"Jimmy, Mommy's come home to stay," she said softly and sat down beside him as Myra and Colleen moved out to the kitchen silently motioning Sherrie to come with them. His eyes followed her and the dump truck lay still under his hand, but that expression didn't change.

"Let's go home and have some lunch, huh?"

He ignored her outstretched hand but stood up obediently and walked to the door, waiting sullenly for her to open it. Jimmy had matured more than just physically in the last month.

18

Laurel's absence had done little to change the beige bungalow. Her yellow drapes were drawn across the glass doors,
shutting them in with a cozy security. She touched the old
refrigerator, ran her hand over the smooth surface of the new
stove. Everything seemed so . . . normal. Maybe she had
imagined everything. It was then she decided to paint the
kitchen a pale yellow.

Jimmy stood patiently at her side, one hand in hers, the
other providing the thumb for his mouth, the plastic dump
truck tucked under his arm.

He did remove the thumb long enough to eat the cheese
sandwich she made for his lunch. But he refused to sit in his
highchair and crawled up on a big kitchen chair. Laurel
wondered when this advance had taken place. She regretted
missing it. The sandwich and milk gone, Jimmy returned to
his thumb. He hadn't spoken, smiled, or shown any enthusi-
asm at her return. He submitted to being undressed but
crawled into his crib unaided and then turned his back on her
to nap.

She'd done her best to hide her hurt and disappointment,
to keep up bright chatter and a smile. But this final rejection
was too much, and she went into the bathroom and wept
into a towel so that he wouldn't hear, telling herself she must
give him time. To his young mind her absence had amounted
to desertion. He'd trusted and needed her and she'd let him
down.

Michael came home with Pat that evening, and Laurel
watched them through the living room window as they

202

inspected the Jaguar. Still wearing their flight suits, they looked strange standing next to a mere automobile. Pat crawled in behind the wheel, shaking his head, his lips pursed in a whistle.

She'd made tacos, a favorite of Michael's, and predinner Margaritas. He and Jimmy watched her suspiciously during dinner as though waiting for her to do something strange and unexpected. Later, while Michael settled on the couch with a newspaper, she bathed Jimmy and read him a story.

His body was rigid as she carried him into the bedroom. But just as she bent over the crib to put him down, she felt warm little arms encircle her neck, cling so tightly she almost lost her balance. So she sat with him instead on her own bed, clinging back, kissing his cheeks, breathing in the sweet freshness of his breath and skin that she'd dreamed of, longed for every day in the hospital, afraid to speak for fear her voice would send him back to that distant, confused child's world and away from her. They remained so for what must have been more than an hour in the dark warm silence, even after he relaxed his hold and slept against her.

Despite the insistent ache between her shoulder blades she would have been content to stay there holding her son while he slept the night, but Michael's tall shape darkened the doorway.

"I think he's asleep now," he whispered and gently disengaged Jimmy from her grasp, laying him in the crib next to the Teddy bear. And then he took her by the elbow, led her from the room, and closed the door.

"He *does* still love me," Laurel whispered, only smearing the tears across her cheeks with her hands instead of wiping them away.

"He just didn't understand that you had to be gone. Jimmy's too young to hold a grudge, Laurel."

But the tears kept coming, and she gave up trying to save her mascara. "Those damn pills are supposed to be happy pills."

She moved into the kitchen to make some coffee and to get away from him, but he followed her. Together they watched the water rise up into the glass dome—an excuse not to speak and then both started talking at once.

"You know, I even missed the sound of this old percolator."

"Laurel, I put in for base housing. We can live better than this. . . ."

"Oh, don't . . . I mean you don't have to on my account. I like it here . . . really."

When they sat in the living room with their coffee cups, it was with the same uncomfortable restraint that had plagued them on Michael's visits to the hospital. She thanked him for the car, but he shrugged it off.

"I got ahold of your parents last night. They'd taken a trip to Canada. Your father said your mother *might* come out Christmas. Do you want her to?"

"It might help me remember if I see her, talk to her. . . ." But Laurel couldn't really care about that now.

Michael leaned forward to wipe imaginary dust from his shoe, giving him an excuse to look at the floor. "It's been rough on you living here, not knowing me from before. . . ."

"Even worse not knowing me . . . what I am." Then the tears came again, and he put his arm around her, letting her huddle against him until it was over.

The next day Michael carried a cardboard box when he came home, and Jimmy, who was himself again but with a little more mischief in him, danced around his father trying to peer over the top of the box.

Michael lowered the box slowly to drag out the suspense and finally set it on the floor. Laurel and Jimmy knelt beside it. There in the middle of an old gray doll blanket sat a fluffy white pup with black splotches indiscriminately strewn across his fur. One spot ringing an eye gave his face a ridiculous unbalanced appearance.

"What kind of a dog is that?" Laurel asked.

"I'd say about every kind. A civilian carpenter smuggled three of them onto the base and was trying to give them away. What do you think, Jim?"

"Puppy!" And Jimmy grabbed the struggling dog by the throat with both hands to lift him out of the box.

"Hey, not like that. Michael, he's too little to have a dog. He'll strangle it."

"I *not* too little."

The puppy was off across the floor, with Jimmy after him, and just made it under the stereo where he set up a furious shrill yapping. From there he headed into the kitchen, around the partition, through the living room and into Michael's bedroom, yapping all the way, his toenails scratching and sliding on the tiles at every turn, with Jimmy screeching his excitement not far behind. Laurel brought up the rear in an unsuccessful attempt to rescue the puppy before her son caught him.

As she passed Michael, she heard his deep chuckle and turned on him. "Just you wait, Michael Devereaux." And then she stopped, startled at the instant change in his expression. "What's the matter? I was only kidding."

"You used to say that, that very way. But you'd shake your fist at me and then giggle." And they stood just looking at each other while pandemonium reigned under Michael's bed.

About midnight Laurel sat yawning on the kitchen floor in front of the box which she'd turned on its side for a doggy bed, but the puppy snuggled on her lap.

"Why not put him in his box and turn out the light?" Michael came in silently on bare feet.

"Because he keeps sneaking into my room and crawling into bed with me. And he snores."

"Want me to stand the next watch?"

"He isn't even cute. All dogs are cute when they're puppies—but not him. He's a mess." And he was, his fur all different lengths, his body already too long for his legs.

"I could take him away early before Jimmy gets up."

"What are we going to call him? We can't just call him puppy."

"You never did listen to me," Michael said with a half-smile that reminded her of Paul. He sat beside her and looked down his nose at the puppy with mock seriousness. "Let's name him Clyde."

"Clyde? That's not a puppy name."

"Well, as you pointed out, this is not an ordinary puppy. And when you go to the door and yell 'Clyde' you can be sure you won't get someone else's dog."

And so Clyde was added to the family and Laurel had another potty training job.

Michael brought home a gold leaf to replace his captain's bar on Friday. He was now Major Devereaux. They celebrated with the Patricks at a restaurant where a man in a full suit of armor astride a white horse escorted them from the parking lot to the door.

It was a gay evening and Laurel got a little high. They barhopped around the city after dinner, and she found herself snuggling closer to Michael each time they returned to the car. He would gaze down his long nose at her and make some sarcastic remark, but there was less coldness in his eyes that night, more of a questioning, calculating look.

Pat kept the party going with his jokes and insisted upon calling Michael "Sir." They were on their way to one more stop before starting home when their headlights fell across a barricade blocking the road. Uniformed men with nightsticks and dark helmets stood guard, ugly gas masks hanging loosely around their necks.

And the party was over. Everyone was quiet as Michael made a U-turn and headed the car toward home. Laurel shivered beside him. Why, just when a little happiness came along. . . .

19

Promotion or no, Michael had to work that weekend. Jimmy and Clyde seemed complete without her, so Saturday morning Laurel put on some floppy jeans and an old shirt of Michael's and brought out the yellow paint she'd bought on a shopping trip with Myra.

A fine spray of yellow dots coated the white metal cabinets, the refrigerator, and her face when she'd finished giving the ceiling the second coat. She was kneeling astride the sink and on top of the counter scrubbing the dots off the cabinets when she heard a furious yapping in the front.

Jimmy slid the door back. "Hippies, Mommy."

Clyde slipped through ahead of his young master, his tail whipping about excitedly. He slid across the floor on a newspaper and his tail landed in the tray of yellow paint. She grabbed him by the scruff of the neck and shoved him out onto the patio.

"Laurel, did you see what's going on out there?" Myra and Sherrie bustled into the kitchen before she could close the door. "You'd better go out and lock that Jaguar. Our yards are full of hippies and there're more pulling up every minute."

Jimmy and Sherrie were jumping and screeching their excitement by the time she and Myra joined them at the front door. Two battered Volkswagen buses plastered with flower decals and four other assorted vehicles filled her yard and Myra's. They watched an old school bus, painted lavender, with curtains at the windows, park across the dirt road and disgorge an unbelievable number of hairy youths to add to the swelling crowds that filled all three yards and much of the road.

"Mommy, what's hippie?"

"They're just people, honey," Laurel answered.

Four more groups came one after the other, parking in front of Colleen's house. Her car was gone. Soon a string of honking vehicles lined the paved road alongside the base in both directions.

"This must be the protest demonstration for Luke."

"But why clear down here? Why not at the main gate?" Myra asked, flattening her nose against the screen above the children.

"Probably just gathering here, and they'll march to the main gate together."

The young people stood or sat in small groups, seemingly relaxed, the growing din owing to numbers rather than needless activity or raised voices. A short gal, too bulky for her low-cut jeans but with a magnificent bobbing chest, walked alone and unhurried between the Jaguar and a bus. She bobbed up the steps in front of them and stared.

Laurel's gasp brought an absent smile to the girl's face. It *was* real, alive—the snake that wound around her shoulders pinning her long hair to her back and bosom. She rubbed the back of its head with a languid finger and it lay still. Under the snake she wore a leather vest without buttons and nothing under the vest but curving breast and pinkish-brown nipple that peeked out when she breathed in and hid again when she exhaled.

"Hi, hippie. Hi, snake." Jimmy waved.

"Hi, kid." The snake girl turned her back to them and sat on the step.

"At least the snake keeps her hair from blowing in the wind," Myra whispered.

"And her vest from getting too far out of line."

Handmade signs and posters began to appear, many of them from the little bus beside the Jaguar. Many slogans and many duplicates, including the familiar, almost hackneyed MAKE LOVE, NOT WAR. But the sign most often repeated was a professionally printed poster with a flyer's helmet identical with Michael's. And wearing the helmet, a grisly, leering human skull. No caption was necessary.

"Oh, Laurel, your car." Myra put her hands to her face and peered between her fingers as one of the youths jumped up on the hood and revolved slowly, his arms raised to command silence. His hair was shorter than most but growing theatrically down the nape of his neck and parted on top so it hung equally on both sides and in his eyes, leaving it free to sway in dramatic emphasis with any forceful gesture. Laurel was thankful for his bare feet as the nose of the Jag bowed under his weight.

Someone handed him a megaphone. "Cool it!"

They gradually gathered around him and just as gradually quieted. Even the snake girl ambled off the steps.

"Now, we form a single line. It'll look longer that way and we keep together to block all traffic. . . ."

"Where's Sid?"

"You mean John. John will meet us at the main gate with students from Tempe and the Chicanos."

A blaring of horns and confused shouting and a pickup truck slowly but persistently forced its way into the crowd from the main road, about ten or fifteen boys packed into the back of it. When it stopped, all but two jumped out and began taking signs from the two who stayed to distribute among the crowd.

"This is our movie—we don't need you," the boy with the megaphone shouted at them.

"You'll just have a fuck-up on your hands without us, man," answered one of the boys in the truck in a rich bassoon of a voice that didn't need a megaphone, a grinning black with one earring and a bush of tiny curls all puffed and rounded on his head. Laurel thought he bore some resemblance to a porcupine attacking a high-voltage wire.

The white youth with him was serious, intense, almost savage in heaving the signs into the waiting hands of his helpers, ignoring the protester on the Jaguar. The new signs weren't going over too well and had to be literally forced on the crowd by the boys from the truck.

BASE OF PIGS; IMPERIALIST—FASCIST PIGS; PIG-AMERICAN MONSTER; WARGASM. One read "F T A" on one side and FUCK THE ARMY on the other with "Army" crossed out and "Air Force" written under it.

A sign carrier pursued the snake girl up the steps, but she refused the sign and called after him, "Go suck your thumb."

The militants were few in number but had a disquieting effect on the peace marchers. The only way you could tell them apart was that the agitators looked more agitated. Laurel put her hand on Jimmy's head and reflected with a shiver that unfortunately agitation was more contagious than peace.

"There's going to be trouble, Myra," Laurel whispered.

"I know. Think we should call the police?"

"I don't think we're going to have to. Listen." Sirens screamed in the distance just as a militant brought a sign down on the head of a hippie who'd refused it.

"Do you think someone else called them or they're just coming to clear the traffic jam?"

The injured hippie sprawled on the ground next to the Jaguar and some of the youths who'd been fading to the edges of the crowd at the sound of sirens moved back into it to stare down at him.

"Let's not have trouble now." The boy with the megaphone hopped back onto the Jaguar and swung the hair out of his eyes by jerking his head. "Move out with your own signs and keep going. The fuzz won't stop you if you're peaceful and the Guard's still in Tempe. Get moving—fast."

Cars and kids choked the road in both directions, and

210

Laurel wondered how the police would get through the mob. The sirens sounded close now but seemed to be no longer moving and she guessed them to be at the outskirts of the crowd which she couldn't see from the doorway.

The noise of the mass of people and automobiles had kept Clyde fairly well drowned out, but now they could hear him again and then suddenly saw him as he sprang around the corner of the house and dived into the first set of legs he met. He looked even uglier with a yellow underside to his tail.

Laurel grimaced as he sunk his puppy teeth into an ankle. The owner of the ankle howled, and then Clyde was lost in the push as the crowd attempted to form lines and move out. From somewhere to their right an injured puppy yelping began.

Jimmy slipped from under her hand and was out the door before she could snatch him. Something was shoving them back and pushing too many of them up the steps, forcing the door closed with Jimmy outside and Laurel in. Now all they could see through the screen were hippie backs.

"Lock the door, Myra. I'm going out through the kitchen and around."

"Hurry. Jimmy could get crushed in that mob."

It looked as if the whole house would be crushed by the time Laurel reached the open gate in the fence between her house and Colleen's. She couldn't see Jimmy or Clyde.

The crowd surged backward between the houses as she moved toward it, and soon she pressed against the tide, immersed in a sea of shouting confusion and stumbling bodies and an odor like that of musty woolens often worn but never aired.

"Jimmy." She was shoved back a step for every three forward, buffeted from one to another. "Please let me through. My little boy's out here." But her voice seemed to bounce off the wall of low murmur that was somehow deafening and hurl back at her.

Laurel had not stopped to ask herself why the crowd

moved away from its intended course, why lines hadn't formed and advanced orderly toward the main gates. Her only thought had been Jimmy. But now as she lost a sandal she sensed the panic around her and looked into some of the eyes close to her; expressions ranged from confusion to hysteria.

It was more than just her own fear, but she found her weakness for it responding to the fear around her. She knew if she didn't find Jimmy soon and get out of there she'd lose control.

Tears blurred her vision and she bit her lip till it bled. She fought herself as well as the crowd—trying to breathe deeply, but the air was not satisfying, not enough.

She cried out as an elbow struck her in the nose and she fell but was buoyed back up by the swaying bodies around her. And then someone stepped on her bare foot and she screamed, trying not to, telling herself she mustn't let the screams out or she'd be unable to stop them. The pain was very real, but she had little time to dwell on it, for she was losing ground. In all this time she'd made it to the front of one of the buses, but now the crowd moved her back without her feet even touching the ground.

The sight of a white helmet moving closer—some kind of an official insignia on it, not on a poster but on a man's head, gave her hope, and she began kicking and clawing her way toward it. She crawled over some of the people in front of her who'd gone down, fighting her way toward the helmet, wiping tears from her eyes with the torn sleeve of her shirt so that she could keep the helmet in sight.

As she struggled closer she could see other helmets, but she headed for this particular one because the policeman wearing it was huge. He towered over the crowd, circling a stick on a leather strap over his head like a lasso. He'd be safe and strong enough to battle them both through the crowd to find Jimmy.

At last Laurel tucked her fingers around his belt and held on as the bodies around her tugged and jostled and tried to pull her free. "Help me. Help me, please," she screamed, not wanting to because it made her sound hysterical.

A heavy hand, dry and hard, gripped her wrist, pulling her fingers away from the belt. The policeman drew her close and shouted into her face, "What's the matter?"

"Help me. My little boy. . . ."

"You on a trip?" His eyes narrowed and studied hers, pulling her closer to him as he swayed in an attempt to keep his balance. "You better come with me." He slipped an arm around her waist and carried her like a long, floppy package, clearing a way for them with the stick in his hand.

"Wait. My boy. Jimmy! Jimmy!" The more Laurel fought him the more the arm around her middle tightened on her rib cage, crushing her breathing. She struggled to turn sideways and slip out of his grasp but couldn't.

They were past Myra's house now and out onto the paved road. Several panel trucks and an ambulance had pulled up alongside the fence that lined the base. Much of the crowd had thinned here, running off, leaving their cars behind.

The policeman dumped Laurel into the back of a panel truck where another armed officer guarded several battered peace marchers. "Think we got a drug case here. Watch her." And he waded back into the mob.

Laurel sat limp and resigned on the metal bench until a stretcher passed the open end of the truck on its way to the ambulance. A boy's shocked eyes looked into hers briefly as he was carried by; blood ran in little streamlets down his face from a wound somewhere in his hair.

The thought of Jimmy lying trampled and bleeding under that surging mob brought her to her feet.

"Get back."

"Officer, my little boy is out there. I have to find him. I'm not a hippie; I live in that house over there and my. . . ."

213

"There's a kid out there? Why do you people bring innocent children into these things if you're going to cause trouble?"

"I'm *not* one of them. I'm. . . ." She followed his eyes and looked down at herself. Both sandals were gone now, one sleeve of Michael's shirt hung in strips, paint smears on dirty jeans. . . . "Just find him, oh, please."

He called to another officer and walked a short distance away to talk but kept his head turned so he could watch the door of the truck.

"Your kid blond with big eyes, yellow shirt? Little?" A fellow prisoner slid down the metal seat toward her. "Don't worry, I carried him out on my shoulders and handed him to the fuzz. He's probably licking a lollipop in a patrol car by now."

"Are you sure? A little boy about two? Thank God."

"Don't thank Him, thank me. Got myself stuck in here for it." Sandy-colored eyes lazily focused on her, "I know you?" He cocked his head comically and pretended to frame her face with his hands. "Yeah, you're uhhh . . . what's her name? Sunny?"

"No, my name is. . . ."

"Mommy!"

"This your little boy?"

And Jimmy was dumped into her lap.

20

Laurel crouched in the corner of the room holding onto Jimmy as though the others were planning an attack, trying not to stare at the boy taking off his pants.

No one else acted disturbed by the strangeness of his actions. They stood against the walls or sat, as she did, on the floor or on the long conference table, their bright costumes giving life to the colorless room.

As much as they frightened her, she had to admit these kids didn't look dangerous. They spoke in whispers or not at all, their calmness unreal after what they'd been through.

Once he'd removed his pants (he wore no shorts) the boy stooped to put on his boots. The loose end of the bandanna wrapped around his head like a sweat band flopped into his face as he knelt to tie them. Then he stood and leaned against the wall, folding his arms and grinning.

"Peenie, Mommy."

Laurel flushed as they turned to look in her corner, smiling at Jimmy's innocence. Friendly smiles, really nice faces if you bothered to look into them. Then why did she fear them? They hadn't been nearly as awesome as the police. Yet she huddled there with her young like a frightened animal cornered by a pack of hounds.

Perhaps it was just that the room was so crowded. Two policemen would come to the door every few minutes and motion four or five young people out. But, just as their numbers thinned, another group would be herded in.

It suddenly occurred to Laurel that the reason the half-naked boy stood where he did—across from the door but to the left of the conference table—was so that he could be seen clearly and immediately by anyone opening the door. His own little peaceful revolt against the authorities, ingenious and somehow pathetic.

The next time the door opened it was to add people to the room. The policeman glanced at the boy without pants and merely shook his head, closing the door.

Laurel recognized one of the youths who'd just entered as the young black with the booming voice and bushy hair, the one handing out militant signs from the pickup truck. He stood with his hands on his hips in the center of the room, revolving slowly to study the faces around him, nodding several times at people he knew.

And then his eyes passed Laurel's face and jerked back to pin her to the wall while he moved toward her. He knelt in front of her on his hands and knees, bringing his face close to hers. "Sunny? Where in hell you been?"

"My name is Laurel." She could find no more than a whisper with which to answer him. Splotches of red danced in front of her eyes across his face as if the sun were playing tricks with her, but there was no sun in this room.

He sat back on his heels moving his head from side to side in slow motion, but his eyes stayed still on hers, the earring swinging in and out of the periphery of her vision. "Oh, nooo, baby, huh-uh. You are Sunny, I know."

Then his eyes let go of her long enough to look down at Jimmy, "Where'd you get him?" Something intimate and possessive in his voice was many times more frightening than what he said or how he looked.

"Is there a Mrs. Devereaux, a Laurel Devereaux in here?"

"Must be the one in the corner. Only one with a kid in this group."

Laurel heard her name, the voices of the policemen in the

216

doorway. Inside she was crying to them for help, but outwardly she sat staring back at the young man in front of her.

"Mrs. Devereaux?" The voice was gentle, close to her.

"Yes."

"Would you bring the boy and come with me please?"

"Yes." But at the door Laurel paused to look back at the dark, expectant face.

"There's no call to be frightened. Your husband has come for you."

In the large outer room small groups of demonstrators were being fingerprinted, emptying their pockets. Michael stood talking to an officer to one side of a central desk.

"Daddy!" Michael took Jimmy from her and then looked her up and down in disbelief. She was aware of her contrast to his tall, groomed handsomeness.

"We're real sorry about this, Mrs. Devereaux. I'm afraid it's pretty easy to pick up an innocent party in confusion like that."

The snap of ice was in Michael's blue-gray eyes. "She does resemble them. Where did you get that outfit?"

"I was painting the kitchen. These were the oldest things I could find."

The sudden relief on Michael's face mirrored that of the policeman's beside him. It was all right to look that way if you were painting your kitchen.

Jimmy didn't remember his new-found friend until they reached the car and started home. "Where puppy, Daddy?"

"The last I saw of him Myra and Sherrie were trying to coax him out from under her car. Don't worry, Jim. He's fine." Michael explained that Myra had called the base as soon as the police began to clear the crowd and she couldn't see Laurel or Jimmy.

Signs of struggle and debris littered the yard. Without expression, Michael picked up a torn poster that had blown

217

up against a trampled shrub near the front step, studied the helmeted skull, and tore it up. Two buses still sat on the lawn.

"Michael, have I ever had a nickname?"

"I imagine so, almost everyone has."

"Have you ever heard anyone call me Sunny? A boy there thought he knew me. Do you suppose he did?"

"I doubt it. Probably mistook you for someone else."

That night Laurel seduced her husband. It wasn't really difficult. He seemed slightly amused by it all. She told herself she did it to erase from her mind the intimacy on the dark face under the bushy hair. But once in Michael's arms she was less sure that was the reason.

His was not a gentle love-making, even when he wasn't angry. He had a knack for keeping her on the threshold between rapture and panic. And he did that very well.

When she'd finished painting the kitchen, she applied for and, after a written test, received her Arizona driver's license. The combination of an extra gear, having to shift gears herself, and the Jaguar's startling acceleration confused her at first. But driving seemed to come back naturally, even if little else did. Traffic paralyzed her until she discovered that other drivers expected her to be a little flamboyant in the red Jaguar. They tended to make room for her.

At her first weekly visit to Dr. Gilcrest she told him of her experiences with the demonstrators and the police. "And two of them called me Sunny. Do you think I should try to find them and ask them about this Sunny? I could put an ad in the personal want ad column or something."

"Why didn't you ask them at the time?"

She sighed and gave him the answer she knew he expected. "I was afraid to."

"And now you wouldn't be afraid?"

"I don't know."

"Do you think you might be Sunny?"

"I don't know that either. I just have to find out. And I want to do something about it, Dr. Gilcrest, not just wait. . . ."

"Why? Are you still afraid your husband will throw you out? Or that someone wants to kill you?"

"I don't think Michael has made up his mind. Part of him will never forgive me and part of him is still searching for the girl he left behind when he went to Vietnam. And I'm trying hard to convince myself that I'm not in any danger. If I could just remember . . . I'd feel easier about . . . everything."

"And what will you accomplish if you do discover you are or were this Sunny?"

"Then I'd find out what I'd been doing for two years and. . . ."

"And what if you don't like what you've been doing? That's really what you're afraid of, isn't it? I hate to see you force this, Mrs. Devereaux. You're not ready to know of your past. . . ."

"But I am."

"No. If you were, you could remember right now. This minute. There's nothing stopping you but yourself. What you really want is to learn of something, some fact which will vindicate you from the unacceptable act of deserting your child. And not just to answer your husband but because you are unable to live with this guilt yourself."

"No!"

He leaned across the desk, smiling his deceptive benign smile, and she stiffened defiantly, knowing he always saved the best till last.

"Mrs. Devereaux, if your past were blameless you wouldn't have blocked it out."

The man was so sensible, reasonable. She hated him.

And so when Laurel went to the desert she did it partly to prove to Dr. Gilcrest and herself that he was wrong.

21

Wind moaned through the cactus with a lonely, depressing sigh. And the desert looked as alien to Laurel now as it had those long months ago when she first remembered seeing it. Again she had that feeling of being alone and lost.

Once the Jaguar had turned off the highway she'd left the world of man and entered the world of nature where she was just one more creature in a vastness of crawling, flying, growing things. This had struck her so unexpectedly that she'd panicked and killed the engine just a few feet across the cattle guard.

A cow with watery brown eyes and stubby horns moved suddenly onto the road in front of her, watched her for a few minutes, and then for no reason jerked its head and ran off. She'd had an impression of being able to see for miles because of the flat landscape and low vegetation, but the animal disappeared completely almost at once.

She drew deep breaths, trying to regain the resolve that had brought her here against her doctor's advice, almost against her own will. The tangy smell of dried weeds prickled the inside of her nose. A car passing on the highway behind her sounded remote, as though on the other side of an impassable curtain.

There was no Harley to force her on today. It was so much easier to run away from something than back into it. . . .

Laurel turned the key and started down the double track,

the growl of the Jaguar reassuring. She wouldn't stop this time but would follow the little road to its end if need be.

She had to make herself scan the roadsides for clues and drive slowly around the unexpected and unnecessary twists in the track. Even here the sun would pick out the shiny metallic surface of an occasional beer can.

A long drive, the tires throwing up swirls of dust behind her, the mountains drawing slowly nearer ahead. It was warm but not warm enough to explain the dampness of her body, the stickiness of her legs against the leather seat. Pain tingled up the back of her neck to her head and stayed there, growing stronger with every mile.

The road ended where the mountains began their rise off the desert floor, as she knew it would.

And there in those sagging buildings the first Paul Elliot Devereaux had met and married Paul II's mother so long ago. They did not look as if they could have helped his rise to fortune.

How could the rough stone ranch house with the caved-in porch have been large enough for Harley's family later? A scruffy big-boned dog barked from the hole that had been a doorway. The squawking chicken jumped to the ground from a glassless window frame. Part of the roof had disappeared, exposing bare rafters. A head with a bright red bandanna peeked around the door of a teetering outhouse on the other side of the rusty pump that sat on a concrete platform. A limp artificial flower hung upside down from the pump handle. Wind creaked the ancient useless windmill to face another direction and blew the smell of the outhouse to her as she sat in the open car.

Two corrals with gateless fences faced the house across the farmyard and a silver metal shed that didn't look as if it belonged. The dog stopped its barking and came down off the porch toward her. A child cried in one of the tents set up next to the weathered picket fence.

Laurel ignored the dog and the people coming out of the

tents as she stepped from the car and walked hesitatingly toward the picket fence. Assorted clothes were thrown over it to dry. The fence enclosed a small rectangle of desert separated from the house only by a well-tended vegetable garden.

That small rectangle was a graveyard. The graves were old but the white wooden crosses at their heads were new.

Those graves didn't surprise her, nor the crosses. But something was wrong. Laurel put her hand on a slivered board of the fence, the windmill creaking and grating above her, and counted. There was one too many. There should have been five but there were six mounds in the enclosure, the one on the end newer than the others in the row.

"Sunny?" The young black stood at her side, a floppy hat over his bush of hair.

"There should be five graves."

"You come to see Sid?"

"Sid?"

"Come on." He took her arm and guided her back around the Jaguar toward the corrals. She couldn't look into the faces around her. Quite a few people had gathered in the yard while she stood at the picket fence.

"I thought you were in jail," she said.

"I had bail. They let a lot go anyway 'cause they ran out of jail."

Four or five old cars, a bus, and a motorcycle sat in the sun behind the corral, facing its open side. Two men squatted Indian-style on the dirt floor of the corral and smoked. At first she could see just their shapes in the relative darkness.

"Sid? Look who's out slumming and in a red Jag yet," her companion said as he released her elbow. He turned to leave and motioned one of the others to come with him. The one who remained raised a hand as if in blessing and said, "God be with you" to them as they left. This elicited a deep guffaw from the black.

"Have a chair." Sid motioned to the dirt around him. He

wore cowboy boots and Levi's and no shirt. His ribs and the bones of his shoulders protruded from under his skin, accentuating his long thinness. Bristly puffs of hair in his armpits matched the black of his untrimmed beard. He studied her from behind oversized wire-rimmed glasses. Sid was the John the Baptist she'd seen on TV . . . and something more. . . .

"Well," he said, stubbing out the cigarette in the dirt. And then he repeated it, "Well," and sat silently waiting for her to speak.

Laurel wished she hadn't come, made marks in the dirt with her fingernail, wondered where to begin. "You know me?"

" 'Bout as well as I know anybody. What do you want, Sunny?"

"One day last April I found myself down by the highway. I didn't know why. Had I been here?"

"Yes."

"With you?"

"Yes."

"Will you tell me . . . about everything? How you met me? What I was doing here?"

"Why?"

"Because I don't remember."

"Sunny, Sunny. Hey, don't cry. It's all right." He reached out a hand to cover hers. "It's all right." But there was something sad in the way he said it.

"Well, tell me please. Even if you don't believe I don't know." She took her hand away and searched in her purse for a Kleenex.

"If you say so, I believe it." He unfolded his long legs and took a rolled-up sleeping bag from a corner, spreading it out for her to sit on. "You'll get your pretty dress all dirty." Then he walked out to one of the cars parked in the sun and came back with two cans of very warm beer.

Next he did a strange thing; he lay out on the sleeping bag and put his head on her lap. And then he began talking as if

223

he often found himself in weird situations, had grown to expect it. "A couple of years ago, I was passing through Denver and saw some kids demonstrating in front of the capitol building. Can't remember why, but I thought I'd help them out so I grabbed a sign nobody was using and joined them." He had a compelling voice, rich yet soft. "We ended up in a park and there you were, looking all sweet and sad. And you said 'Help me.' You looked like a good thing, so I said, 'Okay.' "

There was a shy sadness in his smile and in the eyes behind the orange-tinted glasses that reminded her of Paul Devereaux, as if Sid too shared that sad secret of life. . . . Ridiculous—Paul and Sid were so different, poles apart. He made gentle fun of both of them as he continued the story, holding the beer can on his chest. Once he lifted a dirty finger to touch her cheek.

Occasionally someone would come around the end of the corral and smile and then leave without disturbing them. Flies droned across the streaks of dusty sunlight filtering through the holes in the roof.

His head lay heavy on her legs, but she didn't want to shift her weight and break his line of thought. Laurel had left reality behind when she turned off the highway, and she'd never felt further from it than now, sitting in the lazy warmness, drinking tepid beer and looking down at the strange hair-shrouded face on her lap.

He'd taken her with him to Boulder, a town thirty miles north of Denver, and then west into the mountains where a sort of communal colony of young people had been set up for the summer. (Laurel thought again how strange it was that in a way she'd told the truth at the hearing.) Whenever anyone had asked her name or where she came from she would tell them she didn't know. So they named her Sunny for her smile and accepted her without question.

"It was a kind of slow, soft warm smile that cheers people

224

up, like when the sun comes out after a week of rain," Sid said.

When winter came to the mountains of Colorado, they left for San Francisco and then returned the following summer. He talked of wading in cold rocky streams and walking through thick pine forests and picking wildflowers for her hair. He described an idyllic existence where big children romped in the sun, unharried by responsibility, like the Garden of Eden before the apple.

Sid skimmed over the winter in San Francisco. They hadn't liked it—too crowded—too many tourists gawking at them. So the second winter they'd moved to Southern California. But again they weren't satisfied, so in March they had come to Arizona. In April he'd gone on a pot run to Nogales and when he returned she was gone.

"And that's it, little Sunny." He pulled her head down over his and kissed her gently. He smelled of beer and sweat. "So now where to?" And then he stood and moved to a window hole that faced the farmyard.

Laurel felt too weak to stand. The forgotten headache returned. "Why did I leave?"

"Who knows? You weren't too happy about my John the Baptist thing. We looked around for you, thought you might have gotten lost on the desert. When I couldn't find you, I figured you'd decided to move on."

"Why *do* you do this John the Baptist thing?"

"To stir up the sleeping flowers before they get trampled by Army boots."

"That Negro who came in with me. . . ."

"Who, Rollo? Oh, he's all right, but his propaganda is geared to the peasant mentality. We're not too long on peasants. His stuff turns people off. You never liked him." Sid sat beside her and began rolling a cigarette. He offered it to her, and when she refused, he shrugged and lit it.

"Did I take drugs?"

225

"No. You smoked some, but I can't remember you being interested in the other stuff."

"Those graves out there . . . that last one is new. . . ."

"That was bad. We didn't know what else to do. It's better for you, you don't know about that, Sunny."

"Sid, I have to know everything or I'll go crazy. I did remember that graveyard . . . it kept coming back to haunt me. But I remembered five graves."

"Yeah. . . ." He finally let go of the smoke. ". . . Okay. We found a dead guy just a couple of weeks ago. I don't know how long he'd been out there. The animals'd been at him . . . and the birds. So . . . we buried him . . . it seemed like the right thing to do. . . ."

"You didn't report it to the police?"

"We can't have the police out here, you know that. They're just waiting to get something on us. People come and go around here all the time without saying anything. We wouldn't know if anyone was missing."

"Sid. . . ." Laurel looked away and made designs on the dirt with her finger. "Did we . . . get married? Or anything?"

"We didn't get married." He gave a strange high-pitched giggle. "But . . . mmmmm, baby . . . that or anything!"

She knew what his answer would be. She'd known it when she entered the corral, but it took some time to digest it. Laurel covered her face with her hands. Maybe Dr. Gilcrest was right, maybe she wasn't ready.

"Hey," he whispered, taking her hands from her face and holding them. "What we had was nothing to be ashamed of. It was good, Sunny."

"Didn't you ever wonder about my past?"

"I thought it was something you wanted to forget. And anyway, I never question gifts from heaven."

They sat holding hands in silence for long minutes. She felt the appeal of this soft-spoken skinny boy, sensed something beautiful in his very ugliness. And then she told him about Laurel Jean Devereaux, tears rushing to her eyes when she

226

mentioned Jimmy. He listened calmly, showed no surprise at her strange story.

"How'd you find him—your husband?" Sid asked her when she'd finished.

"I had written his name on a piece of paper and stuck it in the waistband of my slacks. Do you have any idea of how I got that name?"

"No. Sometimes an old paper turns up out here. Maybe you got it there. I still want to know what you want here, Sunny."

"I want to know why I left my baby in the hospital."

A look of disappointment passed over his face and was gone. She sensed his withdrawal. "Maybe you forgot then, too."

Laurel sighed and stood up, brushing the dirt from her skirt. "I wonder if I'll ever know. I have to get back now. Thank you."

"Sunny?"

She turned; she was out in the sun now and it seemed so dark under the roof of the corral she could barely see him.

"Any chance you'll come back?"

"I'm sorry, Sid."

"Don't be. Never be sorry for love, Sunny. I have some of yours stored up inside." His voice came out of the darkness in a whisper. "Some cold night it'll keep me warm."

She left him as she'd found him, squatting on the dirt floor of the corral. And a heaviness tightened around her chest and caught the breath in her throat.

22

Tears filled her eyes as she rounded the end of the corral. She had to blink them away to be sure she saw the blue pickup truck parked beside the Jaguar. Rollo stood with his feet apart, his hands on his hips, facing Harley McBride. Harley wasn't grinning.

A girl with a baby on her hip watched from the sagging porch of the ranch house. Two boys held the barking dog by the neck and several others waited near the pump.

Laurel started running just as Harley took a step toward Rollo. "No, Harley."

Harley stopped and blinked as if he wasn't sure he saw her.

"He's just here to cause trouble, Sunny," Rollo said.

"I'll take care of this, Rollo. Sid wants you now," she lied and took Harley's arm as Rollo backed toward the corrals.

"You know these creeps?" Harley let her lead him over to the picket fence.

"I used to live here."

"So did I," Harley said, still looking over his shoulder at the retreating Rollo, his arm trembling under her hand. "You turn up at the goddamnedest times."

They stood side by side, looking at the mounds beyond the fence. Behind them the dog quieted finally.

"They got no right here." His breathing came hard between his teeth.

"Harley, no one's using this place, and you don't own it anyway."

228

"No, *you* do, Mrs. Devereaux. Were you livin' here with them when I picked you up down on the highway last spring?"

"Yes. Or so they tell me. Harley, why did you come here today?"

"This morning my sister let it slip that they were squattin' here last winter. She didn't tell me then because she thought I'd make trouble. I knew they were around . . . but not right here. I came up to see if they'd come back."

Harley relaxed a little and leaned his elbows on the fence. "This is the first time I been here since they put my old man in that hole. That's my ma next to him and my brother Elvie next to her. Had two brothers in the big war; they never made it back here. First two are the Milners, the folks that homesteaded the place before old Devereaux moved in and married their daughter."

Laurel caught herself nodding at the mention of the Milners, Paul II's grandparents, as if they weren't just mounds in the desert. She wondered what they'd make of the present occupants of the Milner Homestead.

And then Harley noticed the sixth grave. "Hey, what the . . . they been diggin' in there?"

"Harley, that's a grave, too."

"They got no right. . . ."

She grabbed his arm again, for fear he'd start off toward the tents. "Your family buried its dead here and they didn't own it."

"Well, that ain't the same thing." But his guard was down and the grin crept back into his eyes. "How is it when I'm around you the real world just goes away?"

"I don't know. Take me on a walk and show me the old homestead." *And let's get you away from trouble until you've cooled off.*

"There ain't much to look at." But he led her past the garden and behind the stone house. There had been a back porch, too, but it was now a heap of weathered wood and

229

shingles with a flap of rusty screening for the wind to whistle through. A white enamel dishpan, chipped through to the blue in places and partially filled with earth, lay up against a young saguaro.

"What do you do, Harley? I mean for work. You don't seem to have any hours."

"Most anything that comes up at the right time. If it comes up at the wrong time, I don't do it. I been in the Navy a couple of times." He walked along with his hands in his pockets, kicking a rusty can with his boot. "Been around the rodeo circuit some. Used to gamble a lot. Made a fortune once on the market and lost it the same year."

"The stock market?"

"No, greens . . . produce. Buy up a field or two of cauliflower or something and then try to sell at the right time. Paid off Ray's mortgage on the motel and bought my sister a café in Florence. Can't really do it no more. They got fancy regulations and such. Now only the big boys can make it in greens."

"How'd you lose it?"

"Reinvested in a fall lettuce deal. It turned hot when it wasn't supposed to, and I became sole owner of whole fields of green slime." He spread his arms as if to conjure fields of wilted mushy lettuce out of cacti and scrubby trees.

They walked up a mountain path where a large jagged boulder provided some shade and sat on the ground behind it.

"What are you doing now?"

"Living off my investments."

"Your brother's motel and your sister's café?"

"Right." Harley picked up a pebble and threw it at another boulder a few feet away. "You are looking at one of the last of a dying breed of good-for-nothing loafers. Poor but proud."

"Like those kids we just left?"

"I keep telling ya, they're different. Let's talk about you for a change. Only woman I ever met who had to be asked."

"Most of what I know about myself is hearsay." But she told him of her month in the hospital, the demonstration, and her short sojourn in jail, a sketchy outline of what she'd learned from Sid. They sat close together, Harley alternately smoking and pitching stones at lizards. The tiny reptiles were so much the pinkish brown color of the earth and rocks that she didn't see them until Harley startled them into movement.

"Once was I thought I knew what this old world was all about. But somewheres I lost track of it," he said when she'd finished. "What's your big deal husband going to think of this John the Baptist guy?"

"I don't think he'll like the idea much. But don't you think he'll just be glad to know where I was?"

"Might be kind of hard to live with a woman who could just take it into her head to walk out of the house and be somebody else. And even forget how to get back."

Laurel had been sitting there in a warm peacefulness, the real world (as Harley called it) far away and hazy, talking about herself as though she spoke of someone else. But now she was aware of that sense of urgency, a desire to get away from this place and back to her own world of the beige bungalow and safety. She had the creepy sensation that images were trying to force their way up through her consciousness, that she soon would be unable to stop them. She had to be safe at home before they swamped her.

"I have to go, Harley. I left Jimmy with the neighbor and I haven't had any lunch." She started to rise and then sat back down, staring at Harley. Nausea and a sweaty weakness came over her.

The same pinkish rocks and lizards alternately freezing and scurrying . . . the same place . . . but she wasn't seeing Harley McBride. . . .

231

"Hey, this your family? Devereaux?" He pushed a crumpled newspaper at her.

"I told you to leave me alone, Larry."

His long curly hair was tied back with a leather shoestring. His lips looked feminine and pink over the shaggy beard. A beard like Sid's. Why couldn't she convince him that he could never be another Sid to her?

"Just asked you a simple question, Sunny." Larry leaned against the rock and smiled at her. A lizard darted away from his boot as he stretched out his legs. "You'd better read this." He tapped the newspaper and put it on her lap. "There's an article in there about a wealthy Arizona family by the name of D-e-v-e-r-e-a-u-x. Ring a bell?"

"I don't know what you're talking about, Larry."

"No? Well, I'll just tell you, Sunny. I was sitting in the two holer reading the toilet paper and came across this article, and this name Devereaux just kind of jumped out at me and I asked myself why? Well, I have a cousin married a Devereaux, but that wasn't it. Then I remembered a couple of years ago, this man hanging around that place in Colorado where I met you and Sid. . . ."

"Larry. . . ."

"Now wait, it gets better, this story. This man had a picture and he was showing it around and I said, 'That's Sunny,' and I pointed you out. He looked at you and said, 'No, that's *blank* Devereaux.' I don't remember the first name now but the Devereaux stuck because of my cousin. He watched you and Sid for a while and asked some questions and said he was just checking to see if you were all right and I never saw him again and I kind of forgot about it till now. . . . Getting interested, aren't you?"

Sunny picked up the paper. It was really too much to hope for. ONE OF TUCSON'S FIRST FAMILIES. Below the title was a row of pictures with captions. "Paul Elliot Devereaux I, pioneer, land and mining baron of early Arizona, died. . . ." Her eyes moved to the second picture, "Paul Elliot Devereaux II, author and professor of. . . ." Again she was disappointed.

"Janet Hamlin Devereaux" . . . "Captain Michael James Devereaux, Luke Air Force Base" . . . "James Michael Devereaux" . . . . Her eyes left the picture of the baby at the end of the row and came back to the picture just before it . . . those eyes . . . the mouth . . . were they familiar or did she just want them to be?

"Larry, can I have this?"

"Oh, no." He tore it away from her and stood up. "I'm going to keep this, Sunny gal." A slow smile separated his mustache from the shaggy beard. "I can tell by your face that I got the right Devereaux'. Tell you what, you be a little nicer to me and I won't go into Tucson and tell them where you are. Poor little rich girl runs away from home? Something like that?" He started to chuckle. . . . "And to think I almost wiped my ass on your family."

But Sunny didn't care if Larry Bowman laughed at her. She'd find something to write that name on before she forgot it . . . *Captain Michael James Devereaux, Luke Air Force Base.* . . .

"Doe Eyes, you going to sit there dreaming? Thought you wanted to go." Harley stood looking down at her as Larry had. But Harley wasn't laughing.

"I'm starting to remember things . . . being here. Harley, I'd feel better being home right now . . . I . . . ."

"Sure. Want me to drive you?" He helped her up.

"No. Thanks anyway. I don't want to leave my car here."

He held her arm as they walked down the path. The smell of food came to them from the ranch house, and it seemed that the whole tiny community had gathered on the porch and the steps for lunch. Their noisy chatter and laughter stopped as she and Harley passed. Laurel avoided their eyes for fear she'd recognize some of them.

"Got half a mind to round up some of the boys for a little target practice. Might scare 'em out." He opened the door of the pickup and looked past her to the diners on the porch.

"What if one of the women or children got hurt? Wouldn't that make you feel like a big man for the rest of your life? Harley, promise me you won't do it."

"Oh, for. . . ."

"Please?"

His glance came back to rest on her. "Okay," he said softly, a half-grin on his lips that wasn't in his eyes. "But I'm going to have to tell the sheriff about that new grave over there."

"I know."

"You'd better get out of here before I do." Then he bent down and kissed the end of her nose. "Good-bye, Doe Eyes. This time I mean it. Take care of yourself."

Laurel watched the old blue pickup until it disappeared and then the dust clouds that traced its path in the sky above the cacti. Even after the dust had settled and the sun had washed the sky clean again, even then she didn't move.

Laurel. Sunny. Doe Eyes. Which one? Or was she really any of them?

23

"I just couldn't get those kids to stop horsing around and go to sleep, so I took Jimmy over to his own bed. He snuggled down with his Teddy bear and the puppy and went right off." Myra opened her screen door and joined Laurel on the front step. "Don't look so shocked, Laurel, I've been checking on him."

"It's not that . . . I'm just . . . I've had a strange day and I'm not feeling too well."

"Come on, I'll take you over and tuck you in with Jimmy. You probably could use a nap yourself." Myra took her arm and led her down the steps. "You're shaking. Do you want me to call your doctor?"

"No. I haven't eaten since breakfast. . . ."

"That's funny, I could have sworn I heard Colleen drive in and Clyde bark a few times. Then I was on the phone for a while. I was just coming over to see if Clyde's barking woke Jimmy when you pulled up."

Colleen's front yard was empty. "Maybe she left again."

"Must have." Myra lowered her voice as they stepped into Laurel's living room. "All seems quiet here. I hope he didn't wake up and find himself alone. The colonel's wife called and talked on and on about this luncheon . . . I'm on this committee . . . I couldn't very well hang up on. . . ."

"Myra." The tingle started casually at the back of Laurel's neck but grew stronger as it moved down her spine. "Clyde's not barking."

"Puppies sleep soundly some. . . ."

But Laurel ran down the hall and into the bedroom before Myra could finish. She grabbed the edge of the crib to keep her balance. No Teddy bear, no puppy.

No Jimmy.

"Well, I'll be . . . that little squirt must have been playing possum on me. Now don't look so worried. He couldn't have gotten far. Probably snuck in the back door to wake up Sherrie."

Jimmy was not with Sherrie or in Myra's house. He was not in the front yard or the back. Both of Colleen's doors were locked tight. He was not in either of the cars or under the beds. Laurel moved automatically through the search, painfully aware of the silence, the lack of puppy yapping that accompanied Clyde wherever he went.

They ended up in Laurel's living room, Myra shaking her head. "I really feel responsible for this. He must have wandered down the road. Let's split up and you go one way and I'll go. . . ."

"No." Laurel sat on the lumpy couch. "I'd better stay by the phone. There wasn't any note."

"Note? Jimmy can't write."

"But if someone took him and didn't have time to leave a note, he'd call." How could her own voice sound so remote, detached?

"Took him . . . you mean . . . Laurel Devereaux, that is the most hysterical thing I've ever heard. Strange things like that just don't happen . . . or not often anyway. Why would anybody . . . you mean you're going to sit here while he. . . ."

"You . . . wouldn't believe the strange things that happen to me, Myra. I know it sounds ridiculous but. . . ." The telephone's ringing cracked into the room with a sharp raucous sound. Laurel covered her mouth with her hand, muffling the cry that came out on her breath.

"Laurel, it's not what you're thinking." But the color had

disappeared from Myra's round cheeks. "I'll answer it. . . ."

"No." Laurel reached the phone before her friend was halfway across the room. "Hello . . . hello!" Someone breathed but did not speak. "This is Laurel Devereaux, please answer."

". . . are you alone?"

"Yes, I'm alone." And she gave Myra a warning glance.

"If you want to see your kid alive"—Laurel lowered herself slowly to the floor—"follow these instructions carefully." She could barely hear the throaty whisper over the sounds in her head. "Drive down the old road to Tucson. After you pass Florence, slow down but keep going until I contact you. Do *not* bring anyone with you. Do *not* contact the police or tell anyone. Have the top down on your car so that I'll know you are alone. Got that?"

"Drive down the old road to Tucson, slow down after Florence . . . oh, please don't hurt him."

"If you call the police or tell anyone, I will kill him." He hung up with a nasty crash.

She kneaded the crawling skin on the back of her neck. Her legs felt hot and sticky. . . .

Laurel could have sat on the creaky swing, but she sat instead on the wooden steps because the porch light attracted too many creepy bugs to the swing. She curled her arms around her bare, sticky legs and rocked her body back and forth to still her troubled thoughts.

Fireflies blinked at her from the lilac hedge. The heavy heat of a July night weighed on the world till even the massive oaks in the parking lot seemed to sag under it.

Dishes clinking in the house behind her made her feel guilty. She should be helping her mother, but she couldn't summon the energy to stand and walk back into the house.

A tired shuffle behind her and the screen door creaked open and slammed closed, and she knew her father had come to join her. The swing groaned under his weight. Daddy wasn't afraid of bugs. Daddy wasn't afraid of anything. The old resentment rose again inside her. Since she'd started college that resentment had grown harder to put down.

"Dreaming again?" The familiar tolerant note to his voice that he reserved not just for her but for women in general. John Lawrence had little time for the weak. His pride would never recover from the fact that his only living child was female.

"Laurel Jean, don't you think it's about time you got out of that fairy tale world of yours and started coming to grips with this one? You could start by picking a major."

"Oh, Daddy."

"Well, we can't afford to send you to the university indefinitely. You're going to have to decide what you want to do with your life. You can't dream the years away forever." The smell of his cigar smoke hung stagnant on the heat of the night.

"It's a hard decision to make."

"There's no decision worth making that isn't. Can't you just consider it a challenge?"

"It's all so hopeless. What difference does it make what I want to be if someone's going to drop a bomb and wipe out everything?"

"That's what you said when you were in high school and the Russians launched Sputnik. Ran around like Henny Penny with the sky falling in. You're still here, aren't you? Have some faith in God." John Lawrence sighed and rose from the swing to sit beside her. "Look, I know you're tired of hearing about the Depression and World War II. But those were scary times, too. And. . . ."

"Not like this."

"Well, you'd better learn to live with it, it's the only world you've got."

And they were at the impasse again. He would never

238

understand her, and she could never be quite all that he expected. But she loved him and it hurt that the strange frightening barrier existed, had always been there.

Laurel looked over her shoulder into the proud heavy face and whispered, "You'll never forgive me if I don't make it in life, will you?"

"The one thing I couldn't forgive, Laurel Jean, is if you ever stopped trying." He got to his feet and walked back into the house, slamming the screen, leaving behind him the harsh anger of his voice and the smell of his cigar. . . .

Myra stood above her with the telephone receiver in her hand. "Laurel?" The plumpness of her face seemed to sag. "I've called the police, and the control tower is contacting Michael. Don't get up. This is all my fault."

Laurel sat up and, holding onto the edge of the stereo, pulled herself to her feet. "What did you tell the police?"

"That Jimmy had been kidnapped. They're coming right over. Lay down on the. . . ."

"Is that all?"

"Yes, but. . . ."

"Myra, he said he'd kill Jimmy if I called the police . . . or brought anyone with me. I have to get out of here before they come."

"You're not going to do what he said? You're in no shape to drive anywhere."

"He doesn't want Jimmy. He's just using him to get me. Maybe I can talk him into not hurting Jimmy if. . . ."

"Who wants you? Why?"

"He wants to kill me . . . I can't quite remember why or who. . . ." Laurel was out the door and running toward the Jaguar.

"Come back. You can't—"

She couldn't risk waiting for the police even though she knew she was doing a stupid thing. She couldn't risk Jimmy.

This is one time I won't stop trying, Daddy. But Myra was right. She shouldn't be driving. She had to fight fatigue and a funny lightheaded drowsiness as well as city traffic. Once out in the country, she had to fight harder. The road stretched long and straight and endless, the desert on either side a monotone of dun-brown with the green of the cactus muted by drenching sunlight. The sky, an eternity of cloudless uniform blue without even a contrail to liven it up.

Laurel tried not to think of what might be happening to Jimmy; she tried counting fence posts. But that made her dizzy. She knew she was driving too fast. When she passed the turnoff to the Milner Homestead, Laurel couldn't believe she'd been there only a short while ago. Everyone would be gone now . . . she'd known it was wrong, but she'd warned Rollo that Harley planned to bring the sheriff . . . that all seemed so long ago . . . hardly any cars on the road. . . .

The Florence turnoff just ahead . . . she slowed the Jaguar to about fifty. Leaning forward over the wheel in the most uncomfortable position she could find, she analyzed herself. She felt drunk, the high buzzy drunk before the low sets in, and she didn't trust this feeling.

A semitrailer roared up behind her. It bleated a warning and passed, its tailwind throwing the little car about. Sounds—the truck, the rumble of the Jaguar, even the buzzing of the tires on the warmed pavement—were magnified in her ears. And the beat of her heart, the pulse of blood through the veins in her neck, all seemed to make noise. An almost unbearable racket.

Something was happening to her or was about to happen. She should pull over and stop until it passed. But she couldn't. She had to get to Jimmy. Paul's face floated onto the windshield, the sad knowing half-smile under the thin mustache. . . . "Man was nature's one great error . . . the most destructive of her predators . . . a most unnecessary crea-tion. . . ."

Laurel jerked and so did the Jaguar. Two right wheels bit into the shoulder, trying to pull the car with them. The steering wheel fought to free itself from her hands and a concrete abutment above a culvert loomed ahead. She fought the skidding, swerving car back onto the road, missing the abutment by a bare foot. Rushing air screamed through the open car.

Wide awake and tingling now, Laurel slowed the Jaguar even more, searching the sides of the road for some contact with the man who had Jimmy. How would she know? Had she passed them already? What was Jimmy feeling now?

Far ahead, a car was parked at the side of the road. Laurel's legs trembled. Drawing closer, she could see it was a small Volkswagen. She pulled behind it and as she turned off the motor, a puppy's injured yelping replaced the roar of the Jaguar.

The Volkswagen was locked and empty, but Clyde, tied by a short rope to a rear wheel, had almost strangled himself as he'd wrapped the rope around the wheel. He lay still and whimpering as she untied him, and then free, he scampered about frantically, jumping up to nip at her legs and then off to anoint a cactus and back again.

"Clyde, where's Jimmy?" She leaned against the Volkswagen and looked about her, waiting for some kind of signal. The trembling took ahold of her again . . . nothing moved . . . except the puppy. . . .

She watched the old blue pickup until it disappeared and then the dust clouds that traced its path in the sky above.

"Harley?"

"Good-bye, Doe Eyes. Take care of yourself."

Sid's head lay heavy on her lap. He smelled of warm beer and sweat. "What we had was nothing to be ashamed of. It was good, Sunny. Never be sorry for love, Sunny. . . ."

Sunny looked at the note again. "Captain Michael Dever-

241

eaux, Luke A.F.B." She'd walked a long way from the corral, trying to work off her confusion. Should she do something about this before Sid came back or wait and discuss it with him?

"I'll wait. Sid will know what to do." She turned back, taking her bearings from the nearby mountains.

A grunting and crashing across the little gully ahead brought her up short. Two men rolled over each other on the packed desert floor, kicking and jabbing. They came to the edge of the gully and then rolled and slid to its bottom without letting go of each other. A dark stain on the gully's side . . . where they'd marked their trail in blood. . . .

Larry Bowman reached for the other man's throat and rolled on top, his breathing coming in grunts, his hair falling into his eyes.

Sunny could see the muscles in Larry's arm through the tears in his sleeve; his teeth bite at his lip over the dark beard. She couldn't recognize the bloodied face of the man on the bottom, but he soon stopped kicking and lay still. . . .

She stood rooted, unbelieving . . . trying to blink away the sunspots that blurred her vision.

Larry Bowman rose, straddling the still figure at his feet and looked at his hands as if he couldn't believe they'd just strangled a man. Then he pushed his hair back from his face and glanced around him. His glance stopped with Sunny. . .

"Sunny?" He swallowed as though it hurt. His chest heaved. "Sunny . . . we . . . have to . . . talk about . . . this. Sunny!"

She didn't remember turning; she was just running away from the gully and Larry Bowman, crashing through low bushes, in no particular direction, just away from the crashing and running footsteps behind her.

"Sunny!"

How long or how far she ran, she couldn't tell. When she could run no longer, she walked until she had to stop to vomit.

242

The mountains were far behind her and the sun had set in front of her. No sounds of the chase now, but she kept walking until she came to the double track and continued along it, gulping air into her lungs with each step.

A woman's voice behind her said, "Congratulations, Mrs. Devereaux. You have a son."

And Sunny was running again.

24

Laurel sat on the ground beside the Volkswagen, the taste of vomit on her tongue.

The desert waited quietly in the sun.

She pulled herself up by holding onto the car. "Clyde?"

No sound. No movement. No cars on the road. The gaunt saguaros pointed to the sky and waited. . . .

Laurel walked toward them, and it was like stepping into a forest of armed giants, even though they were widely spaced, with large patches of barren salmon-pink earth between them. No trees here and the bushy growth was shorter, greener than that around Florence.

She tried whistling for Clyde, but her mouth was so dry she couldn't make the sound. Had he found Jimmy and Larry Bowman?

A still world, motionless, lifeless. . . .

"Sun-ny . . . Sun-ny. . . ." A mocking whisper. In front of her? To her right?

She stopped and waited, shuddering off the little tingle that raced down her spine. He had her where he wanted her. Why did he taunt her?

"Sun-ny. . . ." Much farther ahead of her now. He was drawing her away from the road . . . so he could dispose of her more easily. If only he would spare Jimmy . . . or was Jimmy already dead? Laurel began running in the direction of the voice.

The toe of her shoe caught in a hole and she sprawled

forward, hitting the packed earth so hard the air in her lungs pushed out of her mouth in a groan. Her thick hair came down over her face. She lay still, trying to pull in her breath through the pain in her chest. Finally she smoothed back her hair and lifted her head.

There were small holes all around like the one she'd stepped in, burrows where animals hid from the sun. Dazed and still fighting for air, she rolled over on her back, the glare of the sun full in her eyes, and stared down at her legs to see if they were broken. . . .

A head with short clipped hair and impersonal eyes peered over the paper sheet that draped her knees. "You've begun to dilate. I expect to see you within the week, Mrs. Devereaux. We'll get a look at that baby very soon now." He stood up and moved to the tiny basin to wash his hands.

Laurel slid her feet out of the stirrups and sat up on the examining table. She winced as the baby jabbed her bladder.

"You've had a healthy pregnancy, kept your weight down. I don't expect any trouble." The doctor turned, drying his hands carefully on the paper towel, his eyes searching her face. "Why so glum?"

"I'm afraid."

"Don't let those old wives' tales scare you. It's not really very bad at all. When the neighbor ladies start giving you a blow-by-blow account of their childbirths, change the subject."

"It's not that. I'm afraid for my baby. I . . . I don't have the right to bring a child into this world . . . not the way it is now."

"Isn't it a little late to be worrying about that. . . ."

Laurel moved her hands along her legs. One ankle was sore, but that was all. The sunlight made transparent green and red splotches dance in front of her eyes. She put her hands to her face and the relative darkness was comforting.

She must keep control, keep returning memory at bay. Every minute she lost in these little excursions into the past might bring Jimmy a minute closer to death. Was he afraid? Was he crying for her now?

Jimmy lay flat, his arms and legs flung outward, his eyes half-open to the darkness. He didn't move. Only a forelock of his hair lifted from his forehead by the wind and then lay back. Moonlight outlined the clean rounding of his chin, the curve of his baby nose, the dull glow of his blond hair. The little dog lay still at his side, the Teddy bear propped up at his feet watching them both.

Shadows moved all around them, dark furry creatures scurrying near and away, then approaching again, drawing closer each time. Another shadow, that of a bird with widespread wings swooped across his face....

The scream stopped halfway up her throat, choking her. Laurel took her hands from her eyes to let the brilliant sun wash away the dark vision and stood up carefully, testing the sore ankle. She could walk on it, but the cars and highway were gone.

"Sun-ny...." Which direction?

She was going to her death on the slim chance that she could save the life of her son. How could she hope to persuade....

"Sun-ny ... Sun-ny...."

Laurel began walking slowly and then faster as she found the pain in her ankle would not hinder her much, listening for the summoning whisper, trying hard not to put a name to the feeling inside her. But the word shaped itself in her mind despite her efforts....

Terror!

She knew the meaning of it, if not the name, even before she opened her eyes. The kind of terror that screams at you to escape first and analyze it later. The room was empty. Good. Maybe, just maybe, she could escape if they thought she was still asleep.

When she sat up and put her legs over the side of the bed she felt the pain. They had hurt her and they would be back. Clothes, she needed clothes. A metal cupboard, the same dead white as the walls. Two dresses, one too big, the other she would take. Underclothes in a drawer under the mirror, shoes on a shelf above the dresses. She must hurry. Time. Not much time. They would come back and hurt her more. Don't think about what they'd done. The pain was in her breasts and even worse between her legs. Don't think. Hurry!

She slipped into the clothes and carried the shoes. Opening the door just enough to peek around it, she looked into a hallway. The room was situated toward the end of the long hall.

Her breathing came in little cries and she covered her mouth with a trembling hand. Mustn't make noise. Hurry!

She was in the middle of the hall when a door opened and a blond woman wearing a white dress and white shoes stepped out. The woman looked startled to see her, was about to speak.

She plunged through the closest door, across the hall from the room she'd just left and couldn't believe her luck. A stairwell.

A sharp pain made her take the stairs slowly, look up to see if the woman would follow. Hurry! She had a chance now. If there was an unguarded door to the outside leading off this stairwell. Dizzy. Tired. Hold onto the railing.

She must not think about what had happened to her. Couldn't quite remember anyway. That was good, plenty of time later. Blood, burning hot and sticky, oozed onto the pad between her legs. . . .

Laurel stood in the middle of a shallow wash; a cool breeze had come up to blow her hair about her face. Weak and tired now. Too much was coming, at the wrong time. Difficult to tell the real from the remembered. Must keep them straight, the remembered no longer mattered. The sun was moving farther down the sky. Getting late. Must get to Jimmy. Very tired.

A dog barked. And kept on barking. Clyde. Where? The sound seemed to come from all around her. Did she really hear it or just imagine it?

"Sun-ny. . . ."

The wind was rising, carrying away the sounds she strained to hear. As she began walking she felt the desert on either side of the wash watched her with an impersonal interest. Would she retain control of herself long enough to save her child? No matter. She was just another animal with the female instinct to protect her helpless young from a predator. Struggles such as this were dramatized daily here.

"Jimmy!" Laurel screamed as she ran and then stopped suddenly.

About ten feet to her right in a clearing between cacti Jimmy revolved slowly, looking about him, dragging the Teddy bear by one leg. His blue corduroy bib-overalls were dirty, and as he moved toward her she could see the clean streaks on his cheeks where tears had washed away the smudge.

He wasn't looking at her and she couldn't speak, couldn't run to him because if he wasn't really there. . . . If she tried to pick him up and he wasn't real. . . .

Time seemed to wait, to hold its breath. He saw her now but still moved slowly as though he wasn't sure she was real either.

"Jimmy?" It was barely more than a whisper but it brought him racing toward her, and she was on her knees to catch him. He didn't dissolve. He was warm and dirty and he clutched her with that silent stiffness that she knew to be his reaction to fear.

She sat back and rocked her body, burying her head in the

248

smooth warmth of his neck and cried out with terror and exhaustion. . . .

"Hi."

Laurel stared over Jimmy's shoulder at the cowboy boots, the rumpled blue jeans . . . the dull blue-black luster of the revolver he held loosely at his side.

"You're one very hard gal to get rid of, you know that?"

She looked away from the revolver and up into the soft hazel eyes of Evan Boucher. "Evan?"

Yes, cut the long hair to collar length, trim the mustache, shave off the shaggy beard, and Larry Bowman became Evan Boucher. She wasn't really that surprised . . . just hadn't had time to work it out herself . . . it didn't matter anymore. . . .

"You know me now, don't you, Sunny?" He sat down in front of her, the gun resting on his lap. "I couldn't believe it when you didn't remember me in Tucson. . . ."

"It was you in the courtyard. . . ."

"I knew you'd remember sometime. But I thought I'd be clever and pin it on someone else, and when I saw how your husband felt about you and when old Professor Devereaux told me about how he'd chopped up his room with an ax and about his hot temper . . . and even showed me the ax . . . well, it seemed like the thing to do. But it was dumb. I'm not really clever." He shook his head slowly and ran a finger over the handle of the gun.

"Even tried to fix your stove one day when you weren't home." Evan grinned and picked up the gun. "But nothing came of it. So you see I'm not very clever."

"Evan, don't hurt Jimmy, please don't hurt him. He's no threat to you."

"Never wanted to hurt anybody." He laid the gun down again. Why was he talking so much? "Didn't mean to kill that guy last spring either. All I did was sell his girl some hash and he came looking for me. They didn't even live out there. Sunny, he just came at me . . . calling me names . . . then he hit me . . . and I hit him and pretty soon . . . he was dead."

249

What was wrong with him? Something different. "You could turn yourself in and claim self-defense. . . ."

"No way. They're trying to pin a drug rap on me now. I'm out on bail because they're looking for someone who'll talk. That's all they'd need. No, Sunny gal, I'm all done being clever."

He was tense, trembling, talking too fast. Could he be high on something? Speed? But Larry Bowman never touched his own stuff. She felt so tired and hopeless. It was hard to think. But, yes, she did think he was on something, probably for courage. He didn't want to kill again, but he had to and he knew it. And so did she.

Clyde wandered into view and started his incessant yapping. Evan swore and aimed the trembling gun, firing it twice, but so erratically that the dust flew far short of the puppy. Clyde ran yelping with fear until they couldn't see him. But they could still hear him.

Jimmy shuddered in her arms.

"Damn dog! I shouldn't have brought him . . . but he ran out the door when I opened it and I let him in the car so he wouldn't start barking again." The two vertical furrows formed on his forehead. "That wasn't clever either." He held the revolver up for her to see. "But a gun isn't meant to be clever. It's straightforward and to the point, clean, fast. . . ."

"Please let Jimmy go. He. . . ."

"No, no, Sunny. You see I have to kill you because you saw me kill a man . . . and I'll have to kill him because he'll see me kill you." He smiled apologetically and turned the end of the gun toward her. "I shouldn't have drug this on so long, I'm sorry, but it's not easy to kill people . . . you know? Sweet, gentle, little Sunny . . . with the big eyes. . . ."

Clyde's barking was suddenly very close, and Evan whirled and fired at nothing, swearing savagely. She couldn't believe he'd turn his back on her, couldn't believe the swiftness of her own reactions when she hurled Jimmy aside, jumped up, and ran full force into Evan Boucher. Her shoulder landed in the middle of his back; the gun flew as he hit the ground.

"Run, Jimmy. Run." Laurel sat on his back, with her hands clamped to his hair, pulling his head up and smashing his face down on the ground.

He bucked her off with one heave and was on top of her, his hands pinning her arms. Blood dripped from his nose and he spit dirt from his mouth.

"Run, Jimmy!" And she just went on screaming, bringing her knee up to hit him in the groin. But he flattened himself on top of her, effectively pinning her legs, too.

Laurel screamed and squirmed, and when Evan let go of her wrist to fasten his hand on her throat, she ripped his face with her fingernails. One of his eyeballs filled with blood.

Just as his other hand found her throat, Michael's enraged face wavered above her. The edge of Michael's hand sliced down.

Evan's body jerked with the cracking sound. The hands at her throat relaxed and he lay heavy on top of her.

Michael lifted the weight off and pulled her to her feet. Laurel coughed, gasped. Her throat burned. He held her upright. Jimmy grabbed onto one leg, his face buried in her tattered skirt.

There were uniformed policemen everywhere. "Who is this man?"

"He's . . . Evan Boucher and . . . Larry Bowman . . . he uses both names."

"He was." The policeman kneeling beside Evan stood up and looked at Michael. "Neck's broken. That's some chop you have, Major."

"Evan killed the man in the sixth grave. . . ." She looked up at Michael. "The fool turned his back on . . . me. . . ."

251

25

The room lay deep in darkness when the sedative wore off and Laurel awoke, cold and alone in the big bed in Tucson.

Michael insisted that she and Jimmy come here to rest after their ordeal. They'd been examined by a doctor and then questioned by the police. There would be a routine hearing into the death of Evan Boucher, but under the circumstances Michael need have little cause to fear. They'd exhumed the body in the new grave at the Milner Homestead but had not yet identified it.

Myra sent her rescuers down the old road to Tucson, and the red Jaguar clued them where to stop. Clyde's barking directed them to the general search area and her own screams to the very spot.

Laurel pulled the covers tighter, but the cold was inside her where she couldn't warm it. She'd been so sure she would die today that it felt strange to be alive. And just as strange was the knowledge that she had been ready to kill, that, given the strength, she would have killed Evan Boucher without hesitation.

She rolled over on one side and then the other and finally gave up, leaving the bed to find a warm robe and fuzzy slippers. But Laurel still shivered as she stepped through the connecting door to Jimmy's room, stepped gingerly because of her bandaged ankle.

The puppy growled as she came up to the crib and then licked her hand when she tried to pat him. Jimmy slept with his knees under him, hunched over the bedraggled Teddy bear. As she covered him, Laurel felt a surge of pleasure just to find her child warm and breathing.

This was an exciting, terrifying world that would often challenge her courage. But her father was right. It was the only world she had. The only world Jimmy had.

Laurel did the one thing her father could not forgive. She quit trying. The detective would have written him that she'd gone to live in a hippie colony in the mountains. To John Lawrence that would be quitting. He hadn't known she'd gone one step further and forgotten what she couldn't face.

Back in her own room, she switched on a lamp and stood staring at the empty bed. She couldn't hope to control this world or even to understand it. She would never understand the violent streak in people, the almost stupid cunning of Evan Boucher, the naked pleasure on Harley's face when he confronted Michael on the desert, the change that came over the gentle Sid when he donned his John the Baptist robes and exhorted others to violence.

And she would never understand Michael Devereaux who was more explosive than any of them. Laurel just knew inexplicably that she wanted him.

She moved into the hall and stood listening to the quiet. Would this house always make her feel so small? Would she have the chance to find out?

Light from the entry hall below gathered around the balcony railing, the carpet and back wall of the upstairs hall.

The door to the salon stood open, and as she started down the stairs, she heard the faint sound of voices, Claire's nervous giggle.

Laurel hesitated at the base of the stairs. This hall was larger than their entire apartment in Denver. The morning Michael kissed her good-bye and left for Vietnam, she'd crouched on the floor of that apartment, feeling the emptiness, realizing that he'd taken his strength with him.

She was so sure then that he would never return.

Paul's voice came to her as she crossed the sunburst. ". . . Not really so surprising, Michael. The female of any species when defending her young is an amazingly vicious animal."

Flames soared and twisted in the fireplace, sending writhing shadows about the far end of the room.

Michael stood with his back to the fire beneath the portrait of his young mother and his younger self, staring into the brandy snifter he revolved rhythmically, absently, in one hand.

"I can't imagine Laurel as vicious or even properly feisty. She's always appeared one of the most helpless creatures I've ever met." Janet sat beside Paul on a couch to the side of the fire. Claire, in a chair across from them, leaned toward Michael.

Only Maria noticed Laurel approach, until she was halfway across the room and Michael looked up from his brandy. Stilling the motion of the snifter, he watched her move toward him without blinking.

"Good heavens, Laurel, you're supposed to be asleep after that sedative. You shouldn't be up. Consuela will get you anything you. . . ."

"No, Janet." She stopped in front of Michael, determined to meet the challenge in his eyes. "I want to speak to my husband. Alone."

A long embarrassing silence followed while the firelight sent contorted shadow patterns across Michael's face and the portrait above him.

"Yes . . . well, I suppose it's well past bedtime for everyone." Paul drained his snifter and rose. "Come along, Janet. Claire."

"Laurel, be reasonable. It's too late at night to have it out now. Michael's tired and. . . ."

"I can take care of myself, Claire." That low warning in his voice as he interrupted her. But he didn't take his eyes from Laurel.

Claire looked from Michael to Laurel and then turned suddenly to follow the others.

Michael slid back the screen and kicked a smoldering log into sparks and flame. "That was a foolish thing you did today, not waiting for me before going off after Jimmy."

"I know."

"I came very close to losing you again."

"Michael, when I went to the Milner ranch this morning. . . ."

"Did you find what you were looking for?"

If only she didn't have to risk telling him. "Yes."

Laurel hesitated, trying to find acceptable words for unacceptable facts. There were none. "You were right . . . about there being a man. I met him today."

Michael turned from her to stare up at the portrait of his mother. And Laurel told him about Sid, unable to read the expression on his proud face.

When she finished, he didn't speak or move. She put her hands out to the fire, but even it couldn't warm her. The sedative had left a dryness in her mouth.

"Michael, you've admitted other women in your life . . . and you knew what you were doing . . . I couldn't remember either of us." She was suddenly aware of the day's struggles, the soreness of her throat, the ache of pulled muscles, the scratches, bruises. A weary hopelessness. Warning prickles played over her skin and her voice caught. "You can't turn me out now. . . ."

"Laurel, listen to me," he whispered and turned to her. "When you walked out on Jimmy . . . when they told me you'd been seen just . . . walking out . . . I didn't believe it. I kept waiting for a letter saying there had been a mistake. Then I thought your folks would find you and talk some sense into you. After a few months of that I was left with no hope . . . just anger . . . that grew and ate. By the time I reached the States, that anger was so powerful . . . and when I saw Jimmy. . . ."

Michael set the snifter on the mantel and ran long fingers through jet hair. "I was ... so ... goddamned mad." He spit the words at her, and she turned away, her hand covering her mouth.

"Let me finish." The resonant voice came close behind her. "Not once ... in all that time ... did I try to find you ... did I even think that you might be in trouble and need me." He turned her to face him. "So don't ask me to judge you, Laurel."

Even in the flickering half-light she could see the deepened lines around his mouth, the gray tinge to the swarthy face. He'd had a few struggles of his own today.

"When you did come back, my anger had turned to hate. I stayed away from you because . . . because it was hard to keep up that hate when I was in the same house with you." His arms moved abruptly and drew her hard against him. He buried his face in her hair, the warmth of his body finally penetrating her as the fire could not.

"I didn't give you a chance to explain. Or myself a chance to believe you." His voice came low, muffled. He tightened his strangely clinging hold. "Then you blanked out on me on the desert that day and I knew what I'd done to you, to us. But I didn't know where to start making it right. ..."

"I don't care about that." She wanted to stay enveloped in this hard warmness forever but she pushed away from him. "What about us . . . now?"

Michael straightened, drew back into himself. "I am every kind of fool and hypocrite, Laurel"—a hint of the old sarcasm, directed at himself this time. "But I don't give up easily." He'd humbled himself as much as he ever would and the familiar challenge crept into the metallic eyes. "Do you?"

"No. . . ." Laurel moved back into the crushing warmth. "Not anymore, Michael."